Stephen Sim lives in Scotland, where he studied at the University of the West of Scotland. This is his second novel in a series of three concerning King Arthur and the sacred artifacts left to Joseph of Arimathea.

Acknowledgements & Dedication

I would like to thank my friend, Carol Hughes for her help and encouragement in the process of writing this novel.

I dedicate this book to my brother, Tom.

GAWAIN AND THE QUEST FOR THE ARK OF THE COVENANT

BY

STEPHEN SIM

'SECOND NOVEL IN 'THE GRAIL QUESTS'

GAWAIN AND THE QUEST FOR THE ARK OF THE COVENANT

THE SECOND NOVEL IN 'GRAIL QUESTS'
Published by Create Space in 2014
Copyright © Stephen Sim
All rights Reserved

No part of this publication may be reproduced or transmitted in any form or by electronic or mechanical means, including photocopy, recording, information storage and retrieval systems, or digital media without permission from the publisher except in the case of brief quotations embodied in central articles and reviews

1st Edition

This book is set in Georgia Type Set
Printed in United States of America
Edition   2014
ISBN 13: 9781500630508
ISBN 10: 1500630500

MAIN CHARACTERS IN THE NOVEL

LADY ELAINE – SISTER OF MORGAN LE FAY
EROS – KING OF THE FAIRIES.
GAHERIS – OLDEST SON OF KING LOT
GAWAIN – YOUNGEST SON OF KING LOT
GALAHAD – RELIGIOUS FANATIC
GUINEVERE – QUEEN AND RULER OF BRITAIN
LADY HELENA – LADY AT COURT
LANCELOT – FAMOUS WARRIOR
KING LOT – KING OF LOTHIAN AND ORKNEY
LADY MORGAN – HEALER AND RIVAL TO GUINEVERE
NEMUE – APPRENTICE TO VIVIENNE
OLWEN – DAUGHTER TO YSBADDADEN
PENELOPE – AMNESIA SUFFERER
PERCEVAL – YOUNG WARRIOR
POLYXENA – SPY AND THE QUEEN'S FAVOURITE
RAGNELL – TREASURE HUNTER
TITIUS – ROMAN COMMANDER
VIVENNE – GODDESS OF AVALON
YSBADDADEN – GIANT
YVAIN – SERVANT TO LADY MORGAN

FORWARD

Immediately after King Arthur's death, a time of unrest and uncertainty gave way to a time of relative peace and calm. This was due to Queen Guinevere's quick reaction to the change in circumstances. She put forward her claim to the throne immediately and confounded many by marrying Lancelot to seal her sovereignty. With their combined forces the couple quickly stamped their authority across the length and breadth of the five kingdoms. Although there were some pockets of unrest they did not come from the quarter most feared, for Lady Morgan was biding her time. She was waiting for her chance to avenge her brother's death and bring those responsible to account. Civil war had been averted for now, however many had not forgotten the circumstances of the King's death and looked to the powerful lady from Tintagol to bring them justice.

The legend that was King Arthur did not leave people's minds so easily. Despite reports of his death being widespread, many sightings of the King were reported from one end of the country to the other. Reports were even made as far away as Constantinople and Rome. It would seem as long as Arthur's body remained missing, people would cling to the hope that one day he would return.

The whereabouts of the sacred hoard kept by Joseph of Armathea, which many believed included the vessel known as the Holy Grail, remained a mystery. Stories abounded across the Christian world as to the location; many sited the hoard in the land of Moses, others in the land of the old pharaohs, and some speculated Joseph brought it with him when he came to the land of the Celts. Stories of great healing were often attributed to the sacred chalice, but stories of deaths by plagues were equally attributed to the object known as the Ark of the Covenant (Ancient of Days).

The strife to keep the Celtic world from falling into foreign hands did not end with the death of King Arthur. His successors were faced with an unprecedented increase in numbers of immigrants which brought about a resurgence of power of the Angle and the Saxon peoples to Britannia. For the next forty years, just at a time when the Celts were fighting petty wars, the incomers grew and intermarried with the locals to bind them forever to their new home.

The struggle for power after Arthur's death began a process that would eventually lead to the break up of the five kingdoms.

It was not uncommon for women to become chieftains and to hold power for their area, although it was unusual for a Queen to rule all five kingdoms but it was not without precedent. So when Guinevere took power not many complained and even fewer tried to stop her.

Belief in Gods has been at the heart of all civilisations since man first learnt to walk. Even in ancient times there has been a need to believe in magic and to believe in something that can not be explained. It is my belief that magic should never be allowed to die from our everyday lives, for without it we become dull and bereft of imagination.

So welcome to the fantastical world of; Kings and Queens, chivalrous men and gracious ladies, magical swords, giants, dragons, fairies and arrogant Gods!

Stephen Sim. 2014

*Avalon's island, with avidity
Claiming the death of pagans,
More than all in the world beside,
For the entombment of them all,
Honoured by chanting spheres of prophecy:
And for all time to come
Adorned shall it be
By them that praise the Highest.
Abbadare, mighty in Saphat,
Noblest of pagans,
With countless thousands
There had fallen on sleep.
Amid these Joseph in marble,
Of Arimathea by name,
Hath found perpetual sleep:
And he lies on a two-forked line
Next the south quarter of an oratory
Fashioned of wattles
For the adoring of a mighty Virgin
By the aforesaid sphere-betokened
Dwellers in that place, thirteen in all.
For Joseph hath with him
In his sarcophagus
Two cruets, white and silver,
Filled with blood and sweat
Of the Prophet Jesus.
When his sarcophagus
Shall be found entire, intact,
In time to come, it shall be seen
And shall be opened unto the world:
Thenceforth nor water nor dew of heaven
Shall fail the dwellers in the ancient isle.
For a long while before
The day of judgement in Josaphat
Open shall these things be
And declare to living men.*

Chapter 1

'Make an ark of wood that cannot be eaten by worms, and overlay it with pure gold. And thou shalt place therein the Word of the Law, which is the Covenant that I have written with mine own fingers...'
(Kebra Naast - Chapter 17).

It was a cold morning as the lady stood on the hill-top and looked down upon the forest below. A frost sprinkled its silvery mist over the land as the late autumn sunshine made the green and brown landscape sparkle like a thousand candles. The lady turned her head towards the river, from where all the noise was coming from. She was startled to see people running, shouting and carrying buckets of water towards a villa that was on fire. The lady turned her head in the opposite direction to see a group of fine looking boats glide slowly down the river. The conflicting sight of turmoil and calm was somehow unsettling to the lady. Why were her thoughts so confused she wondered? And why was she standing on some hill-top in the early morning?

 A sharp breeze awakened the lady from her thoughts and to the realisation that the clothes on her back were totally inadequate. As another shiver ran through her body she looked down at her scant attire. She saw that she had no shawl and that her dress was thin and not meant for outdoor wear. This discovery clearly surprised the lady. She then looked down at her feet and saw the reason why she was so cold, for she had no boots or shoes on her feet. Using her fingers she examined the rest of her outfit to find that she had no undergarments on either. Wherever she had come from she had clearly left in a hurry without thinking. The lady wanted to get out of the cold and into the warmth of her abode, but where was that? She had no idea where she was, and more alarmingly who she was.

When it finally dawn on the lady that she had lost her memory, she became profoundly interested. So much so that she forgot about the cold and sat down on a bank by the river, to contemplate. After some meditation the lady began to recite the letters of the Latin language aloud. Pleased with her effort, she announced without effort the most important towns of the country; Eboracum (York), Cantuaria (Canterbury), Lundonia (London), and Caerleon (Chester). She was proceeding to another such exercise, when something touched her upon the calf of the leg. Sitting at the lady's feet was a small rough-haired dog. With his eyes dull and his coat thin and ragged, the pup looked in a pitiful state. For a moment the two regarded each other in silence. Then the dog rolled over and put his paws in the air.

'Where have you come from?' the lady asked.

The dog whimpered a little.

'You poor fellow, what a state you are in.' The dog's sad eyes seemed to concur with the statement. The lady got to her feet. 'It's obvious we must find you some food.' She looked along the river path and sighed. 'It must lead somewhere,' she muttered as they started off down the path together.

The lady walked at a steady pace and after awhile she saw a row of pleasant looking houses a little back from the river. She looked down to see the dog, but found the little fellow was no longer by her side. Peering back into haze of the dawn she could not see him. She retraced her steps and after a little while she came upon the poor vagabond, nose down on the turf whimpering. 'At the end of your tether, old fellow?' the lady whispered. 'Never mind I can carry you the last of the way.'

The lady stuttered in her attempts to remember a name that was on the tip of her tongue. Why couldn't she recall, she wondered? Could the person maybe live in one of those houses she had come upon? She picked up the small dog and returned towards the affluent dwellings.

It wasn't until the third house that a man came upon the lady and her scruffy companion. The man saw from the rear of his villa two lost souls approach his domain and came out to meet them.

Castor was a retired wine merchant from Gaul who had made his fortune and was now bored with his solitary life. He was going bald and was seen as being a little eccentric by the rest of his neighbours. The moment he set eyes on the pitiful sight before him he came down the steps towards them. 'What has happened here, is the dog sick?' he asked.

'I found him along the riverbank. He is so thin I fear he is close to death.'

'Oh surely not, all he needs is a good meal inside him.' Castor opened his arms to take the dog from the woman. She gave over the tiny bundle and looked relieved to see the beast in safe hands.

'Come on in, I shall see about food for you both.' He turned his back on the woman to walk into the villa. When he realised the lady hadn't followed him he glanced over his shoulder. 'Come now, it's a lot warmer inside.' The lady hesitated for a moment before following the man into his home.

The house was lavish compared to most abodes, but all the lady knew was it was warm compared to the cold of the morning. It seemed like no time at all before Castor's guests had eaten their fill and were purring with contentment. The dog immediately after finishing his feast, found a quite corner to snuggle up and quickly fell asleep. The lady also felt sleepy but tried hard not to succumb. Without an explanation the man was forced to ask the lady who she was and where she had come from. To his surprise the lady could not give him an adequate answer.

'You mean you don't know your name?'

'No my lord, but I don't mind somehow.'

Looking at little befuddled, Castor scratched his bald head. 'What are we to do then?' he inquired.

'I am entirely in your hands,' the lady advised him.

'Well I can see you are not a peasant from the clothes that you wear.'

The lady looked over her garments again and found that although her dress was not made for the outdoors, it was nonetheless made of the finest silk. 'I must be rich I suppose, but I cannot say.'

'We must find out who you are. I'm sure someone is missing you and will be searching for you as we speak.'

The lady managed a weak smile. 'You have been so kind,' she said. 'One day I'll pay you back, but until then can I possibly stay here?'

'You are most welcome to stay...' Castor's voice wavered and the lady felt a little embarrassed.

'If you could find me some clothes and some boots to wear...I could leave you in peace...'

The man was most apologetic. 'No, no dear lady, I would not cast you aside in your present predicament. It is just that I live here alone and I am worried about your reputation.'

The lady sighed with relieve. 'Right now that is the least of my problems I can assure you.'

Castor got to his feet and put his finger to his lips. 'Yes now, what can I give you to wear, let me think?'

As the man went further into the villa to look for clothes, he left the lady alone to think. The woman became curious so she got to her feet and wandered around the man's room looking for a mirror of glass, or silver, so as to see her reflection. The rooms were spacious and had marble and stone floors, many with beautiful mosaics, so characteristic of the late Roman period. The furnishings were few but of good quality; there was as an oak chest, a sturdy desk, a wooden sofa, and a tapestry depicting two lovers drinking from a single bowl. Behind a crimson drape the lady came upon a silver mirror polished and shiny. She picked up the object which was light to the touch and stared hard back at her own reflection. What she saw startled her, for her face had many lines, although she felt quite young inside. She took her hand and explored the contours with great care, finding ever line fascinating and rather wonderful. Somehow she knew this was a face that had known great strife and great pain.

After putting the mirror down again she returned to her seat and waited patiently for Castor to return. The more the lady thought about her situation, the more the appeal of remaining unfound became attractive. Her worn out face told of sadness but with no past behind her, the lady could think of a possible fresh start to her life. She hoped no one was missing her and no one had a claim on her.

The facts were not so clear-cut. The lady had not completely lost her memory. She had lost only part of it. For her, her personal past was blotted out. She could remember nothing that she had ever done or ever suffered. She could remember no acquaintance, local or personal, animate or inanimate, which she had ever had. With these important exceptions the rest of her memory was pretty sound. What general knowledge she possessed was, more or less, at her disposal. Names that were household names such as; King Arthur and Queen Guinevere she recalled, even places, like Lundonia she remembered hazily. If the lady's memory was playing up, her instinct was nonetheless sound as a bell. Her instinct told her to leave the past behind. If someone came looking for her then fine, she would return to her past life. Something sinister had happened to her, she was sure of that and for that reason she was content to let her past remain dead.

*

Elaine was desolate, now that her two young friends, Olwen and Gallia, had left to take care of their own affairs. She felt like a prisoner in her sister's home, for she had been forbidden to venture beyond the castle walls. So what if she was a ghost, the world would have to learn of her resurrection sooner or later. She could not hide for the rest of her life.

This was not the life that Vivienne had promised her, this was not the life that her new found hunger craved.

Since her time recovering with that lady, Elaine's capacity had grown as had her powers of perception.

Lady Morgan was set free by Guinevere after King Lot and representatives from the High Council petitioned for her release. The Queen had not forgotten the trick pulled on her by the lady from Tintagol and was even more watchful than before. Lady Morgan wasted no time in paying a visit on her future husband, King Ursien in Gore. She was accompanied by Lot, his sons and Lady Helena who was in disguise. This left Elaine restless and bored with her tedious daily routine. She was impatient to escape her confines so that she could experience adventure and romance for the first time.

Elaine shut her eyes and placed her head upon the back of a hardwood chair and sighed. She was all alone in the great hall, with only the sound of distant footsteps to disturb her concentration. She turned her thoughts to the Island of Foaine and to her new found friend and confidante. The lady's eyes remained closed as she saw the lady of the lake ascend from the water. Without the Goddess opening her mouth, her voice entered Elaine's consciousness. 'What is it? Why are you contacting me?'

Similarly Elaine communicated without opening her mouth. 'I am no use to you here. I can not help Morgan, for I am kept a prisoner in my sister's castle.'

'Surely you have not softened your resolve already. The man who killed you is free and unpunished.'

'I can not get anywhere near him.'

'With the Queen's business in Lundonia over, she will return to Caerleon. You must find a way into that great fortress and set the seed of disharmony. If you can not manage entry yourself, perhaps you can transfer your thoughts onto another. Your mind is strong enough to transfer your hate to someone else.'

'My hate does not consume me as you predicted, I still struggle to believe the man is guilty.'

'I have another suggestion. Take on a disguise and infiltrate the Queen's household, say as a lady-in-waiting. That way you could overhear things, things that they speak of in private. Perhaps they will reveal their murderous past to one another in their matrimonial bed.'

Drops of perspiration began to drip down Elaine's cheeks. The thought of her past admirer in the arms of the Queen made her blood boil. It was this thought, put deliberately into her head that strengthened her resolve to take action. 'I will do what you suggest, but what will I say to my mother? How can I escape my confinement?'

'I will send Eros to you. He can help you with your deception.'

'Thank you, my lady. I hope I can be of use to you and my sister.'

Vivienne re-emerged into the pool, while Elaine opened her eyes in the great hall. A wave of exhilaration came over her. Was this what men felt when they went into battle she wondered? If it was, it made her jealous of their freedom and power. She could not understand this restlessness, for in the past she led a quiet peaceful existence. Her body felt it was no longer her own, but belonged to someone else.

Eros was the King of the fairies and as great in his world as King Arthur had been in theirs. He would help her to do the impossible. He would help her to be in two places at the same time.

Chapter 2

*'For sweetest things turn sourest by their deeds;
Lilies that fester smell far worse than weeds.'*
(Shakespeare's- Sonnet 94)

It was that part of the night when all good people should be asleep when Lady Elaine welcomed her late night visitor. Her guest was no bigger than her hand, but what a mischievous little fellow he was. Eros flew around the room gleefully doing summersaults and spins to entertain his now favourite human. Elaine too looked excited and clapped her hands in gentle merriment at his antics.

Elaine got out of her bed and sat on the edge of the divan looking up at her tiny friend. 'I cannot be in two places at the same time, can I?' she inquired.

'You can and you shall, but your conscience and spirit will be with your fake body, while I shall inhabit your true one.'

Shaking her head, the lady still looked confused. 'Surely that's impossible. For one thing whose body will I be inside?'

'The lady is in no need of her body anymore,' the fairy replied.

Elaine gulped. 'You mean I shall be inside a dead person's body?'

'It's only a shell. All human bodies decay and rot, but our lady loves the shape of humans so much she collects the most beautiful in a special place only she frequents. You will feel only your own sensations and not that of anyone else's. So do not be afraid.'

The lady screwed up her face. 'It doesn't seem quite decent; it seems sacrilege to do such a thing.'

Eros smiled. 'You are confused because you believe in the religion called Christianity. There is no single God, not like the one spoken of by the being called Jesus. No punishment will be meted out to you by him and no harm will befall the body you will inhabit.'

Elaine's face told of her bewilderment, but Eros just laughed.

'Shhh....Someone will hear us.'

'No one can hear us. I have suspended time so we can complete our transformation.'

'I am scared,' admitted a now pensive looking Elaine.

Eros flew in front of the lady's nose. 'You need not worry. It will be wonderful, I promise. I always wanted to know what it was like to be a human and now I shall find out. Tell me about this eating thing, is it really enjoyable?'

'Oh yes it can be extremely nice, but a word of warning, do not over indulge.'

The fairy looked perplexed. 'Surely you would want to do something that was pleasant a great deal.'

'No, you do not understand. Your stomach will ache and you will become sick.'

'Sick?' asked a curious Eros. 'What is this thing you call sick?

'I cannot explain. Just be careful not to eat too much.'

Nodding his tiny head the fairy agreed, and then instructed the lady to lie down on the bed.

'I am worried in case I get lost,' Elaine admitted.

'You humans seem to worry a great deal. Have no fear my children will accompany you through the night until you reach the castle in Caerleon. You will be quite safe. No one can see you.'

Eros buzzed around the room one last time, enjoying his last moment as a pixie before landed upon Elaine's chin. 'Just shut your eyes,' he told the woman. 'Think of something lovely like the flowers around our lady's pool and before...'

His words died away and without being told the lady opened her mouth so that the tiny fairy could jump into her body. There was a strange tickly sensation as if she had eaten some tasty brew, before a great pain racked at her insides. She gasped for breath, opened her eyes and raised her upper body. As she rose to her feet she turned to see herself laid out on the bed before her.

Elaine's hand touched her head but she was afraid to speak. Eros, now looking exactly like the Lady Elaine, rose from the bed and came to reassure the lady that all was well. Not convinced the real Elaine began to shake, but Eros put his now human arms around the lady and gave her a hug.

'Ye gods, this is nice,' he exulted.

Looking pleased with this new sensation he re-enacted the embrace several times.

'Oh you humans, how lucky you are to be able to experience such a marvellous feeling.'

After trying several times to speak, the lady finally uttered a few words. 'I feel strange,' she complained.

'You must take a look at your new body, it is quite nice, but I prefer this one I have to say.'

Eros, as Elaine, showed the lady the reflection of her new face from the mirror by her bed. She was suitably impressed, for her skin was young without wrinkles and her bones were nicely set.

The lady then used her fingers to explore every crevice that made up her new face. She looked no older than twenty and despite Eros's claim she had to admit she was more beautiful. Yet it was not a face of an innocent, but that of clever and worldly young woman. It appeared obvious to her that this woman had led a very different life from the privileged one she had enjoyed.

As if he could not help himself, Eros embraced Elaine once again. As she pulled her body away from the exuberant fairy to look at her new self again in the mirror. 'How odd to see oneself,' she admitted.

A smiling Eros assured her that he would not do anything that would compromise their plan. Elaine wondered. Just how would he react around her family and friends? Would they guess something was amiss? Would they just think she was still unwell?

Eros could see the lady's questions and thought to reassure her. He was in for a surprise though, for as he was about to embrace the lady again she stood back and complained. 'No more hugs and don't go around hugging people all the time for they will think it's rather strange.'

With a look of hurt upon his face the fairy agreed. 'You must go now, but you must return in seven days time.'

The lady agreed, but had one last question. 'What if I don't return by then?'

'I'm not sure what will happen, but my mistress made it quite clear you must.'

Elaine smiled. 'I will. Enjoy your stay…what am I saying…just don't do anything too extreme.'

The room was suddenly engulfed with tiny flying objects that swirled around the two women. Just as Elaine was about to fly away with her pixie friends, Eros made one last inquiry. 'What will you call yourself?'

Elaine could not think. 'What was the lady's name?' she asked.

After a moment's hesitation the fairy revealed it was Polyxena.

*

Castor had made such inquires as he could to locate anyone connected to the lady without success. He was about to leave to inform the local prefect when he came upon a pleasant scene.

The lady and her dog were playing happily together in his hall. Both had recovered and both looked well and content with their lives. The lady heard his footsteps and turned her head to see him approach. 'Ah, just the man we were looking for,' she explained. 'We need someone to be our judge in our important decision.'

Castor looked intrigued. 'If I can help you in any way, I shall.'

The lady smiled. 'We have decided that we can not remain anonymous any longer.' The terrier moistened his lips. 'You see it's not only unfashionable but inconvenient. I propose to give us both names, but we need an arbiter to convey that my choice is both honest and without prejudice.'

'Have you decided yet?' the man inquired.

'We are in agreement on one—Caesar.'

The dog rolled over upon his back, and the lady patted him affectionately around his neck.

'Caesar is an unusual name for a woman,' Castor joked.

The lady laughed. 'I have struggled to find a name for myself, but the dog seems to love the name I have picked. What do you think?'

'Caesar it shall be. As for your name, I propose you accompany me to the local prefect and find out your real one.'

The lady frowned. 'Please do not think me ungrateful, but I would rather you stop looking for my past and let me get on with my future.'

'You could be married. I see you have a ring on your finger...that...'

'I told you it means nothing to me...I would know if I was married surely.'

'You can not be sure of that. Come with me at least...I promise not to just hand you over. We must try and find out what really happened to you, don't you think?'

A now solemn looking lady agreed. 'Still I must choose a name...I have racked my pitiful thoughts, but I can not find a name that suits me.'

Castor said he was not good at names either, but did offer up a suggestion. 'I always thought Penelope was a nice name,' he said.

The lady saw Castor go red in the face, and knew the name had significance for the man. It made her feel good that the saying of her new name might bring him a little happiness. 'Penelope...Yes, call me Penelope from now on. I feel the name fits me well.'

The man agreed and offered to wait until the lady got ready to leave. All three left the villa soon after to venture into the heart of Lundonia, to a place called Westcheap.

Chapter 3

The sun was fresh up from the morning sky, when a small boat navigated through the narrow channel from one world to the other. Gaheris had given the charge of his lady, to Eberth, a tall muscular mute from the Orkney Isles. The tall Pict had the nick name of the Bull, for obvious reasons. He was diligent in his duty and never left the lady's side. Olwen complained at first, but soon the two communicated admirably well with each other through a series of signals and signs.

Also on the boat were Lady Olwen's trusted servant John and a young warrior from Listinoise, called Perceval. The young man looked little more than a boy with his freckled face and innocent countenance. A friend of Gawain's, he had volunteered to undertake the mission knowing of its dangers. Although young he had already attained a reputation for bravery and daring and had on more than one occasion saved a friend in battle.

The small band of adventurers sailed into the unknown territory wondering if their undertaking would lead to glory, or death. To rescue a normal man from the dreaded island would have been hazardous, but to rescue a giant without awakening the Gods seemed an almost impossible task.

Gaheris was conversing with Perceval in the stern of the boat. 'You have seen many amazing things in your short life, but what you are about to witness will astonish you.'

Looking suitably enthralled Perceval requested more details.

'You will see soon enough. Just remember the beings that will appear before you will be phantoms and cannot hurt you.'

'Yes, but others you said were not phantoms.'

'They will not hinder us. Remember we care only about the giant and getting him to safety.'

'What about the Gods?'
'They should be busy elsewhere.'

*

'Are you still going ahead with your reckless plan?' asked Vivienne.

'Why?' said Gwawl. 'Have you changed your mind and want to come with us?'

The Lady of the Lake shook her head. 'It is madness; you'll blow yourself up and all the islands with you.'

Gwawl stared at the lady. His manner was threatening, but the lady remained calm.

'We are running out of time, thanks in no small part to your actions.'

The look on the lady's face implied innocence. 'I really don't know what you are referring to?'

'I'm referring to the return of our treasure. There were a few items missing, such as the chalice...'

'Well we all know who holds that object now. Lady Guinevere cannot control its power and with her spirit she never will.'

'I think Gwawl is more interested in finding out what happened to the cylinders,' Pwyll informed the lady.

'That is a puzzle,' the lady admitted.

'Not to me. I'm sure you hold the items in question.'

'A little insurance policy perhaps,' hinted Rhiannon.

'Lady Morgan gave over every item she rescued. It is a shame the cylinders weren't with the rest of the treasure.'

'I assume the lady had no idea what was inside the cylinders? asked Nuada.

Vivienne answered that the lady was only interested in the welfare of her sister.

'How is her sister?' asked the reserved Mider.

Mider seemed genuinely interested in Elaine's fate, so Vivienne saw no reason not to reassure him that she was well and fully recovered.

Gwawl was getting impatient. 'What is you want my lady, apart from wasting our time today?'

'Your temper hasn't improved with age, I see,' commented Vivienne.

The Gods all stood around a large round table where no one being had an advantage. Their equality had the opposite effect to what the lawmakers had intended. No one being had power over another it was true, but this only led to bickering and fights for supremacy.

Pwyll, rather like his enemy, was suspicious of the lady's motives for calling the meeting. He addressed the lady again with another question. 'You have taken upon yourself to instruct a young maiden in our arts. Pray tell us why you have done this?'

'You are referring to my apprentice Nemue I assume.'

Pwyll acknowledged he was.

'I cannot stand by and watch this intolerant religion destroy everything that has come before.'

Rhiannon responded bitterly. 'All this has been agreed already,' she thundered. 'These creatures need a simple message, one that is easy to follow and obey. All present agreed that they would never again interfere in human affairs, but you think you can ignore our rules and do whatever you want.'

The lady of the lake smiled. 'You forget I am the one dedicated to remaining. If I want to communicate with creatures other than my pixies, I don't think anyone here should object.'

Pwyll agreed with his wife. 'Rhiannon is right to be annoyed. Every time we interfere some sort of catastrophe occurs. I think I speak for everyone around the table, when I say that we can not allow you to continue to teach Nemue.'

'The girl already holds too much power,' expressed Gwawl.

Vivienne felt surrounded by enemies, only Mider and perhaps Nuada remained neutral, the rest were against her. The reason she called the meeting was twofold. She wanted to give Gaheris time for his expedition and she wanted to find out which of the Gods conspired with Guinevere. If Gwawl was interested in Nemue, she concluded he probably was the one in contact with the Queen. She was sure a God had instructed Guinevere in the use of the chalice. For no human, unless pure in heart, could touch the object for more than a moment without experiencing terrible pain. 'I wish to bring to the council's attention, one of us that we have seen fit to abandon. I wish to appeal again for his reinstatement,' Vivienne suddenly announced.

'It's too late for his reinstatement. However I too am a mother, so I understand your anguish. I plea to all those assembled, for his past crimes to be exonerated.'

If the lady was shocked be Rhiannon's sudden announcement, she nevertheless quickly accepted it. 'I am moved by Rhiannon's words and accept her kind offer, but will you not welcome him back to our lands?'

'He is better suited to remain with the humans,' stated Pwyll.

*

Olwen and Eberth were last to ascend from the boats onto the island. The fearful girl bit her lip so bad that it began to bleed. 'I hope my father's mind is intact, for the noise alone would drive you mad,' she complained.

Eberth bowed his head in agreement and used his hands to communicate to the lady to take hold of his shirt and not to let go of it for a moment. The lady was glad to agree to his order.

The large Pict was tall and strong, his frame actually lifted the girl off her feet and into mid-air. She was quite safe though, for no man or ghost was going to hurt her as long as the loyal Eberth had his strong arms around her frame.

The island was just as Gaheris had remembered it, sinister, gloomy and full of pitiful sounds of torment. The other men all looked terrified, even the brave Perceval, but King Lot's son was steadfast in his resolve. 'Follow me and do not look at the ghastly sights around you.'

'Are you sure these phantoms cannot hurt us?' asked Perceval.

'I'm sure, as long as we close our minds to their despondency and darkness.'

The men all ran behind Gaheris, who never faltered in his approach towards the desolate castle. His strides were bold and his sword was drawn ready for action. The men had one or two encounters with the ghostly spirits of the island, but they did not succumb to temptation and managed to keep pace with their leader. Eberth and his charge made up the rear.

Gaheris reached the castle gate to find the drawbridge up and their entry blocked. This was a blow, but it was quickly remedied by the athleticism of the agile Perceval. He climbed the outer wall like a monkey, springing from one foothold to another and from one handhold to the next. Everyone stood and watched, hardly able to believe what they saw with their own eyes.

'Where did he learn to climb like that?' whispered Gaheris to the others.

'I think he's half man, half ape,' answered John.

Within a short space of time the young man had reached the battlement and disappeared from sight. A short time later the drawbridge opened and the men entered. What they found was pretty much what Arthur and Gaheris had found a year earlier.

The place was littered with debris, cobwebs and the musty smell of death. Gaheris led his men to the largest room in the castle where he had found Ysbaddaden before. He entered the room full of hope, only to be disappointed when he found the place empty. The man had not counted on this and for a moment he looked lost, but quickly regained his wits and gave orders for his men to pair up and search every room in the castle. He was paired with John and they climbed the ragged stone stairs to the rooms above. These rooms he conceived would have been bedrooms in the distant past, but now they lay crumbling wrecks. Damp pieces of mould gathered at windows and in between the stones, to give the place an earthy look. It was as if the place was growing from within, becoming a part of the wildness around it.

Rooms were occupied by what Gaheris had called phantoms; ghost-like creatures that were white in appearance, but incandescent in substance. He believed these beings were the lost souls of men and women who had somehow wronged the Gods. Their punishment he perceived was to roam the abandoned island in torment.

John, after encountering such a creature, swung his sword in its direction only to hear the blade swish through the air and the creature to dissipate before his eyes. Gaheris told him to save his energy, as he might need it, fearing the Gods might come upon them at anytime. They climbed up eventually to the towers and to the smallest rooms in the castle.

There were four towers in all, small, cramped and isolated compartments all in better repair than anywhere else. Gaheris whispered to John to be quiet as both men listened for any sound. The distant echoes of phantoms could be heard, but there was a closer sound too. Gaheris swore he heard the breathing of a human being.

With his sword drawn, Gaheris entered the room first. He was in for a surprise for instead of the giant, a small boy lay asleep in the corner nearest to the window. A slit of light shone down upon his face from the opening, making his features clear to the eye. He was young, no more than twelve, his face was sharp, his bones almost issuing out from his cheek. His breath could be heard quite clearly, it was low but powerful.

Gaheris approached the boy and without ceremony shook him out of his slumber. The boy's eyes blinked, before he stared back at the two men standing before him. The boy spoke in the plain clear language of the Romans. His Latin was spoken in perfect diction. 'Who the devil awakens me?'

The boy scratched his head, but before he could close his eyes again Gaheris had taken hold of him and raised him to his feet. 'Where is the giant?'

The boy, still a little sleepy, said he was gone.

'Gone where? Gaheris asked.

'They took him...'

'Who took him?'

The boy tried to break free from Gaheris's grip, but without success. 'Let me go,' he shouted. 'I'm tired, I want to go back to sleep.'

'You can sleep all you want after you tell where Ysbaddaden is.'

'I told you they took him. The Gods needed him for something so they came and took him away.'

'Where did they take him?'

The boy shrugged. 'To their land I suppose.'

'But he couldn't walk, his legs were broken.'

'They must have fixed his legs somehow, for I saw him walking quite freely.'

'Did he not protest, put up a fight?'

'No, he seemed happy, well who wouldn't be to get off this island.'

John approached. 'Who are you, boy?' he demanded.

With a look of defiance the boy gave his name as Abdur.

Gaheris stood thinking, while John studied the boy's expensive attire.

Abdur wore the dress of an Eastern dignitary, with his colourful silk gown, soft shoes and strange pointed headgear. The men had travelled to many places, including lands as far as Persia, where they had encountered similar types of garments. It was the shape of the boy's eyes that startled the Celts and not his mode of dress. His eyes were elongated in shape and quite different from anything they had ever encountered before.

Gaheris, after his contemplation, looked at the boy with interest. 'You do not come from this part of the world. So why are you here?'

Abdur sighed. 'It isn't for the company that's for sure.'

'You must be a prisoner. What do the Gods want with a boy such as you?'

'I have nothing except the clothes on my back, but my father is...'

Gaheris waited patiently, but the boy was reluctant to give the name of his father away.

'Is your father about to pay a random for your safe return?' John asked.

Abdur said yes, but with little conviction.

Gaheris kneeled down to be at the same level as the boy. 'We came to rescue the giant, but since that is not possible we can rescue you instead.'

Abdur put his hand up to his mouth. 'Did I say I wanted to be rescued?'

'You like it here, with all the noise and the strange creatures...'

'No, but they made it clear that they would punish me if I tried to escape.'

'They can't punish you, if they can't find you,' stated Gaheris.

The boy agreed that was so.

Perceval entered the tower, to report that the men had found nothing. 'What have you found though, is it human or something more exotic?'

The boy turned his body to stare at Perceval. 'You should address me as Prince Abdur. You should all address me in this way.'

Perceval laughed. 'I think I'll call you little toad.'

Abdur looked mystified. 'What is this thing, a toad?'

'It is a slimy beast with big sad eyes that jumps about our waters.'

The boy did not understand, but cursed Perceval for his insolence.

Gaheris addressed his men and spoke in Common Celtic. 'The boy is coming with us. We are leaving this foul place to go in search of Ysbaddaden...'

Abdur interrupted his statement. 'Please speak in a civilised tongue. I can not understand your barbaric language.'

Perceval looked at the boy. 'It would appear our little toad is in need of some manners.'

'We don't know what island Ysbaddaden will be on,' John commented.

Gaheris agreed but said they would try them all if need be.

John stared at Gaheris. 'The lady will be disappointed.'

'Yes indeed. I will be looking for you to agree with me when we see the lady.'

John's face looked blank. 'Of course we are all in your hands.'

'This island was not guarded, but the others will be...'

'If you mean to forbid Olwen to go any further you have my support,' stated John.

'I wish her to return with the boy to the mainland.'

'I am not going anywhere with any girl,' Abdur complained.

'You do as you are told, toad,' cried Perceval.

'I might just stay right where I am.'

'You'll do that. We'll send up a couple of ghosts to keep you company.'

Gaheris addressed Perceval. 'He's coming with us. I'm not leaving him here.'

'You're the commander, whatever you say.'

Chapter 4

The local prefect, stationed at Westcheap was a man revered for his tenacity and good sense, by the name Leogran. He listened to everything that Castor had to tell him with a certain degree of suspicion.

The lady, now called Penelope, felt uneasy, for the man's eyes never wavered from hers the whole interview. She wondered if he recognised her and sat in a constant state of fear of exposure.

Leogran got to his feet and began to walk around the room. To the surprise of his visitors the man seemed uninterested in the whole affair. 'I'm not sure what you expect me to do? I have not enough men to enforce the law as it is, yet you bother me with trivialities like this.'

Castor left his seat and followed the man. 'I can assure you it is not a trivial matter for the lady,' he advised.

The prefect turned and walked up to Penelope. 'You do not speak, why is that? Do you have nothing to say? Or are you frightened in case there is something in your past that you might deliberately want to keep hidden?'

'That is outrageous,' cried Castor. 'You can not talk to a lady like that.'

The lawman looked at Castor. 'A lady you say. Where is your proof, by your own admission you know nothing about the woman.'

'I know a lady when I see one.'

Finally Penelope spoke. 'It was not my idea to come here today, but I came because this kind man wanted me to. It now occurs to me that I can not live off his generosity forever. I must make my way in the world and that is perhaps where you can help.'

The lawman looked interested. 'Go on.'

'You say you have not enough staff, perhaps you could find me a job here.'

Castor butted in. 'You can not work for such a man, I will not allow it.'

Penelope smiled at her benefactor. After pacing up and down, Leogran laughed. 'Just what can you do, my lady?'

'Oh, you might be surprised. For instance I can speak several languages, such as your own Saxon tongue, Goidelic, and even Roman Latin. This might be useful when it comes to dealing with the many different peoples that frequent this town.'

This was a good point. Lundonia although not populated as it once was, was still a metropolis that many different peoples frequented. This increased the chances for crime, that and the fact that it was also on a busy river. The lady could indeed be of great help, but the law enforcer was still suspicious.

'Huh! Not a lady he says. When has the peasantry learnt to speak Latin?' Castor proposed.

'Indeed. How is it you can remember languages, but nothing from your own past? It seems rather a convenient loss of memory to me.'

'I will not allow you to continue to insult this lady,' shouted Castor.

Penelope managed to calm the man down and did not seem to take offense at the remark. 'If I knew the workings of my own memory then I would not be in the predicament I am.'

'If I have insulted you in any way, I apologise. In my work I tend to see the worst in people...'

'That is not an excuse,' muttered Castor.

'I will have to think about your proposition, my lady. In the meantime I will make some inquires, although you have given me little in the way of details to make of a search. Still I will do what I can.'

Penelope seemed satisfied, although her companion was not. 'Just remember sir, we pay the King's taxes to ensure you do your duty.'

'I do not have to be reminded of that I assure you.'

'When shall I call again?' inquired Penelope.

'Leave it for a few days.'

The lady thanked him while Castor grunted a sort of acknowledgement as they were both shown out of the building by a clerk.

*

Elaine was accepted into the Queen's service, although not as a lady in waiting, but as a simple drudge of a kitchen maid. Much to her dismay she found herself cleaning kitchen utensils and being at the mercy of everyone in the household. She could not venture anywhere near the quarters of the nobility let alone anywhere near the Queen. She was so tired by the end of the first day that she nearly collapsed from exhaustion. Finally as the day came to an end she was allocated an area in the kitchen to sleep and given a blanket. As she curled up, she was determined not to sleep, but the lady was too tired and drifted off.

Elaine was awakened by the snoring of one of the other servants and realized her time for exploration was upon her. She got to her feet and sneaked out of the kitchen without awakening anyone. She climbed the stairs timidly, hoping no one would see her, for she dreaded being caught by the guards. With her nimble feet and quick eye, she managed to avoid detention. Finally she reached the corridor that belonged exclusively to the Queen and her friends. This had four guards, two at either end. 'How am I to get past them?' she mumbled to herself.

The lady had forgotten she had powers. She was nervous at the thought that her magic could hurt innocents. Still if she was to be any good at being a spy she would have to learn the art of deception. She closed her eyes and wished that all four guards would simply fall asleep. After concentrating for a short time the lady opened her eyes again and looked down the long corridor. What she saw confounded her, for all four guards were curled up on the stone floor fast asleep. Her pathway now free, the lady tiptoed along the passage listening for any sound from within the rooms.

One room after another Elaine heard no sound, until she heard the powerful refrain of the Queen herself. Guinevere was shouting angrily at someone within her room. Elaine then heard Lancelot's angry voice bellow. It had a cutting intonation to it, sharp and powerful. 'Now you tell me,' he cried. 'You wait till we are married to inform me you will not sleep with me.'

There was a moment's silence, before Elaine heard the most chilling laugh she had ever heard. Guinevere had obviously found Lancelot's statement amusing for she seemed to convulse into hysterics. Her laughter put a shiver down Elaine's back and she wondered how the man would react to it.

It was the Queen who spoke first though and her tone was dismissive, full of contempt. 'You fool. I thought everyone in the land knew of my preference.'

There was an eerie quiet as Lancelot seemed to be contemplating how to react to Guinevere's information. The pause frustrated Elaine and while she waited a sudden thought occurred to her. What if she could see beyond doors and walls? She stared through the thick wooden door and into the bedchamber itself. What she saw was Lancelot and Guinevere in close proximity, wielding a sword a piece at each other. This was not what she expected, but a sense of glee entered her slender body. Revenge might be nearer than she thought. This very night perhaps without interference the lady's two foes might well destroy each other. Through her new found power of magic she was able to see the whole play unfold.

Lancelot's face was red with rage, while the Queen looked in total command of her senses. She had her chin a little in the air, a gesture of defiance and resolution. Lancelot was filled with jealousy, for the Queen had refused his entry to her bed. There was a red drape covering the front of it, acting as a canopy withholding an occupant's identity perhaps.

The man could not see into it, but he suspected a man was in his place. Lancelot was now beside himself with rage. 'Who have you got in your bed, wench?' he demanded.

'Do not treat me like one of your common whores. I am your Queen so address me as such.'

'I will address you as I please.'

With a sneer upon her face, Guinevere's sword was raised a little and barred the man from passing her. Lancelot also placed his sword nearer to the Queen's. There was an impasse. Lancelot looked past the Queen to the unknown occupant on the bed and his temper snapped. With a sudden cry he yelled his abuse and clashed his sword against Guinevere's. To Elaine's surprise the Queen did not give in, but swung her sword against Lancelot's in return. Both parties then engaged in a sword fight that lasted some time, but ended when Lancelot finally forced the lady's sword from her grasp.

Pushing his way past the Queen the man grabbed hold of the occupant around the arms and forced them forward into the light. What the man saw was not what he expected, for it was not a man at all, but a terrified young woman of about sixteen. The lady grabbed hold of a bedcover to hide her nakedness, but her form was now indelibly stamped upon the man's mind. He turned his head and stared at Guinevere. The look on his face terrified Elaine, but it did not have the same effect on the Queen. She had the same look of defiance she had earlier and perhaps a look of victory too.

Elaine waited for Lancelot to run Guinevere through, but he seemed rooted to the spot, his head full of doubts and questions.

'You depraved woman,' he finally uttered.

The Queen, to the man's disbelief, came to her own defence. 'How dare you seek to judge me,' she spat. 'You who have countless songs sung of your many conquests and no doubt you have countless bastards the length and breadth of the country?'

Guinevere moved towards Lancelot and as the man stood staring, she turned her face to look upon the frightened girl huddled in a corner. 'Let me introduce the Lady Megan, she is young and sweet tempered.'

Lancelot was not in the mood for such posturing and pushed his way past Guinevere towards the door. In a panic, Elaine ran from behind it towards an inlet nearby. She was fortunate that the man did not see her, but Lancelot's mind was so confused at that moment that probably he would have missed her if she was standing right in front of him.

With Lancelot gone, Elaine thought to make her escape. Just as she was about to step out into the corridor the figure of the frightened Megan exited the Queen's room. Guinevere kissed the girl on the forehead and whispered something, probably of a conciliatory nature, and the girl scurried away down the aisle.

It suddenly dawned on the Queen that none of her guards were in attendance so she wandered down the passageway in the opposite direction from the girl. Guinevere came within a few paces of Elaine before stopping and turning her head to peer into the crevice. Even in the dimness of the light, Guinevere recognised the lady standing just a few paces away from her.

'Is it really you? You've come back to me...but they told me you were dead.' Guinevere gasped for breath. 'Are you real or are you just an apparition?' she inquired.

Now caught, Elaine took a pace forward into the light. She was amazed to see the Queen's reactions to her. Guinevere's eyes shone like stars as she smiled on the face of the woman she knew as Polyxena. 'You are real, tell me you are real.'

'I am real, my Queen.'

Guinevere embraced the young woman and held her close.

The whole encounter felt bizarre to Elaine, as her mind and her body experienced conflicting emotions. Something about Guinevere's touch disturbed her but was strangely familiar. It was at this first encounter that the notion first hit Elaine that there was something of Polyxena still remaining within her body. Confused, she did not know what to do or what to say, but luckily the Queen took her by the hand and led her away.

Looking a touch afraid, Elaine studied the Queen and did not utter a word. Guinevere took her silence as some sort of censure and thought to reassure her. 'You saw the girl?' the Queen queried.

Elaine nodded.

Guinevere smiled, but beneath the smile was a hint of fear. 'She means nothing to me. You know I never sleep, it's my way of getting through the night.'

A thoughtful Elaine remained steadfast in her stare.

'Tell me what happened?' asked an impatient Queen.

Having no idea how Polyxena had died, Elaine was lost for words for the moment. She thought to change the subject. 'You did not wait long to replace Arthur,' she commented.

'Politics is an ugly matter. I had no choice but to marry the man.'

'He forced you?'

'Don't be so naive. No one forces me to do anything.'

'But he means nothing to you.'

'He means less than nothing to me. He doesn't know it yet, but his days of playing King will soon be over.'

'You have no more use for him then?'

'He has served his purpose, but his men I still need.'

'Surely you have everything now, what more do you wish for?'

Guinevere could not contain her feelings and whispered in Elaine's ear. 'Forget about politics, forget about Lancelot, and forget about the girl. Just hold me close and tell me you still love me.'

Elaine should have felt revulsion, but the touch of the woman far from being repugnant actually excited her. These strange feelings made her feel panic and she pushed the Queen away from her. Still fearful to speak, she retreated to a corner of the room where she found a trunk to sit down upon.

Guinevere took her time before coming over to her. She inquired again as to what happened to the young woman, but again she got no answer. 'I made enquires the length and breadth of our lands, but the only story I heard was of your execution in Carthage. Why were you in such a place? I did not expect you to follow the man across oceans.'

Elaine had no answer of course, for she could not know to what the Queen was referring. If she was clever though, perhaps she could discover what plan Guinevere had given to her spy.

'I followed your instructions just like a good servant should...'

Guinevere sat next to Elaine on the trunk. 'You hurt me when you speak so. We are equals, my love. My wealth and power is also your wealth and power.'

'So you tried to find me?'

'Of course I did. I sent out spies everywhere and one such spy swore they saw you hang in a square in Carthage. Is this not so? Did you not suffer from such a fate?'

There was no way of knowing if the lady did in fact die by hanging, but it was soon established that she did. Guinevere placed her right hand upon the lady's neck and gave a shriek of horror. 'Oh no, my love I see it quite clearly, the red around your neck.'

Elaine touched her own throat and felt a slight imperfection. It had never occurred to her that this was the reason for the lady's death.

'I will make it up to you I promise,' said the Queen.

'If I were to ask you for something would you agree to it?'

Guinevere was passionate she would.

'When the time comes to do without his services, will you give Lancelot to me?'

Guinevere studied the woman before her. She had no idea what the lady might want with Lancelot. Fearing that she might have feelings for him, she was reluctant to give into her whim.

'What do you want with him?'

Elaine spoke calmly. 'Do you believe in vengeance?'

'You know fine well I do.'

'Then you will understand that the man has to answer for his crimes.'

'If he has committed a crime against you, I shall gouge out his eyes for you.'

The strange brew of love and hate stung Elaine. She wondered why Guinevere could process two such conflicting passions. It was clear whatever love she had in her bosom was directed at one being only and that being was called Polyxena. Elaine at this moment in time was this woman, and so the recipient of the Queen's love. It seemed a pity not to make the most of the situation. Who knows what secrets she might find out? It might mean getting unbearably close to the lady and that might be hateful. The information she might receive could bring about the destruction of the Queen and put her sister on the throne in her stead. Still how far was she prepared to go to bring about the lady's downfall?

'You mean to kill Lancelot?' asked a curious Guinevere.

She hadn't thought about it in such cold blooded terms, but if he was guilty of hideous crimes then yes, she wanted him dead.

'Will you do this for me?'

Guinevere smiled. 'You have my word, he is yours to dispose of as you see fit.'

'Thank you.'

'You must tell me everything that happened?'

Elaine agreed she would, but said she was tired.

'You must rest. Here take my bed it...'

Elaine shook her head.

The Queen realized the suggestion was in poor taste and laid out the divan instead. This was pulled out from a wall and made a comfortable substitute bed. With a cover placed over her, Elaine tried to sleep while the Queen continued to look upon her from a nearby chair. Elaine tried to comprehend just what had occurred. Within a short piece of time, she had gone from the lowest person in Caerleon to the second most important.

Chapter 5

At last it was time to eat thought Eros, for a beam of light entered into the chamber and the sound of movement suggested that the servants were about their business. But still he waited, what seemed like an age, before someone came upon him.

Eros sat at the biggest table in the great hall and demanded something to eat the moment a steward appeared. The poor steward, a stout man called Gerald told his mistress what was on offer for the morning meal. The lady was not impressed and began to rhyme off her demands. 'I'll take everything you just mentioned, but I wish to taste the meat of the partridge, and that of the chicken, oh and also that of the boar...'

Gerald suggested leaving both the boar and the partridge until later in the day, for he insisted these dishes were never meant for consumption in the morning. Eros was having none of that. In a tone the poor steward had never heard from the lady before, Eros insisted on large potions of everything. Gerald agreed to bring them, but muttered profanities as he left her to go down to the kitchens.

An impatient Eros, stamped his hand down on the table several times, before Gerald and two other servants arrived with the provisions. They brought from the kitchen the pheasant meant for the evening meal, along with two chickens, the legs of the boar, some sweetmeats, bread, oats, milk, and some wine. This last item was the latest demand from Eros and one that Gerald brought reluctantly. He and the other servants laid all this in front of his mistress and waited for her reaction.

Eros clasped his hands together and his mouth began to water in anticipation. He tackled the pheasant first. He looked up at Gerald. 'How do I eat it?' he asked.

More confused than ever, the man mimicked the breaking of the meat with his hands. Eros was still unsure, so the man used his own fingers to prize apart the meat. He gave a large piece of it into Eros's hands and who then placed into his open mouth. The portion of meat rather entered and fell down the lady's gullet like a rock falling down a cliff. Without digesting the item the meat lodged half-way down the lady's throat.

Gerald came to her assistance immediately as she began to choke. Using his many years of experience he went to the lady's back and put his arms around her stomach. He then lifted Eros to his feet and tried to wrench the stuck portion up and out of his mouth. By this time Eros's face had turned a crimson colour as he gagged for all his worth. At last, after several attempts the man made Eros spit out the defending matter onto the floor. Eros coughed and coughed and Gerald sighed in relief. It was then the Lady Ygerne entered with Morgause to witness the extraordinary scene.

'My goodness, what has happened?' she asked.

The steward was quick to reassure her. 'Everything is fine my lady, a piece of meat got stuck in Lady Elaine's mouth that is all.'

Lady Ygerne came to help her daughter and comfort her. 'I must say it looked rather worse than that. I thought for a moment you were about to die again.'

Catching his breath Eros agreed with the lady.

Morgause looked at the feast assembled on the table and was less conciliatory. 'Feeling hungry this morning I see?' she suggested to Elaine.

With his face returned to its normal colour, Eros's ignorance showed in his reply. 'I was feeling a little bit hungry this morning.'

Morgause opened her eyes wide. 'You are acting rather strange.'

Lady Ygerne remained concerned. 'Why don't you stick to your normal meal in the morning of oats and milk?' Looking lost Eros agreed. He scoured the table looking for the items mentioned. It was her mother who personally served her daughter. 'You look a little pale, my dear. Perhaps you should stay in your room today?'

'No,' screeched an animated Eros. 'I can not be locked up in this castle a moment longer.'

Morgause sat down to her meal, looked across the table at her sister and asked her not to shout. 'You must venture forth sometime I guess. Why don't we go for a walk after breakfast?'

Eros nodded his head and took his first taste of food. The milk helped to slide the oatmeal down his throat and to his amazement it tasted good. There was something peculiar about the sensation. He licked his lips of some milk, before pouring more onto his plate. His timid first encounter over, the pixie was ready to try lots more. After his third helping, Lady Ygerne interfered. 'You better stop or you won't be able to move, let alone walk anywhere.'

As he left the table with Morgause, Eros was already thinking of his next meal. He turned his head as the sight of pheasant and other meats vanished from his view. 'Shouldn't we take some food with us?' Eros inquired of Morgause.

'What! You're not still hungry?'

The pixie assured her that he was.

Morgause sighed. 'Well I suppose we could take a basket and venture a little further afield.'

'Yes,' agreed a jubilant Eros.

'Okay, but not too far,' Lady Ygerne warned.

'We'll stay away from crowds,' promised Morgause.

Morgause and Eros walked around the castle, before taking a path that led to a nice old well, next to a stream. Suddenly the lady hesitated as she realized what she had done. She tried to retrace her step, but Eros was enchanted with the location and would not budge.

'There are nicer places a little further,' said Morgause.

'I like it here. I find this lovely and peaceful. Shall we have our food now?'

Morgause reluctantly agreed. She took out the assortment of meats and laid them out on a large cloth. No sooner had she finished, that a ravenous Eros began to gorge his face again.

'Take your time. You'll make yourself sick otherwise.'

A smiling Eros seemed unconcerned and drank some wine to wash down his gluttonous extravagance.

'I don't know why you look so pleased with yourself, I'm sure you're going to suffer for your behaviour.'

Eros suddenly looked worried. 'Am I behaving strangely?' he asked.

'Extremely so, but then again everyone in this family behaves strangely. Why should you be any different?'

The sun came and went thanks to the disturbance of the clouds, while the leaves silently fell all around them. It was as peaceful and serene a scene that anyone could possibly wish for and yet there was an atmosphere between the two sisters. These tensions Eros immediately picked up upon and after breaking wind for the fourth time inquired as to why the lady was so pensive. 'Do you miss your husband?'

Morgause looked annoyed at her sister's question. 'It might seem strange to say so, but I do.'

'Is it the sex you miss?' Eros inquired.

Taken back with the candour of the question she opened her mouth, but couldn't find the words to reply.

'I would like to know what it is like to copulate.'

Morgause almost choked, as she tried to reconcile this new Elaine with the one she had grown up with. 'What do you mean? What has happened to the nice innocent sister that I know so well?'

'I am still the same, but because of my strange experience I feel I must start enjoying the pleasures of life.'

Morgause reached over and took a leg of chicken away from her sister. 'You can not stuff anymore into that stomach of yours without it bursting.'

Eros did not protest, but asked his impertinent question again.

'You are in strange frame of mind. Have you been messing about with Morgan's herbs?'

From the look on Eros's face, Morgause realised she did not comprehend her question. 'Why are you interested...I mean did you not have relations with Lancelot?'

The fairy knew the answer to that question, because he had inquired about it with Lady Elaine. She had told him the question would not come up, but he was curious of all human activity so the lady told him the truth, that she had never had sex with anyone.

'You are old enough to experience such an event, surely someone wanted to...'

Eros shook his head. 'Is it pleasant?' he queried.

Morgause said it depended on certain things.

'Depending on what things?'

'Oh, whether you love the person or not, whether you are attractive...'

'Your husband is very...'

'Very what?' inquired Morgause abruptly.

'Manly, I suppose is the word. Does he not hurt you?'

'He is a bit of a brute, but he can be surprisingly tender.'

'So that is what I should be looking for, someone who is tender and a bit of a brute?'

Morgause went red in the face and tried not to laugh. 'I think it's time we found you a husband.'

'Good. Can you do that before seven days passes?'

'What is wrong with you?'

Eros lent forward and whispered something in Morgause's ear. The lady looked shocked, but after a few moments she began to laugh.

'Who is this woman lying beside me? I do not recognize you. Please tell me I misheard what you said.'

'I think I would like someone to...before it is too late.'

'Is this because you died or nearly died...oh God help me here, this must be some strange dream.'

'Can you tell me, where I might go to experience such an encounter?'

'You expect me to know of such places? '

There was just a hint of cognition from Morgause that alerted the fairy.

'I promise I will go there myself and will not tell a living soul.'

'You tell everybody everything. It's just your nature.'

Eros broke wind again, but this time the colour in his cheeks changed. A sudden greyness came over them. A second and a third burp followed, before a huge amount of substance exited his mouth and spilled out onto the cloth.

'I did try to warn you,' pleaded Morgause.

Eros thought he was finished now and that the awful pain in his stomach would ease, but two more bouts flared up and this time an even greater amount of sick fired out over Morgause who had come closer.

'That's great, we both stink of it now,' Morgause complained.

'Oh, I will succumb,' Eros moaned. 'What is happening to me?'

'You ate like a pig and now you stink like one.'

'I will never eat again, never.'

'I feel that way about wine sometimes, but I always seem to return to, as if to punish myself.'

'Is that why people eat, to punish themselves?'

*

King Lot and Lady Morgan arrived at King Ursien's castle to be greeted with a great deal of pomp and ceremony. Lot was pacing up and down in a bedchamber, muttering to himself and glancing over at Morgan who was placing a wet poultice on Lady Helena's forehead. 'We can not stay here,' he declared.

Helena closed her eyes and seemed to drift off to sleep, while Morgan turned to face her brother-in-law. 'She needs to rest,' she whispered. 'Besides, has not the King made us extremely welcome?'

Lot grunted a reply.

'Gawain and his scouts have every entrance covered. No one can come upon us without warning.'

Lot started his pacing again.

'Do try and calm yourself,' Morgan advised the man.

'Why would Ursien suddenly become our friend? I don't like it. He's always been too frightened of Guinevere to risk her anger.'

'He won't betray us.'

'How can you be sure?'

Lot stopped his pacing and came over to where Morgan was sitting. He sat beside her. 'Don't tell me you have made some deal with the man?'

'I have, but don't look so worried. I've decided to form a partnership with him.'

Lot voice dropped to a whisper. 'You can not trust him my lady, he is as devious as a fox.'

'After what happened at the execution even I can see why the Queen has to be stopped.'

The man looked at Morgan and gave a huge sigh. 'So he has joined our ranks?' Does that mean he will fight with us against the Queen?'

'He will join us yes. First he wants some assurances.'

'What kind of assurances?'

'Oh the usual kind, he wants more than his fair share and...'

'And...Go on?'

'There is one thing he wants more than anything else.'

Lot shook his head before flooding the air with obscenities. 'I'll kill him first,' he ranted.

Morgan took hold of the man and made him calm down. 'This is my decision.'

'Has someone forced you?' the man demanded to know.

'Circumstances have forced me,' replied Morgan.

'I don't understand?'

'I have accepted his offer of marriage.'

'You must be mad.'

'We need his forces if we are to defeat Guinevere.'

Lot mulled over Morgan's announcement before continuing to disagree. 'We do not need him my lady, we can...'

'It is done now. I will do my duty by him but nothing more. In return all his men will be at my command.'

A startled King Lot saw the lady's resolution. 'You mean to declare war on the Queen?'

*

Cadfan, a clerk in Leogran's office, made his startling report to his superior.

'You are sure this is the same woman that two days ago was standing in my office?' asked Leogran.

'Yes sir, I have been most thorough. We have been interested in this woman for a long time. She is something of a magician when it comes to avoiding our custody. Even now we have no real proof against her, only unsubstantiated accusations.'

'I knew there was something wrong the moment I set eyes on her. Now why would this woman want a job with us? I have half-a mind to give her what she wants, and maybe that way we can catch her at whatever game she is playing.'

'You expect her sometime today?' asked Cadfan.

'Yes. Let her think we do not know who she is. That way her guard will be down. I will offer her a job, a job that you will supervise at all times.'

Cadfan bowed his head.

A short time later the prefect was interrupted by the arrival of Penelope who was escorted into his room. The lady came alone which pleased Leogran and made it easier for him to relax and tell the lady his lies.

After being given a seat, Penelope asked the man if had found anything out about her. The law enforcer told her that he had made no progress regarding her background.

'So no one is missing me or looking for me?' the lady asked.

'If someone is looking for you, he or she, has not come to any of the judicial bodies in Lundonia or surrounding area to inquire after you.'

This was indeed true. No reports of a missing woman fitting Penelope's description had been reported. The woman was rather relieved at hearing this, she dreaded coming across some stranger who claimed to know her. It was good to be able to feel free, unhindered by the past and only interested in the future.

'Have you considered my request?' Penelope inquired. The man was shrewd enough not to appear too keen. 'I have, but I'm not sure you realize what the job would entail.'

'I am intelligent and willing to learn.'

'I will be scrutinizing everything you do.'

'If I can not do the job then you can always dispense with my services.'

Leogran was pleased to have roped in his prey, now he would have to wait before reeling her in and hopefully all her associates along with her.

Chapter 6

Perceval regained his breath and marvelled at the beautiful surroundings before offering his help to Gaheris. The man pulled his compatriot to his feet as they both stood in awe of the place that the lady of the lake called home. The air had a strong sweet aroma to it and the water splashed delicately upon the grassy banks. It was the sound that alarmed them for it had a strange whining timbre that seemed to gain in intensity. 'What is that?' asked Perceval.

'Damned if I know.'

The noise seemed to gather, as if some hive of insects had suddenly engulfed them. It was only when Gaheris reached out his hand that the man realized that tiny beings were in front of his eyes. The whining continued unabated until as by some magic it suddenly dulled and moved away. Perceval like his friend saw something extremely small fly into his view. He also reached out his hand but was startled when a voice fired a salvo of abuse at him.

'Careful you stupid fool. Do you want to break my wings?'

The voice was childlike, with a higher than normal human pitch. The men both heard the statement and almost fell to the ground in shock. Both men were unable to stop staring at the single tiny creature before them.

'You are not real,' declared Gaheris woefully.

The creature fired more abuse at him. 'Not real he says. I have been around a lot longer than you have, my clumsy human.'

'Then who or what are you?' Gaheris asked.

'More insults. I am a Queen…and this is my domain.'

'Ah, but I know who lives here, my tiny friend.'

'I take it you have come looking for the lady of the lake, but I have lived here a lot longer than she.'

'Do you have a name?' inquired Perceval.

'Of course I have. 'Do you?"

'My name is Perceval and my friend's name is Gaheris.'

'Gaheris...you say. I know this name...you are a relative of Lady Morgan?'

'I am...but you have not told us your name.'

'It is Sybil. What do you want?'

'Where is the lady of the lake?' asked Gaheris. 'We need to speak with her.'

'You should not have come here unannounced, the lady will be annoyed.'

'Is she not here?' queried Perceval.

'She is never away from this place long, I expect her back soon.'

The whining increased again as more fairies surrounded the humans as their curiosity got the better of them. The noise was deafening and only eased when the lady of the lake suddenly emancipated herself from the lake. She did not look pleased as she saw two human males standing talking with her fairies. 'Who dares to invade my sanctuary?' the lady shouted.

'It is Gaheris, lady, forgive us for coming unannounced.'

The lady had missed one full day of peace and quiet in her lovely waters so as to help these pitiful humans yet here they were in her home without permission. The lady wanted to punish them for their unforgivable intrusion. 'You should not have come here.'

'I am sorry my lady, but Ysbaddeden is no longer on the island of the dead.'

'I see, so you thought I would be able to tell you where he is?'

'All we know is that the Gods took him away...but we do not know where.'

The lady pondered. She addressed Gaheris. 'Come with me for a swim, you can leave your friend with Sybil.'

The man did what he was asked. The two very different beings swam in the magical pool in close proximity to each other. A sudden sense of calm and wellbeing came over Gaheris in that swim. By the time it was over both beings felt different from the experience. The lady saw how the water had relaxed the man and was happy to converse with him finally. They paddled together away from the noisy flying pixies.

'I do not know where he is, but we shall look in the pool to find out.'

Gaheris saw exactly what the lady saw. He recognised Mider as he appeared on the island to visit Ysbaddeden in the castle. Mider placed his hand upon the giant's legs and within a few moments the giant rose to his feet and began to walk about the room. The look of joy on Ysbaddeden's face warmed the man's heart. He remembered how forlorn the giant had been and how sad, but now it appeared the Gods were giving the large man back his life. With a wave of the lady's hand, she made the water ripple away one scene for another. This time the giant was working deep down in a cave, shifting through mountains of dirt. He was creating a long narrow passage that rose upwards from the burrows of the earth to the ground above him. The job he was doing would have taken thirty or forty men to do in the same time frame. The only reassuring aspect of this picture was that Ysbaddeden was still looking content. He worked away without resting, but with a smile on his face.

Once the picture had vanished Gaheris asked the lady the question. 'Do you know where this place is? Can we rescue him there?'

The lady was unhelpful. 'Yes I know where they are keeping him, but I will not help you in this matter.'

'Why won't you tell us?' pleaded Gaheris.

'Do not be insolent. I can not help you at the moment, but maybe...'

'Is he being held against his will?' the man asked.

'In a manner of speaking perhaps, but again it could be that he has made a bargain with the Gods.'

'What kind of bargain?'

'I cannot say, but he does not look to be unhappy.'

'You refuse to tell us where this place is?'

'All I can do is plea for his early release. Will that appease you?'

'What work is he doing?'

'You ask too many questions, human. Leave me now and if I learn anything else I will pass the information on through Nemue.'

The lady signalled to Sybil, who flew over to her. They conversed in their own language before the fairy guided Gaheris and Perceval away from the island.

*

Elaine, posing as Polyxena, within a few days had transformed herself completely. She had become a successful spy and had gained the confidence of the most powerful woman in the land. She was now in a position to pass on valuable information to her sister, concerning the Queen's future plans. Elaine was on her way to King Ursien's castle in Gore, to tell Lady Morgan of her new position and to offer her services as a double spy.

The journey from Caerleon, through the Bedegraine forest was uneventful but slow. It took her two days before she entered the outer wall of Ursien's castle. She was excited about the prospect of being able to help her sister, but there was a problem. With her face changed would she be granted an audience?

The lady was there officially as the Queen's spy, and Gruffydd was already in position to keep an eye on the household. Gruffydd had done his part, by assuring her a role as a lady's maid. In fact he did so well that Polyxena was assigned to look after the sickly Lady Helena. On the first day of her service she entered the lady's bedchamber, to see Morgan bathing her lady's forehead. Unfortunately her sister had others around her. Surrounding the sick bed were her sister's servant Yvain, King Lot, Gawain and another she did not know(Titius) all crammed into the confined space.

The people in the room were her family and friends and yet she hesitated to speak her mind. It would be difficult enough to convince one person, let alone four of her true identity. So she would have to somehow get people to leave the room of their own free will.

All the occupants of the room appeared suspicious of the new maid, none more so than Lady Morgan. 'Who are you?' she inquired as Polyxena approached the bed.

'I am the new maid,' Elaine announced.

'What happened to the last one?' inquired King Lot.

'I'm sure I couldn't say.'

The new servant's voice further aroused suspicion. This young woman spoke well, in a clear cultured manner.

'Do you live inside the castle?' asked Morgan.

'I do, my lady. Now if you would allow me to clean the room and make up fresh bedcovers for my lady.'

'We are not leaving her alone with you,' stated Gawain. Elaine looked at her nephew with a kindness she had never shown before. 'You do not think I would harm my lady, do you?'

'We do not know who you are,' the young man retorted.

Luckily sense prevailed and Morgan took the maid's advice. She addressed all the men in the room. 'The maid is right the room needs air and not men cluttering it. I will stay, but everyone else must leave.'

The men all looked annoyed, but none challenged the lady and all left without question. Elaine volunteered her name and began chatting with the women on everyday matters. She did not forget her duty either and set about replacing old sweat cover sheets with clean fresh ones. She was ably helped by Morgan until all was done and dusted. It was after she had finished her chores that the lady sat down on the bed next to Morgan. 'I must speak with you, my lady. It is most important.'

Morgan listened to what the maid had to say.

Elaine tried to speak in her own voice, but the sound that came out was still that of Polyxena's. 'Sister it is me, Elaine, I am in disguise.'

Morgan stared at the woman, but did not offer an opinion.

'My voice is different I know…and my face…and I look younger, but it is all the work of the lady of the lake.'

'How do you know about the lady of the lake?'

'It's me, Elaine. I made my recovery on the lady's lake...'

'You are clearly not my sister, so who are you? More to the point what is it you are after?'

Elaine gave a huge sigh. 'Eros, the King of the fairies...'

'You know about the fairies?'

'Yes. Now do you believe me? Eros is inside my body and I am using this one to spy on Guinevere.'

Morgan shook her head, but took her sister in her arms. 'It must be so, but you should stay well away from that woman.'

A smiling Elaine disagreed. 'It's better that I don't. She knows about your proposed marriage to Ursien.'

'That can not be possible...I only agreed yesterday.'

'She has spies everywhere...including in this castle.'

'Then she knows everything.'

'Yes, but I can tell her whatever we want her to know. We are in a unique position to feed her misleading information.'

'It is too dangerous.'

'I am working as one of her spies. We can feed her lies and she will believe every word that I tell her.'

'I doubt that...the lady trusts no one...'

'She trusts me...she trusts me above all others.'

'You're speaking like a fool. How could you suddenly become the lady's confidant?'

'That is easy to explain. The Queen has...an unhealthy attraction for her own sex. This on its own would be useful, but better still the lady's great passion at the moment just happens to be me.'

'Whatever do you mean?' inquired a shocked Morgan.'

Elaine was amused at her sister's reaction to the news that Guinevere was a deviant. 'You should see your face, sister. You're supposed to be the worldly one, and I'm supposed to be the innocent. 'Our great Queen sleeps with women and not with men.'

'That is disgusting, I'm sure you're mistaken.'

'I saw it with my own eyes.'

'But our brother would never have allowed such a thing.'

'Perhaps he did not know?'

'He was married to her long enough, surely he would have found out.'

'Perhaps he did. But he could hardly announce to the world that his wife was being unfaithful and intimate with another woman, now could he?'

'The longer I live, the more shocked I become at what takes place at court.'

Elaine smiled in agreement. 'We must use this weakness to our advantage, sister…'

Morgan stared hard at the face of Elaine and tried to imagine her, as her sweet innocent sister. 'I don't believe I am hearing what I'm hearing…you're not suggesting you become intimate with Guinevere.'

'Heaven forbid, but I can use her to gain an advantage for you.'

The idea seemed to be abhorrent to the lady. 'If the woman ever found out your true identity she would kill you on the spot.'

'I have fooled her already…she is blinded by love.' Morgan's hand went up to her head. 'My head hurts,' she proclaimed. 'You have giving me a headache with all this nonsense. I forbid you to go anywhere near that evil woman again.'

Elaine had always been slightly intimated by her illustrious sister, even now with her new found power and importance, she felt intimidated. 'I will not stop,' Elaine pronounced. 'I will continue until I see you sitting on the throne instead of that woman.'

Morgan spoke softly. 'Please let's not argue, I'm only thinking of you. Guinevere is capable of anything, including murder.'

'I know. She was responsible for Arthur's death and the others on that boat…'

'We suspected that, but without proof…'

'She admitted as much to me…'

'It's still not proof. It's only your word against hers.'

'Let me continue to spy on your behalf?'

'I want to see the real Elaine again, not this face and not this body...'

'I promise to return to Lothian in five days, it just gives me enough time to return to Caerleon to misinform the Queen.'

Morgan seemed adamant. 'No. If you must inform the lady of anything you must do it by raven and then return home immediately.'

Elaine was adamant. 'I must do this,' she decreed.

Morgan tried to talk some sense into her sister.

'Think dear sister, what a chance we have to create a disorder in our enemy's camp,' Elaine advised.

'I cannot bear the thought of anything happening to you.'

'Nothing will happen to me. Shall I inform the Queen that the marriage is a fraud and will not happen?'

'I doubt she would believe that.'

'I'll make her believe it. I'll tell her that I overheard you discussing it with Lot.'

'You were never interested in power and politics, why this sudden interest?'

Elaine couldn't answer this, but assured Morgan that she would return to Lothian immediately after delivering the message.

Reluctantly Morgan agreed and the sisters began to talk on more every day affairs. Elaine studied Lady Helena before asking of her welfare.

'The lady is much better and will soon be back to her old self.'

'I have never met the lady.'

'I have only recently, but from what I hear she is strong willed and used to getting her own way.'

'She is quite a beauty...'

'That is why so many men hover over her all the time.'

'Don't tell me Gawain has lost his heart?'

'Yes, but he has a rival.'

'How very exciting, oh to be that young again.'

'Standing there, you are that young again.'

'That is true, but there is something disconcerting about being inside this body.'

Morgan moved close to her sister. 'It is not natural...I will not say it is unholy, but I fear the use of such magic.'

'I sometimes feel that someone other than me inhabits...'

'Tell me whose body is it you inhabit?'

'A woman called Polyxena. She was once in the service of the Queen. I believe her to be a capable spy and perhaps even an assassin.'

Morgan sighed and embraced her sister. 'I will not be happy until I see the face and body of my dear Elaine once more.'

After the embrace, Elaine left the room while Morgan thought how much simpler their lives once were.

Chapter 7

When Gaheris and Perceval returned to Lady Morgan's home in Tintagol they expected to see Olwen, John and Eberth. They were shocked to find that the occupants of the small boat had not returned. Gaheris was frantic and set out immediately to return to the land of the Gods. His new friend volunteered to come with him.

They sailed by the new tide and re-entered the channel that led to Annwn, the island of the dead.

This time their presence was noticed by the imposing figure of Mider. He stood upon the water like it was land and barred their progress. 'What brings you to our islands?' he demanded to know.

Showing no fear Gaheris stated he was looking for a small boat that carried his woman. 'I feel she has lost her way and has gone into your territory by mistake.'

Mider managed to hide a smile. 'This boat, does it contain others?'

'Yes, a small boy, a deaf mute and a servant.'

'You will return from whence you came.'

'But I can not abandon my betrothed.'

'The lady you seek has been reunited with her father and has given me a message to pass onto you. She wishes to accept our protection until her father finishes the work he has started.'

'I wish to believe you, but I need to see the lady to make sure she is in no danger.'

'You doubt my word?'

'I fear for her safety, she is fragile in body...'

'Your love is touching, but the lady has made a bargain with the Gods. She is safe and takes care of her father. As I have said, both will be returned to your world soon, safe and without injury.'

'I must see her to be reassured.'

Mider looked annoyed and blew from his mouth a breath that almost capsized the boat, sending it backwards through the air. The God took a few paces forward. 'Do not get me angry. The lady will be returned to you unharmed as long as you stay away from these islands.'

Much shaken and wet the men nonetheless repeated their defiance. Perceval entered into the discussion. 'You might be a God, but why should we take your word that the lady is safe.'

Mider screwed up his face and blew fire from his mouth. The flames engulfed the boat, starting several small fires on deck. The men ran about trying to put out the flames and after awhile eventually succeeded. They were black from the fumes and weary from their endeavours, when Mider lifted them high in the air by their collars. He suspended them above the ocean and spoke once more. 'I should smash both your heads together and let you sink to the bottom of the sea...but I shall be lenient.'

The men gasped for air as they struggled to shake themselves loose and make themselves heard. The voice of a muffled Gaheris screeched a reply. 'I must see her...you are not human...so you do not understand. I will gladly die if I can be assured my lady is well and unharmed.

'I do not give my word lightly. If I say she is well then she is.'

'And the others?' muttered Perceval.

'The boy has returned to where he belongs, while the silent one is constantly by the lady's side.'

'And the other man?' asked Gaheris.

'He is safe but under lock and key.'

'Why should he be treated differently?' inquired Perceval.

'Like you, he behaved inappropriately and became a nuisance. Only after much pleading from the maiden did we agree to spare his life. Now if you do not agree to go back to you own lands, I will inform the others to kill your friends, starting with the lady.'

Still swinging in mid-air, both men gave into the God's threats. Mider placed them down upon their boat with some care, before swiping the boat with his mighty hand sending it hurling back from whence it had come. Lucky to be alive both the men re-gathered their thoughts and stared at each other.

'I don't know about you, but I hate being told what to do?' groaned Perceval.

'I never liked it. We should wait until dark and try again.'

Perceval nodded his head. 'Do you think he was telling the truth?'

'It is possible I suppose.'

'If they have Olwen's father, she would not jeopardise his safety.'

'What can they want with them I wonder?'

*

The one thing that played on Guinevere's mind was the whereabouts of Lancelot. His absence was troubling, for she could not afford to lose his support. She sent out scouts and messages to all her outposts to see if she could track him down. Her rashness was now a cause for concern. It was Germanus who brought her news. His network of spies covered ever abbey, church and prayer house in the land. Lancelot had been spotted entering the abbey at Glastonbury.

Through Germanus's instructions, a spy had been detailed to keep an eye on Lancelot. This spy was an assassin by the name of Sextus, a man used before by Germanus.

In disguise, Lancelot stayed at a small inn, not far from the abbey and paid several visits a day to the place. He appeared a most devoted member of the church as he prayed like a man with something on his conscience.

Sextus followed Lancelot into the abbey and knelt some distance behind him. He kept his eyes on the man but could not hear his murmurings. Lancelot's mood was sombre as he prayed to his God for forgiveness for his past crimes. As Sextus watched from his good vantage point, he saw a new figure approach Lancelot and kneel beside him. This new figure wore a hooded cloak, but by the way the person moved Sextus was convinced that it was a woman. He cursed his carefulness, for not being closer to the man, and sought to move forward. He moved a few paces down so as to hear their conversation.

It was the hooded figure whom he heard first. 'But for Lady Morgan I would have removed the lady's head from her body.'

'Do you come from that lady?'

The lady waited a moment before answering. 'Why do you assume that I come from her?'

'Who else would have an interest in removing her?'

'You might be surprised.'

Lancelot went to remove the lady's hood from her face, but the lady put her hand up to stop him.

'Don't you know it is discourteous to cover your head in church?'

'I am not of your faith. I couldn't care less what is good etiquette in your place of worship.'

'If you are not here on behave of Lady Morgan who do you speak for?'

'You have no need to know the identity of my employer.'

'How so,' asked an impatient Lancelot.

'Your brief association with Guinevere has not turned out quite how you thought it would. I am surprised you have not killed her already and taken the High Throne for yourself.'

Lancelot muffled a laugh. 'You sound just like her, another woman with ice in her veins. I am not some cheap assassin, ready to throw away all my principles...'

'Principles,' the woman scorned. 'The man speaks of principles after what he has done.'

Lancelot grabbed the lady's arm. 'What do you think you know?'

'I know everything. I've seen every murderous blow and treacherous deed. Arthur died quickly, but Agravain didn't, and as for the pitiful Helena I doubt she will ever be quite the same.'

'Damn you woman, what do you want?'

'I want to offer you the High Throne.'

The man stared through the darken veil that was the lady's disguise to see only the brightness of her eyes staring back at him.

'I believe you must be mad,' he declared.

'In return I want your assurance that Christianity will return to being a small banned religion and that Wicker will be decreed the official religion once more.'

'I have no love for either,' declared Lancelot.

'Then it doesn't matter to you.'

'How can I be crowned the leader of my people...when she still lives?'

'Of course you can't.'

'You want me to kill her then?'

Lancelot could just about see a smile from beneath the lady's veil. 'Would you really miss her?

'You must think me a despicable person,' suggested Lancelot.

'I think you are a capable of great things and terrible things.'

'To kill is easy for a soldier, but to commit treason...'

'Really, don't make me laugh...you dispatched your friend easily enough.'

'It was not easy,' declared the man.

'This I promise will be easier for your conscience to accept.'

'I must make it look like an accident...'

'I would do it myself, but I can not get close to the lady.'

'If I do this, I want complete control...'

'You shall, providing you keep your promise to crush Christianity.'

Lancelot bowed his head. 'I shall do so. It will not be easy to kill the Queen.'

'I have a poison that is tasteless and undetectable.'

'You want me to kill like a woman?'

'This way it will appear that she just died in her sleep.'

'No one need be accused of murder then?'

'It is the quickest and cleanest way.'

From beneath her cloak, the lady handed Lancelot a small vial. 'Just a couple of drops in her mouth will do the trick.'

Lancelot took the vial from the lady and stared a long time at it. When he eventually looked up he found that the lady had gone.

Sextus waited until the lady had left, before hurrying away from the Abbey. His news was urgent and had to be sent to Germanus immediately. Unknown to him the lady in the Abbey had always been aware of his existence. She waited outside and followed him to his room, without being seen.

After bribing the landlord, the lady quietly entered his room to find the man securing a piece of parchment to a leg of a raven. He let the bird go and got to his feet, pulling a knife from his belt as he did so. 'You?' he acknowledged sounding startled.

The lady moved silently into the room and glanced at the knife. 'I'm afraid I cannot let you send your communiqué,' she advised.

Sextus moved his knife closer to the lady. 'Are you going to stop me?' he threatened.

The lady laughed. 'I have met your type before. Your puny knife does not worry me.'

The man lunged forward, swinging his knife at his opponent. To his surprise the lady moved swiftly out of the way of the weapon and laughed once more. 'People pay you money for doing this?' she mocked.

'How do you know me?'

'I make it a habit to know my enemies.'

'I do not believe we have met before.'

'You work for them. That is all the information I need to condemn you.'

'I work for myself.'

'I cannot take the chance in allowing you to live.'

It was Sextus's turn to laugh. 'What are you going to do? Are you going to tickle me to death with your jokes?'

'I'm going to let you kill yourself,' the lady said coldly.

The lady took two steps forward and stared into the man's eyes. To his surprise he found his muscles unable to move. His mind issued the command to strike the lady down, but the signal from his brain failed to register. He found a voice in his head giving him instructions. These instructions were startling, as they were perverse. 'Take the knife and turn it the other way.' He did what the voice in his head told him. The blade of the knife was now pointing towards him. The voice continued to issue him with further instructions. 'Now you will take your other hand, grab hold of the knife and with all the force you can muster you will force it up into your own breast.' Still in a trance Sextus carried out the instructions and committed suicide.

This was an involuntary act, but if anyone had witnessed it, it would have appeared that the man simply committed suicide. In reality it was the lady who had killed the man, through the power of her own will. The lady wasted no time in catching the raven and recovering the parchment. She read the message before destroyed it with fire. She looked down at the corpse and muttered a final farewell. 'See you in hell, my friend.'

Chapter 8

'For two days you have not eaten a thing. You're making yourself ill,' complained Morgause.

Eros had taken to his bed after his violent sickness. He made everyone's life a misery with his constant complaining.

'Just take a little beef broth my dear,' Ygerne pleaded. 'It will settle your stomach.'

Eros groaned. His stomach was now empty and filled with air. 'You mean to kill me with your damn food,' he muttered.

Morgause looked at her worried mother and a certain amount of anger entered her body. She addressed her mother. 'You must get some rest. I will stay and look after Elaine.'

Ygerne admitted to feeling tired and accepted her daughter's offer. Morgause waited until her mother had left the room before turning upon her sister.

Eros was still groaning and making faces when Morgause rounded on her. 'Now you listen to me. You will eat the beef broth and if you do not, I will pull your hair like I used to when we were children.'

Eros was shocked at the lady's violent announcement.

'You wouldn't hurt a poor sick woman?'

'You are acting like a spoilt child in need of a good beating.'

'Barbaric,' uttered Eros.

'Barbaric or not, you are getting up and getting dressed and coming for a walk with me.'

'Must I?'

Morgause's words sounded a little more conciliatory. 'You will feel better for it, I promise.'

Eros agreed and timidly sat up in his bed to sip his broth. Morgause kept her eyes on her the whole time. Eros wondered if the lady had worked out the deception. Who would she tell? What would she do? He could almost see the human's mind at work as the woman studied his every action. He was somewhat surprised with yet another emotion, this emotion was anxiety. A horrible feeling swelled up inside of him, a feeling somewhat akin to the sickness that had led him so low. How do these humans function he asked himself?

The walk that the sisters took rather resembled the one they took a few days earlier. The area around the stream was quiet and peaceful, but Morgause deliberately chose it. She wanted to get a reaction from her sister for this was the last place that Elaine should have felt happy being. 'You like this area?' Morgause suggested.

The fairy liked it because of the stream, the well and the sweet noise that the birds made. 'It is peaceful and the air is sweet with the smell of apple-blossom...'

'Don't you feel a little uncomfortable?'

Eros said he did not.

Morgause sat down by the stream and threw a pebble across the water. 'If it was me I would never venture near the place.'

Something in the lady's tone alerted the fairy to be on his guard. Something regarding this place Lady Elaine had not told him about. 'You know how I love the water...'

'Yes, but it was here that...'

Eros waited, but Morgause never elaborated. A silence hung in the air as the sisters' eyes met one another.

'Who the devil are you?' cried Morgause.

It never occurred to the fairy that their little deception might be discovered but now that it had it came as something of a relief.

'I am Eros, King of the fairies,' the King said in the voice of Elaine.

'Where is my sister? What have you done with her?'

'Nothing dear lady, she is quite well. This whole enterprise is entirely something invented by of her. She felt like a prisoner and so with my help she has liberated herself...'

'She was not a prisoner…she was not safe to roam the area…'

The lady was getting animated so Eros tried to calm her down. 'She is quite well and probably enjoying her little adventure…'

'If anyone recognises her she will be accused of witchcraft and hung.'

'Have no fear on that. She looks different, not like her true self.'

'What are you saying? Elaine is someone else?'

'No, she is herself, but lives in someone else's body.'

Morgause put her hands over her face to muffle her screams. 'What more magic, is this family raving mad. She will get herself killed and you will be complicit in her death.'

The fervour with which these words were spoken alarmed the fairy. 'I am only doing what was asked of me. Do you think I like being trapped in this sickly shell? It is a hideous body, prone to all kinds of ailments. Why do humans put up with such suffering? I do believe I am coming down with another ailment.'

'Nonsense, you look perfectly healthy.'

'Healthy! I almost died when all that strange substance came flowing out of me.'

'Did Elaine not warn you about over eating?'

'Yes, but I had never eaten anything before.'

'Nothing?' asked the lady. How do fairies get their substance then?'

Eros wasn't sure what the lady meant. 'We do not need substance. We do not eat, drink, or sleep, we are just alive.'

'How odd that must be.'

'No. Not as odd as being a ghastly human.'

'Tell me more about Elaine and her enterprise. We must make sure she is safe for she is the delicate one.'

'Yes but the body she now inhabits is stronger and younger.'

'Where has she gone?'

The fairy knew the lady would not be happy, but he could not withhold the information. 'She has gone to spy on Queen Guinevere at Caerleon.'

Morgause rose to her feet in a panic. 'I must go and help her. She will be found out.'

Eros shook his head and disagreed. 'She is cleverer than you think. She will return here in a few days time and all will be as it was.'

Morgause suspected the fairy was withholding something. 'What is it you are not telling me?'

'It's nothing to fear. The lady must return within seven days of taking on her new identity.'

'What will happen if she does not?'

'I don't know, but the lady of the lake was quite adamant that she must.'

'I should go to her.'

'That would be pointless. She will return soon, I am sure of it. I certainly hope so before I die from some other human affliction.'

*

Penelope was conscientious in her work and made friends with her colleagues easily. Even the suspicious Cadfan could find no fault in her attitude and application. The work itself she found interesting and her expertise with languages was quickly put to good use. Immigrants and locals often got into fights with one another and Penelope, as interpreter, became a peacemaker. She made friends easily and was quickly becoming invaluable to her new employer.

Cadfan stood in Leogran's office to make his report. A report that was short and praiseworthy. This was not what the prefect had expected. 'I assume someone has been following her all this time?' Leogran asked.

'Yes, but she is in contact with no one except the man who brought her here.'

'The man called Castor Bernard. What have you found out about him?'

'He is a retired wine merchant from Gaul, a well respected man who has never been in trouble with the authorities before.'

Leogran hummed. 'He could be smart just like the lady...'

Cadfan interrupted. 'We could be wrong about her?'

'You believe her story?'

The man nodded his head.

'You believe her when she says she has lost her memory?'

'Yes, I have spoken many times with her on the subject. I feel that no one could keep up the pretence for so long.'

Leogran studied his deputy. It was clear that the man was quite taken by the lady. 'Your recommendation,' he inquired.

'I think we should forget about her past, whatever that might be, and consider her future.'

The prefect knew immediately what was on the man's mind. 'You think she is ready for field work?'

'I do, sir. Her unique talents could be put to good use.'

'What is our progress with the Mador case?'

'We have no proof so far to bring him to trial. Much of the problem stems from people's fear of the man. His men terrorise the locals and no one will speak out against him.'

'This is not something I can tell the Queen. She wants the man disgraced and found guilty in front of all his peers.'

'For the moment we can't prove he has done anything wrong.'

Leogran beckoned for his colleague to come a little closer to him. 'If the proof is not forthcoming then we must find some,' he suggested.

Cadfan went red in the face. 'I'm sure that won't be necessary, it's just a matter of time before we find him out. '

'I can hardly keep telling our Queen to be patient. We must bring this man to his knees.'

'We could try something less orthodox,' suggested Cadfan.

Leogran looked intrigued.

'We now have within our ranks someone who is well equipped to mingle within the hierarchy of society.'

'Are you suggesting the lady becomes the Duke's mistress?'

'Certainly not,' a shocked Cadfan spluttered. 'But with a little training the lady could make a valuable spy...'

'The Queen has her own spies.'

'He has been known to succumb to the charms of a good looking lady...'

'You mean to set a trap?'

'If the lady gets close to him maybe she can find important information.'

'I will give you my blessing, but the lady has yet to convince me that she can be trusted.'

'I will keep you informed of any developments.'

*

His misery was manifold. He knew that his wretchedness could be laid entirely at his own feet, but that did not make him feel any better. He had given up all hope of redemption and had begun to wander through the countryside in a state of constant melancholy. He felt like a man trapped between two opposing worlds, that of the living and that of the dead. When the man closed his eyes he struggled to find any peace, for it was then that his demons emerged. Each night he saw the face of his beloved and each night her strong stare told him of her wrath.

Merlin had awakened with this image once again stamped upon his mind and it physically made him sick. He belched up the bile that came from the bowels of his soul and cursed his very being.

With no food to eat he wandered along the trail until he came upon a fresh water stream. He used his hands to drink the fresh substance and splash it onto his dirty face. It was only after this rude awakening that the man came to look upon his new surroundings. He knew the area around Cornubia, from his previous roving. It was an area barely touched by man and its unspoiled splendour appealed to him. He could not say why he had chosen this place over another, but it had the advantage of being well away from Lundonia and his recent troubles.

As far as he was aware no one was looking for him and that brought him a little comfort. With the vast forest before him he did not expect to encounter many people, but he was wrong with that assumption. He had barely ventured forth into the vast greenwood when a figure came out from the trees to confront him. This figure looked a poor wretched creature, as he crouched forward to peer up at the old sorcerer. The man's face was so grotesque in its ugliness that Merlin almost recoiled from his sight. He stood his ground however and inquired if he could be of any service. This seemed to amuse the fellow, for he smiled at Merlin with his crooked black teeth. 'It is I that can do something for you,' the man replied.

Merlin now looked amused. 'Pray tell me how you can help me?'

The man stumbled forward a few paces closer. The sorcerer now saw the man's face more clearly and he could see the man's skin was flaky and grey. This made him look so frail that he wondered if the man was not long for this world. His clothes such as they were, fitted so tightly that they seemed to constrict his movement. It appeared to Merlin that the man had stolen someone else's attire to keep out the cold.

The man's black teeth protruded from his lips again. 'Every man should have a purpose,' he stated.

Merlin did not contradict the statement, but waited for the man to elaborate.

'You want to turn your back on all your responsibilities and live out your life as a vagabond?'

'What business is it of yours?' asked Merlin.

'I, like you, tried to hide from my problems. It only leads to disaster, my friend.'

There was something familiar to the man's voice, but the sorcerer was sure he had not set eyes on him before. 'Do I know you sir? Have we met someplace before?'

'I have not seen you in a long time, but yes we have indeed met before.'

'I do not recall...'

'I am a pitiful excuse for a man now, but I once was a great Lord and you were my teacher.'

This puzzled Merlin, for the only students he ever taught were King Uther's children.

'Who are you?' he asked.

'That does not matter, what matters is that you turn away from this course of self-destruction you have set upon.'

'Why should you care if I destroy myself?'

'Until a short while ago I did not care...in fact I would have welcomed your destruction, but now I know that vengeance is a blind and foolish thing.'

'I think you should stand aside and let me pass...'

'For you have somewhere to go?'

'Again, I say it is none of your business.'

The man put his skeletal hand upon Merlin's. 'I forgive you,' he said. 'Now it is time for you to forgive yourself.'

Merlin quickly withdrew the man's hand from his own. 'I do not know what you mean.'

'Look into my eyes my friend... can you not see who stands before you?'

Merlin stared into the pitiful face of the man and saw his pale green eyes stare back. In an instant he recognised something in them. These were not the eyes of some frail old man, but those of a strong young man with plenty of life still left in him. The stare was frightening in its intensity and Merlin was forced to look away.

Merlin started to mutter to himself. 'It is an apparition it will go away, just don't look at it.'

The frail man gripped hold of Merlin's face with both his hands and with surprising strength made him look upon him. The face with all its lines and scars began to transform slowly into a face that the sorcerer recognised. It was the face of a young King Arthur. 'I am mad, mad, I can not be otherwise,' spouted Merlin. 'Only madmen see ghosts...'

'I am not a ghost, or an apparition, but your salvation.'

Merlin closed his eyes. 'Go away. Go away I have no right to salvation...'

'You can help make this land a better place, but you must forget the past.'

'Please leave me alone. How can I forget the mistakes I have made in life...I must live with them.'

'You have a role to play in this land.'

'What role is there for a drunken old fool?'

'You must help my sister to gain the throne away from Guinevere and for our peoples to return to the old religion.'

This did not seem like the words of the King thought Merlin, but more the words of his mother, Vivienne. This he thought must be one of her tricks and yet he wished for forgiveness more than he could put into words. 'Be gone with you,' Merlin shouted. 'Leave me to my misery.' He put his hands up before his face as if to protect him from the vision. A few moments later he slowly let his arms drop to find the phantom gone.

Chapter 9

Elaine saw the mighty towers of Caerleon from her horse and marvelled at its splendour. She was in a happy mood for the news she would divulge to the Queen might well precipitate that lady into taking immediate action; an action that would be premature and extremely costly to her chances of holding onto the throne.

With Ursien's allegiance assured, a war now would favour Lady Morgan and her forces. Elaine's lie would convince Guinevere that the time was right to strike. What Elaine didn't know was that Lancelot was about to abandon the lady as well. At this particular moment in time Guinevere was extremely vulnerable. Like so many things in life a cruel twist of fate was to change everything, for the lady never made it as far as the castle that day.

As her small party of men exited the forest of Dee, they were met with a band of robbers who came at them from all sides. The Queen's men put up a fight which resulted in their deaths, while Elaine in all the confusion tried to escape by making her horse gallop towards the castle. Two men rode after her and one jumped from his horse onto her horse, causing the lady to tumble to the ground. As she fell, Elaine hit her head on a rock and was immediately knocked unconscious.

Guinevere waited until first light before sending out her guards to search the immediate area for Polyxena and her party. She had received news from her friend that she should arrive the night before, so when she did not she became worried. The Queen was aware that feelings still ran high concerning King Arthur's death. The sight of her own guards would often stir a certain amount of animosity around Caerleon and other areas of the country closely associated with her dead husband. Guinevere feared

Polyxena's small party had been attacked because they wore her colours of black and red. So she took it upon herself to lead the first search party.

The area the fifty or so men had to cover was vast, but not overly populated. The locality was beset mostly by mountains, streams and farmland. Only the forest of Dee broke the hilly landscape and it was there Guinevere started her search. It made good sound reasoning, for it would have been through the forest that Polyxena and her party would have to come.

Guinevere was the first to spot the site of the ambush, when she came upon one of her men lying face down in the mud dead. She made her guards leave their horses and search the area thoroughly, slowly but surely they came upon more men, until all six dead bodies were found.

The Queen was not a person who panicked, but the thought that her friend was dead made her feel sick. She regained her composure and issued orders for her guards to continue with the search. It occurred to her that maybe the bandits had captured Polyxena and might try to find out who she was. After all she carried the Queen's colours so they might assume she was a person of importance to Guinevere herself.

It was one of her solders that alerted her to a possible trail. The Queen studied the route with the man and commanded the rest of her men to follow. To her relief it quickly became clear that the trail was made by one person. If that person was Polyxena, why was she going in the opposite direction away from the castle?

*

Now much recovered, Lady Helena was anxious to leave Lady Morgan's protection and start her life over. She wished to escape Britannia altogether and start again with a man more than twice her age. He had not confided his true feelings, but his rescue and his manner suggested he loved her. The wilful side of the lady's nature had returned along with a healthier complexion. Nothing was going to stop her from getting the man she loved, not even if it meant breaking Gawain's heart. Yet something was troubling her, something she couldn't shake off. Everyone was kind but a lingering question hung in the air. No one had asked her about the allegations, not even Lady Morgan. Did they just take it for granted that Guinevere had made them up? Or did they think she was capable of love potions, magic and cruelty?

She could sense Titius was becoming restless also, but the man had not made his intensions clear to her. She dreaded him telling her he was leaving and going back to the army, or waking up one morning to be told he had left the night before.

Helena could not take the suspense any longer and had arranged a meeting by a quiet corner of Ursien's estate. The area was peaceful and the sound of water running from the stream nearby helped soothe the lady's troubled mind. Time dragged on and still Titius did not come. Helena's anxiety returned, but then she spotted a figure in the distance coming towards her.

At first the lady thought it was Titius, but as the figure drew nearer it became clear it was a younger man. The figure of Gawain quickened his pace as he approached. Immediately Helena sensed something was wrong. 'What is it? What has happened?'

Gawain, after catching his breath, stated nothing was wrong. He could tell by the lady's expression that he was not the man she was expecting, but still his love remained unbowed. Common sense should have told the young man to hold fire in expressing his feelings, but he was in love and possessed no sense at all. 'I'm glad to catch you alone,' he began.

Still thinking about Titius, Helena acknowledged Gawain's remark with a nod of her head.

'I do have some news for you,' stated the young man, 'although I hesitate to announce it.'

Helena's instincts told her the news was concerning Titius. 'Has he gone?' whispered the lady.

Gawain nodded. He waited for the lady to react, but she stood in silence.

At the worse possible moment the young man revealed his true feelings for the maiden. 'I am sorry,' he began, 'but he does not love you the way that I do. If he did he would not abandon you this way...'

Helena was so deep in thought that she barely heard Gawain's statement.

The young man continued. 'Let me take care of you. We can have a happy life together.' Gawain paused and hesitantly dropped down on one knee. His mouth was dry like sand, but his resolve was absolute. 'Will you marry me?' he stammered.

It seemed like an age before the young woman came to her senses and realized what was taking place. If her mind wasn't so occupied with her true love, her reaction might not have been so blunt and discourteous. 'Get up off your knees,' she commanded. 'I can not believe you could be so thoughtless. This is not the time for such nonsense...' Gawain got to his feet and with his right hand wiped his brow. He had suffered with a fever, a fever like no fever he had ever known, but now he had passed its crisis point. The lady had responded to his love with distain and contempt; so be it then, if she felt nothing for him then he would go as far away from her as he could. At that moment he wished never to see the lady again, at that moment he wished to slide his sword through the heart of his rival's body. He swore under his breath that if he ever came across the man again he would do just that.

*

The morning had passed and the mid-day approached when at last one of the Queen's men shouted out. 'Look, your grace there, down below, a body.'

Guinevere peered down an embankment to see nestled around many different coloured leaves, a shape. The contours of the shape resembled a human form. Only the head could be seen clearly, the rest of the frame was hidden by foliage of leaves and the debris from a fallen tree. Guinevere was first to leap down the embankment despite calls from her men to be careful.

On coming before Polyxena, Guinevere clasped her lover's head in her arms. She placed her ear up close to Polyxena's lips and listened for the sound of her breath. At first she heard nothing, but the sound of her men descending the embankment and noise of the birds chirping. Then a gentle whisper of breath registered upon the Queen's ear. She gasped from relief, before allowing one of her men to examine the lady properly. He declared the lady had probably collapsed through exhaustion.

Guinevere supervised the construction of a litter by her men and before long it was ready for use. Just before the body was lifted onto the contraption, Polyxena opened her eyes and looked up at Guinevere. In a weak sounding voice the lady asked two questions. 'Where am I?' and 'Who are you?'

*

Gawain had left his home in a rage, but not to go in search of Lady Helena as everyone assumed. He wanted to find some kind of release for the pain and anger that consumed him. Just like his father he was a man of the earth, a man of primitive drives and desires. He felt like killing someone, anyone, just so his frustration could be expunged from his body. A nice war or a stupid argument would suffice. After a few days and nights carousing he found his way to one of his favourite taverns on the border of Corbenic and Gore. The place was known for its riotous clientele of cutthroats, bandits and prostitutes. He entered the place like a man looking for a fight and before long he had his wish.

Several brawls later Gawain was suitably blooded and drunk, but still standing. The day was drawing to a close and the night had come in, when the man observed a new party enter the tavern. The party was made up of one man and two rather striking looking young women. Gawain studied the group for awhile before sauntering over to where they sat. One of the women was particularly attractive; she had long shiny black hair, red cheeks, striking speckled brown eyes and lips that were painted the colour of her cheeks. The man had never seen a more provocative looking woman in his life.

Gawain introduced himself and offered to buy drinks for everyone. The offer was graciously accepted and the landlord set about providing the table with more strong liquor. Gawain sat next to the attractive woman and began to pay the young lady many compliments. The lady was called Ragnell, and her companions, were called Morholt and Rosalinda. They were not local, but were travelling around the country in search of a precious item, the lady confided in him. Ragnell flirted with King Lot's son, teasing him about his manhood and his strength. She championed Morholt, and boasted that he was the greatest fighter in the eastern land where they came from. The lady predicted Gawain would grovel at Morholt's feet before the night was over. Such a challenge was an insult to the young man of course and before long the two men were locked in combat thanks to the interference of the young lady.

Their fight quickly spilled out of the tavern onto the grounds. The two men, who had barely exchanged two words together, fought with their bare hands. They punched, clawed and tore at each other until their bodies reeked of blood. The men's hands, arms and face were now covered in a combination of blood and dirt as they battered each other like two wild dogs. It wasn't long before a large crowd gathered to see the sport in the open air. The atmosphere was gladiatorial as it was virile as both men sought to inflict damage on each other. Gawain took a bite out of his opponent's arm, making him scream in pain, while Morholt crunched his two mighty fists against Gawain's side sending him to the ground with a thud. If the fight was vicious it was nonetheless fair and not likely to lead to anyone's death, but that was to change. Ragnell, who had been keen on a fist fight now decided to increase the danger by producing a dagger from her belt. She threw it to Morholt and egged him on. The man caught it safely, but seemed reluctant to put it to good use. Ragnell then reached into her friend's belt and produced a similar blade and threw that one to Gawain.

Ragnell and Rosalinda began to argue. 'Do you want them to kill each other?' asked Rosalinda.

Ragnell only smiled.

Rosalinda tugged at her companion's dress. 'We must stop them before someone really gets hurt.'

Ragnell paid little attention. Rosalinda tugged harder at her sleeve and Ragnell was forced to pay her notice. 'What!' she complained.

'This has gone beyond a piece of theatre and fun, men might die.'

Ragnell looked into her sister's eyes. 'Yes, isn't it thrilling?'

'You can not mean that. What has either of them done to you?'

Ragnell forced her friend's hand from her dress. 'Just watch and enjoy.'

'No I will not. I will put an end to this madness now...'

To Rosalinda's horror Ragnell slapped her in the face.

As one fight neared its conclusion another began. The two women pushed and shoved each other until Ragnell took hold of Rosalinda's hair and wrestled her to the ground. As the crowd veered from one fight to the other, it soon became clear that the sight of two women fighting was deemed of greater interest as many in the crowd gathered around the women instead.

Neither fighting men were put off by the sudden interruption. Gawain finally got the better of Morholt thanks to an audacious thrust from his blade that cut the man across his face. The blood spurted into the air and several in the crowd gasped in horror at the sight. Morholt dropped his dagger and tried to stop the flow of blood from his face by covering the wound with both hands. The man was vulnerable to a fatal blow from his opponent, but Gawain was no murderer. He threw his dagger to the ground also and came to offer his services to Morholt. His opponent rebuked his offer by spitting his blood down at the young man's feet. A woman came forward and offered Morholt her apron. This was placed over the cut as Morholt walked away towards his horse cursing as he went.

If one fight aborted rather suddenly, the other continued without interruption. It was the savagery that amazed the crowd as they watched two young maidens fight like wild animals in the dirt.

Both women had long flowing hair, and both tugged at each other's locks as if their lives depended upon it. Ragnell had pulled many blonde strands from Rosalinda's hair in a fit of anger. This only made her opponent all the more determined to repay the favour. Rosalinda surprised everyone present by pulling her friend's hair back so hard that Ragnell screamed in pain. Once she had let the hair go, she followed up her attack by a thunderous slap across the lady's face. Again some of the crowd shrieked. Rosalinda's anger looked unlikely to be appeased, but Gawain stepped in between the women and pulled them apart.

Even when he had done this, both women swung blows in each other's direction. Finally Gawain restored order when he slapped both women across their faces. Both women looked at the young man in disbelief. 'You...you beast, I will have your head on a pike for that,' spat Ragnell.

Her statement was met with much hilarity by the crowd who had enjoyed the night's entertainment, but were now becoming cold from the night air. They began to flock back indoors laughing and chatting at what they had just witnessed.

The four gladiators were left alone to pick over their wounds and curse each other for their injuries. With the blood now stopped from his wound, Morholt was the first to reach out his hand in friendship. He addressed Gawain. 'I have no quarrel with you. Perhaps we can forget the whole matter?'

Gawain said he would gladly forget the argument. He went as far as to joke that he could not remember why they had started to fight in the first place. Both men laughed as their ill mood began to disappear.

Rosalinda stood looking at the nasty gash upon Morholt's face and set about helping him. She took him to a nearby stream and with the use of a piece of cloth from her dress bathed his cheek with due care. This left Ragnell and Gawain alone to ponder over their misbehaviour.

Ragnell was the first to make a conciliatory announcement. 'I am not really a bloodthirsty fiend,' she said.

'You would have my head on a pike, would you?' Gawain mused.

Chapter 10

In the pitch darkness of the night, Gaheris and Perceval found themselves stumbling about an area crowded with guards. They assumed that Olwen and her friends must be close by and were ready to put in force a quick rescue attempt if the chance arrived.

As they broke cover and approached a series of shacks they spotted a figure they were familiar with. The figure was coming away from one of the cabins and moving in their direction. They sought cover to hide, but no cover was at hand. The figure was that of young Nemue, friend to Lady Morgan. 'What is she doing here?' whispered Gaheris to his companion.

'Doesn't she work for Lady Morgan?' asked Perceval.

'We will soon find out,' asserted Gaheris.

Nemue couldn't help but see them. She glanced behind her to see if anyone else had spied them. Believing no one had, she took both the men by the arms and marched them away from the cabin towards the shelter of the old stone wall. She made the men slide back to where they had been hiding and to the relative safety that it gave.

'What are you doing here?' the young woman demanded to know.

'We have come to rescue Lady Olwen,' answered Gaheris.

Perceval stared at the woman. 'Why are you here?'

'I've come to do the same as you. If you want to keep your lady safe, you must do as I say.'

Sounding impertinent, Perceval asked why they should.

'Because you will get everyone killed if you do not.'

'What do you mean everyone?' asked Gaheris.

'It would take too long to explain, but you must trust me...'

'Who do you work for?' queried Perceval. 'And don't tell us it is the Lady Morgan...'

'I wasn't going to. I'm working with the lady of the lake. I am her...'

Nemue stopped short of revealing just what her relation with the God was.

Perceval remained hostile. 'You are her what?' he quizzed.

'Why are you interrogating me? You know I am on your side...'

'I only know you through Lady Morgan and her servant Yvain,' stated Gaheris. 'Are you not his girl? Now that I think of it, I have not seen you together for some time.'

'We had a fight, but I still love him. I know that we will soon be together again.'

'How very touching,' remarked Perceval. 'Now tell us again why we should trust you?'

Nemue sighed. 'There are bigger things at stake than your friend's life.'

'There is nothing more important to me than the life of the lady,' stipulated Gaheris.

'I know that, and appreciate it, but she is quite safe.'

'I must see her to make sure...'

'I will bring her to you. Stay here and do not approach the shack...'

'She is well?' asked Gaheris.

Nemue smiled and nodded her head. As she began to move away, Perceval caught her arm. 'Why is it safe for you but not for us?'

Gritting her teeth, Nemue used her right hand to force the man to release his grip on her. She opened her hand to reveal a painted symbol. The symbol was in the shape of a circle and featured a figure, part woman and part amphibian who was ascending from a lake. 'The lady of the lake has made me her pupil. This symbol allows me to walk freely amongst the Gods and their lands. The guards know who I am and will not challenge me, but if they were to see either of you they would surely be a confrontation.'

Gaheris acknowledged the lady's statement and was content, while Perceval remained suspicious.

'I will not be long,' Nemue stated, as she pushed past Perceval and headed back the way she had come from. As she retreated, Perceval whispered to his friend. 'I do not trust her.'

Gaheris shook his head. 'You worry too much, she is a friend. She loves Olwen almost as much as I do.'

'You see all women as perfect creatures and not as they really are. Your gallantry is commendable, but I hope it does not get us both killed.'

Nemue and Olwen left the shack together but seemed in no hurry to find their friends. They strolled about their immediate area before coming close to the wall where Olwen slipped down behind it to see her lover and his friend. Gaheris and Olwen embraced and whispered sweet mutterings to each other, before the man introduced his friend.

'Where is the other woman?' Perceval asked her.

'She is keeping watch. We have little time...'

'Why?' pleaded Gaheris.

'You must trust both of us. Nemue has explained to me why we must remain for now...'

'I cannot leave you here alone...'

'I am not alone. My father is here with me.'

'With the cover of darkness we can all make our escape,' Gaheris suggested.

'No my love, we must wait...'

'Wait for what?'

'My father must do something for the lady of the lake and then she has promised us her protection.'

'Can we trust this God?' suggested Perceval.

'Yes, I believe so,' whispered the girl.

'And John, is he okay?' asked Gaheris. 'We heard he was imprisoned.'

'He is, but the lady of the lake promises to have him released soon.'

'We will stay nearby just in case you need us,' proposed Gaheris.

'Please be careful, my love, the Gods can be cruel...'

'We will be diligent...'

Perceval promised the lady to take good care of her prize.

Nemue then ducked down behind the wall to hasten the lady to leave and to return with her. After hugs and kisses between Olwen and Gaheris, Nemue returned to the cabin while the men sat in quiet contemplation.

*

The lady known as Polyxena, rested all day and half the night before opening her eyes again. She opened them to find herself stretched out on a divan with the imposing figure of Guinevere bending over her. Who was this woman?' she wondered.

'Do you remember anything yet?' Guinevere asked.

Polyxena shook her head. 'Do I know you?' she inquired.

'I am your Queen and your friend,' Guinevere replied.

Polyxena tried to rise from the divan, but the pain in her head made her recoil. Guinevere, leaning forward with a poultice in her hand and placed it on her lover's head. 'You mustn't try to move. My physicians tell me that in time your memory will return, but for now you must rest...'

The lady tried a second time to rise herself up, but again she felt the jolt of pain. She sighed and rested her head back on the pillow. 'I have something important to tell someone...but I cannot remember what or who...'

Guinevere continued with her soothing tone. 'Rest my dear...we will talk tomorrow...'

'How do I know you?' queried Polyxena.

Guinevere was tender with her response. 'We have a special working relationship together,' she said softly.

Polyxena asked for clarification. 'Does the Queen usually take personal care of the people in her employ?'

'You are not just in my employ.'

'I do not understand?'

Again Guinevere showed patience. 'Tomorrow I will tell you everything about our past.'

Feeling groggy, Polyxena asked one last question before closing her eyes again. 'Are we sisters by any chance?'

Once she was sure the lady was asleep, Guinevere bent forward, kissed the lady on the cheek and whispered her reply. 'We are closer than even that.'

*

Penelope had met the target of the authority's investigation, the Duke of Mador. To her surprise the man was most charming, praising her looks, and in her ability to speak many different languages. She had been briefed as to what her mission would entail, but she quickly realized that she would have to allow the man a certain amount of intimacy in their forthcoming relationship or she would get precious little information from him.

She was employed in Mador's castle in Mercia as no ordinary servant, but as a companion to his dysfunctional daughter, Megan.

Megan had been found wandering the streets of Caerwent crying and talking nonsense. A friend of Mador's had recognised her and had taken her to his home. Her talk sounded like that of a mad person and so he contacted her father. Mador had no idea what had befallen his daughter or what had happened to his young wife, but he was keen to reclaim his kin. So he travelled to Caerwent to fetch her. When he found out the true condition of his flesh and blood, he immediately was forced to employ someone to look after her.

The first two employees left after a series of tantrums from the young lady, this made him decide to employ someone older and wiser. Penelope's good sense struck the right cord and thanking his good fortune the man quickly offered her the post of lady's companion. This was strictly speaking a misleading title, for in reality she was part physician, part nurse and part jailer for the unhappy child.

Several days into her new job and the lady felt surprisingly well placed to prise valuable information from her new employer.

Far from feeling repelled by Mador's advances, Penelope felt empowered by her control over the man. He wasn't dangerous she perceived, at least not to a woman of her maturity. Somehow she knew she could manipulate the man into doing whatever she wanted. To her surprise she enjoyed the game she was playing with him.

The fourth night in his employ the man thought to try his luck at gaining intimacy with his new servant. He waited until his daughter was asleep before applying Penelope with wine, but the lady could handle her liquor and did not become intoxicated as he expected, on the contrary it was Mador who became inebriated and started to say things that perhaps he shouldn't. This played into the lady's hands as he declared his association with the Queen and the unlawful acts he had carried out on her behalf.

'I know a great secret,' he began, 'one that might topple the great lady from her high and mighty throne.'

'It's a good thing she has such a loyal friend in you...'

'She is not in the least bit grateful you know.'

Penelope shook her head and whispered how terrible it was that the Queen had not seen fit to reward him for his devotion.

'She has cast me off as if I was an old shoe...'

'You can never tell who your true friends are?'

Mador nodded. His eyes opened wider, as he slipped his hand in between the lady's legs. The couple were curled up together on the lady's divan drinking wine from large goblets and swapping stories of intrigue.

Penelope had taken full precautions by wearing a chastity-belt, borrowed from a lady friend of Cadfan's. The man was too drunk to realise this at first, but when the lady failed to become excited he tried a little harder. Finally he became aware of the obstacle to his desire and he almost burst into tears with frustration.

'Does no one love me,' he cried. 'No one gives a fig for me...not my errant wife or my ungrateful daughter, not even the Queen. Now you seek to make fun of me...'

'No, kind sir, but I can not allow just any man to take advantage of me.

'I'm not just any man,' Mador pleaded.

'I have to be careful...'

'Some man must have a prior claim on you?'

'I wear the contraption to ward off men who would abuse their position and their wives.'

'Men like me you mean?'

'Yes to put it frankly....men like you.'

'And I thought you liked me?'

'I do, but we must get to know each other a little better...'

'Does the thing have a key?'

'Most definitely, but I forget where it is.'

Mador stumbled to his feet and suggested they both look for the object.'

Penelope wanted the conversation to return to the Queen and promised she would find the key, if he revealed the lady's secret to her.

A promise was sworn that he would before the man sat back down again. 'She has many secrets that one, but I suspect like half the populace you already suspect her of murdering the King.

Looking startled, the lady swore she was shocked at the suggestion.

'She had tried many times before. Why do you think the King had stayed away for so long?'

'Is that your secret? Do you have proof of this ghastly deed?'

'She never puts anything down in parchment that might one day incriminate her. She is too smart for that. No, my secret does not concern the King, it concerns Lady Morgan instead.'

The lady knew the secret, whatever it was, was not going to be given up without some reward. So she agreed to allow the man to kiss her on the mouth.

Trying to appear sober the man leant forward and kissed the lady with as much passion as he could muster. He slobbered his moist lips against hers leaving a repugnant taste on the lady's mouth. He tried a second time, but Penelope repelled his advances by putting her hand in front of her face.

'What proof do you have against her?'

'Oh, that can wait. Give me another kiss?'

'Tell me everything about your great secret and I will tell you where the key is.'

'You are quite a tease.'

'Do we have a deal?'

Mador put his arm around the lady. 'One more kiss and then I'll tell you all,' he promised.

Penelope allowed the man his kiss. He felt the lady's resolve weaken and was now eager to impart his knowledge so that he could gain his reward.

'I have written evidence that the Queen tried to kill Lady Morgan, that and two witnesses who might be willing to testify against her on the matter.'

Penelope gave the impression the information was disappointing. 'Is that your great secret? This written evidence, does it have the Queen's signature or seal?'

'It has neither...but why are we talking of such things when we could be enjoying each other.'

'I'm enjoying our conversation, aren't you my lord?'

'Yes, but words alone are not enough...'

Mador tried to kiss the lady again, but like before she kept him at bay. He was becoming impatient and a little more aggressive in his amorous advances. The lady however was more alert and in control of the situation. Penelope left the man's clutches to get to her feet and pace up and down the room. The man was too drunk to go chasing after his lady, so he tried to entice her back with promises of trinkets and gold. His suggestions were beyond contempt to the lady, but she pretended to be impressed.

'Tell me more about this document you claim to possess. Tell me why you think it's so important?'

Mador gave a huge sigh and tried to get to his feet. He stumbled at first, but eventually managed to stand in front of his lady. 'Why do you ask so many questions?' he inquired.

Smiling, Penelope was quick to come up with a smart reply. 'I have to know whether you are the kind of man I can entrust with my own little secret.'

'Secrets, secrets...what's so important about secrets anyway?'

'My secret may not make your rich, but it just might save your life.'

'Damn stupid wench, stop talking in riddles.'

Penelope made the man sit back down again, while she sat next to him. 'I will make a bargain with you. You give me the parchment and the names of your two people you mentioned and I will reveal the secret that will save you from the gallows.'

'You must be mad or something...this is not how servants behave to their masters.'

'I admit I am no servant. I am perhaps the only person alive that can save you from death, so do heed what I say.'

Mador's hand scratched his head as he began to mumble to himself. 'This is not how I imagined tonight...'

'Listen to me my lord, I wish you no harm, but others do.'

The man blinked and looked befuddled. 'Who wants to harm me?'

'Can't you guess?' the lady suggested.

The man's thought processes took a moment to ignite, but after awhile he began to nod his head. 'You mean the Queen, don't you?'

At first Penelope said nothing, but only moved her head a little.

'I am her most loyal subject, why should she turn against me?'

'I can not answer that. The prefect at Westcheap has been given orders to find evidence against you. The lady means to destroy you.'

'How do you know this?'

The lady was reluctant to inform the man of her own part in the affair. 'That doesn't matter. 'You must give me all the evidence you have against the Queen. In return I might just be able to get you out of this mess.'

Mador fetched the parchment and handed it to Penelope. She studied the contents quickly and wondered why this piece of scroll was worth anything at all. 'I fail to see how this implicates the Queen in anything unlawful.'

'On its own, it is worthless but with my two witnesses and Lady Morgan's memory of certain events... I think it could prove most damaging.'

'I want the names of your witnesses?'

'You shall have them, but how can you save me from the Queen's bloodhounds?'

Chapter 11

This was his last day working on the site and Ysbaddaden felt relieved at the prospect of finally going home. His daughter, Olwen was still frightened the Gods would kill them all. But for the intervention of Vivienne her fears might have been realized. The Goddess had travelled with her usual band of pixies to the third island of Avalon to make her special appeal for their release. A short time before the lady's arrival Mider had captured Gaheris and Perceval and had thrown them in the same gaol as John. After a cheerful reunion the three men sat together and tried to plan an escape.

 The Gods were planning to leave so they were in good spirits and gave into the Lady of the Lake's pleas. They promised to release all their prisoners and tried to coax the lady to come with them. The lady refused and warned them that what they were about to do was both dangerous and foolhardy.

*

Gawain was awakened by the sound of thunder, or what he thought was thunder. He was lying face down on the floor of his room naked. His hand moved slowly to the back of his neck where he felt a wet substance trickling down his back. He quickly perceived that someone must have hit him from behind and that he had been knocked unconscious. Groaning and complaining, the man got to his feet and began to look over his surroundings. There was no sign of his three companions and worse still, after checking, he realized that his prize possession, Excalibur was gone. He had been robbed of his money, his weapons and his jewellery.

 Still groggy, the man stumbled from one corner of the room to another, picking up his clothes as he found them scattered about the place. The man cursed his robbers and swore he would find them and take his revenge. With his head aching he was further annoyed by the thunderous noise from outside. People were awake and abroad despite the fact the sun was barely up over the horizon. He heard shouting, swearing, screaming and went to investigate.

As he left his room he became aware of the smell of smoke and of several small fires burning above him. Everyone was scurrying about, trying to exit the place before the roof fell down on top of them. Gawain ran out into the fresh air barely clothed, only to be met with what appeared to be arrows of fire raining down from the heavens.

At first he thought the place must be under attack, but he quickly realised that the flames were not arrows, but pieces of debris falling from the sky. Some people were trying to run away from the scene, while others were on their knees praying to their God for salvation. Gawain was hit by an object and was forced to turn over several times in the dirt before he was able to extinguish the flames. He was to find out later that more than twenty people had died that morning from this strange phenomenon and hundreds more were badly burnt. He was lucky for although he had suffered some burns, his quick reaction had saved him from serious injury.

After recovering his senses the man sought answers and walked towards the dirt road that led to the Bedegraine Forest. He had not walked for long before he became aware of a great light up ahead. He had seen fires before, but this was different for the whole forest seemed to be ablaze. Although many furlongs away from the heat, the fire made the man turn around and briskly march in the opposite direction.

For a few moments he had forgotten all about his attackers, but now that his head had cleared his thoughts turned to tracking them down. This would be a lot easier if he could find a horse, his own had been stolen and all the horses around the area had run off once the fire had started. Forced to walk, the man retraced his steps down the dirt road and made for the largest town in the area, Caerleon. He hoped that was where his robbers were heading, he also hoped he might be able to buy a horse but then he remembered he had no money to purchase anything. He saw many people walking back and forth along that dusty road, many burnt or with blood injuries. All of them seemed dazed and unable to comprehend what had just happened. Gawain felt their sorrow, but he had other matters on his mind too. He was determined to find Ragnell and to take back Arthur's great sword from her.

*

Penelope quite by chance had stumbled upon valuable information that could destroy the Queen. This information was not what her masters had asked for, they were hoping for information that would destroy Mador. Her experience at manipulating the man had convinced her that in her past life she must have been either a prostitute, or a spy. Neither occupation alarmed the woman for it seemed to her that both professions embodied a good deal of excitement.

Because Mador was drunk, Penelope coaxed the man into further indiscretions and convinced him to get written statements from his two witnesses. He grumbled but agreed.

The next day she went with him to Camlan in the west to make sure he went through with his plan. She was not present at the secret locations but stayed at an inn nearby while he gained Fergus and Angharad's testimony. She had not decided what use she was going to make of these statements and the witnesses. Rather like Mador she thought of them as a kind of insurance against bad times. She had learnt a lot about the Queen and her treachery, but not that much about Mador's unlawful activities. What little she had found out she gave to Cadfan later that day. It added to the prefect's already heavy file of circumstantial evidence. She had taken instructions from her employers to set up a meeting with Mador and a corrupt administrator who for a price was prepared to provide papers and a new identity for the man to escape the clutches of Guinevere. He was about to disappear, or so he thought, but what was not clear to Penelope was what the man was going to do with his daughter.

Her assignment continued and her involvement in Mador's family life went on. That involvement meant dealings with the troublesome Megan and her unstable mind.

As day turned to night, Penelope found herself alone with the despondent young woman. Mador had been called away on some business matter leaving the two women alone to entertain one another. Penelope had tried throughout the night to lighten the atmosphere by being cheerful and pleasant, but Megan seemed to be in a world of her own. Penelope felt, as the night went on, a certain anxiety as Megan's conversation flashed back and forward from the present to the past often in midsentence. Most of what the child said made little sense. Although at times she could converse normally, at other times she would speak of matters that Penelope knew nothing about.

The ladies were both sewing; Megan was making a scarf and was embroidering a design upon it, while Penelope was less ambitious and was repairing a man's breeches. Megan looked up from her sewing to address her companion. 'You remember the time I saved the Queen's treasure…you were so proud of me. I thought she was the most beautiful woman I had ever seen…how she praised me…I thought she loved me…but she is a snake incapable of love.'

Penelope was a passive listener often nodding her head, or replying with a yes or a no. She was intrigued by the girl's ramblings and wondered if any of her statements had an inkling of truth to it.

Megan continued. 'Does he still molest you?' she asked. Glancing across at her charge, Penelope asked who the girl was referring too.

Looking at little ruffled, Megan raised her voice. 'Why the brute that is my father of course.'

'Your father loves you…'

'No he doesn't. He is incapable of loving anyone.'

Penelope tried to reassure Megan, but the girl was adamant that her father was a monster. She leant forward and lowered her voice. 'Just be careful,' she whispered. 'He is capable of murder.'

'Don't talk nonsense,' Penelope stated.

Megan remained close and continued to whisper. 'He killed my mother you know.'

Shaking her head Penelope took hold of the girl's arms and assured her again that her father was a kind man.

Megan laughed. 'He is a monster who planned to sell me off to the highest bidder.'

'You mustn't say bad things about your father.'

'He does still beat you, doesn't he? Is that why you are afraid to speak against him? You can tell me everything you know, we are sisters after all.'

'We are not sisters...'

'Yes, don't you remember? We promised each other to be sisters and to look after each other. That way he couldn't hurt us...and then the Queen intervened and set us free. Surely you remember that?'

Penelope said she did, but of course she had no idea what the girl was talking about. She thought it better to humour the young woman rather than to contradict her. What she did realise was that the ramblings weren't as wild as they sounded. Megan's mind was unhinged, but her memory was not. The tale she weaved was factual and her animosity to her father was justified. It was just that her mind was a little muddled. She thought Penelope was her step-mother Hester and that she was still living as his wife.

Megan left her chair to kneel before Penelope. 'I have a plan,' she muttered, 'I intent to set us both free again.'

'Perhaps, I am quite happy here...'

'You can not be...he beats you with belts...'

Penelope saw the panic in the girl's eyes and sought to comfort her. 'He doesn't. He wouldn't dare...'

Megan shook her head. 'I saw it...the lines all over your back...it was horrible...'

'No, I can show you it is not so.'

The girl waited for Penelope to loosen her dress and to offer up her back for inspection. When she did not Megan began to help her undo the ties.

'Wait,' cried Penelope. She loosened her dress, pulled it down a little to reveal her unblemished back. 'See he does not hurt me.'

Megan saw the smooth skin and gently touched it with her hand. 'He is behaving...perhaps he doesn't want to kill you too.'

Now upset herself, Penelope held the young woman close. 'No more talk of this...you must have dreamt the whole thing.'

'Oh, Hester am I going mad?' asked the terrified Megan.

The name registered with Penelope, for she had heard Mador mention it as his errant wife. This realisation sparked a kind of awakening within the woman. What if Megan's ramblings weren't so fantastical? What if the man had killed his wife and had killed his first wife, Megan's mother? He could be a lot more dangerous than she had first thought. Her instincts told her that such fear did not come without some justification. She would wait until Megan felt better before questioning her on these matters further. She hoped she would be able to differentiate facts from fiction from the girl, so as to build a clear picture of Mador's past. His daughter might have real evidence that could put the man behind bars, or even have the man swinging from the gallows.

*

Germanus was waiting patiently for the Queen to leave Polyxena's side so that he could talk with her. As the Queen approached he became worried for he had never seen the lady look so white and listless. She walked to her throne chair and sat staring into space. He came up to her and knelt before her. This was a reversal of their first encounter.

'You bring me some good news I hope?' queried Guinevere.

Looking suitably miserable the man did not answer at first.

'Has your man deserted his charge?' asked the Queen.

'He has been most reliable in the past.'

'Thankfully, I have my own spies and they have found out what yours could not.'

Germanus had felt the Queen's displeasure before, but his patience was running out concerning his position at her court. The Pope was impatient for some reward for the money and time his envoy had spent on the land of the Celts. Any day he feared his recall and the censure of his master.

Guinevere continued with her vitriolic tone. 'My husband after praying in various churches, drinking in various taverns, and whoring in various brothels, has decided to join me again here in Corbenic.'

While sounding relieved Germanus hinted that they had other business to discuss.

'Can you produce the armies of the Franks?' the Queen demanded to know.

'They're suspicious, my lady.'

'What have they got to be suspicious about?'

'They are not convinced that Arthur is dead. They still fear him, even from beyond the grave...'

'You're telling me they think he's still alive?'

'They think he will return, kill you and retake their lands again.'

'Gutless, spineless men all of them.'

'I did warn you at the time...'

'Yes. Let's change the subject, how is the boy?'

'He is becoming a problem. He wishes to leave on some holy crusade...'

'He'll leave when I tell him.'

Guinevere studied Germanus. 'Perhaps he is not the only one that is impatient about leaving me?' she asked.

'My reports to the Pope do not make for exciting reading. It is his eminence that is becoming impatient.'

'Does he ask for your return?'

'No not yet, but I feel he could if my mission here does not begin to bear fruit.'

'When you write to him next you can placate his eminence by telling him that this is not the time for war.

Germanus, being an ex-soldier nodded in agreement. 'You have another source of power, why don't you use it?' suggested the man.

The Queen knew what the man was referring too. 'I've tried many times, but I cannot control the vessel's power.'

'Maybe you need an expert to unlock the chalice's secrets.'

'What would you have me do, go to Avalon and ask the Gods for their help?'

'You need someone who can read the inscriptions on the base, someone who can read the God's language.'

Looking more disgruntled than ever Guinevere scolded her compatriot. 'If you could read the damn object why haven't you done so before now?'

'I cannot, but I think I know someone who can. She is a witch and still wanted for her acts of witchery against the state and your good-self...'

'She is hardly likely to come forward to offer her services then?'

'No she is not fond of either of us. However I know the one person in the world she does care about.'

'Who is this witch that you are speaking of?'

'You know her as the witch from Dalriada, the young woman called Nemue.'

'You don't really expect me to let that woman anywhere near me, do you?'

'That won't be necessary. I'll handle the young woman. All I ask in return is for you to relinquish me from my duty as guardian to Galahad.'

'Is the young man so objectionable?'

'I was never meant to be a nurse-maid.'

'From this night forward you no longer need to teach or look after the young man.'

Germanus managed a slight smile and seemed relieved.

'I hope you can find someone to continue his indoctrination.'

The indoctrination the Queen referred to was more a character assassination than a religious doctrine. 'The young man is aware of the facts concerning his conception and his abandonment?' she asked.

'He is quiet in nature, but every time I bring up the lady's name his mood darkens.'

Guinevere's tone lowered. 'I want him to hate her, like I hate her.'

'I think his hatred can never match your own...'

'You are wrong...I shall take over your assignment. I will have him anxious to take his revenge before long.'

Germanus suddenly felt a longing to escape the Queen's presence. Her loathing for her enemy was filling his being with a sourness that did not fit his character.

Chapter 12

It was late before Polyxena ate a little supper, in the Queen's private bedroom, and felt well enough to talk. The lady's memory remained obstinate, but at least her head no longer hurt her.

Guinevere's instinct told her not to push her friend with questions. She believed that in time she would be her old self again, but she should have known that Polyxena needed answers.

The women spent the night strolling around the grounds of the castle in peaceful contemplation, until the light gave way and they were forced to move inside to the courtyard. They sat on a wooden bench just big enough for two people. The bench was designed for intimacy and the two women were so close that their bodies touched one another.

The Queen had to fend off question after question concerning their association, until finally she was forced to give into the inevitable.

'How did we meet?' asked Polyxena.

Guinevere smiled. 'You came before the High Council on criminal charges.'

Polyxena stared at the Queen and shook her head slightly. 'You are telling me I am...what...a thief?'

Continuing to smile, Guinevere stated in a matter of fact way that her friend was not a thief, but a murderer.

For a moment, Polyxena gulped some air and pleaded for Guinevere to explain.

'This was two years ago and even then I recognised something special in you.'

Polyxena did not ask what Guinevere meant. 'Who did I murder?' she asked.

'You've had a troublesome upbringing, working for your father in a profession that belittles women.'

Polyxena waited for Guinevere to confirm what she already suspected. 'Tell me everything,' she pleaded.

'You must realize that you told me your past bit by bit and that the whole story only you can know.'

'But I don't know...so tell me everything you can.'

Guinevere appeared reluctant to go into detail concerning her friend's childhood, what little Polyxena managed to prise from her implied abuse from both her mother and her father. 'You ran away from them when you were fourteen and joined a travelling troop.'

'Don't tell me I was a juggler, or an acrobat.'

Guinevere smiled. 'I never saw you in your earlier occupation, but you told me you were a jester.'

Polyxena began to laugh. 'Me?'

'It is not as fantastical as it might sound. You have a way with words that is both witty and sardonic. It is a part of you I find refreshing and honest.'

Polyxena continued to smile. 'If you asked me to be funny right now, I doubt I could.'

Guinevere reassured her that in time all her memories would return. If it did not, then the physicians who advised her would all have their hands cut off.

The young woman thought she had misheard, but when she looked at Guinevere's eyes she realized the Queen meant what she said. 'How did I come to murder someone?'

Your father left your mother and moved to Cantuaria, where he witnessed one of your performances one night. He saw his chance to make more money from you and tried to persuade you to work for him again. You refused and an argument ensued. Many witnessed this and testified upon it, when you were put on trial.

'So I killed my father?'

'Certainly everyone on the High Council thought so...'

'Then why did I not hang.'

'You have me to thank for that.'

'You thought I was innocent?'

'On the contrary, I knew you to be guilty.'

'Then why?'

Guinevere's stare made the young woman blush.

'You save me so that...'

'So that you could work for me, but something extraordinary happened.'

*

Having walked for most of the day, Gawain took his chance, when nightfall came, to steal a horse from a small livery. He was not a thief so he made a promise to himself to return the beast, when his business was finished. The trail was now cold and the chances of finding his robbers seemed slight, but he carried on in pursuit of them nonetheless.

He stopped at an inn on the outskirts of Caerleon, to see if anyone had seen the people he was stalking. To his surprise and relief many said they had. They all complained about the behaviour of one of the young women in particular.

Gawain learnt from people's descriptions that the woman was indeed Ragnell. One elderly man seemed to enjoy complaining, calling the whole youth of the day degenerates. 'She came in to our quiet inn with one purpose,' he stated, 'and that was to start a fight.'

'And did she?' asked Gawain.

'Oh yes, she flaunted about the place catching the attention of all the young men, but she was only interested in seeing them fight over her. Several tussles happened, but one almost ended in tragedy. Two local lads, old friends fought first with fists then with daggers until one of the young men suffered a serious wound. You can still see his blood stains on the ground leading up to this place.'

'Did no one call for the authorities?' asked Gawain.

'Yes we did, and we managed to hold the troublemakers for a time...but then that fiend of a woman managed to shake off her bonds and free the others.'

'Did you see her with a sword,' the young man inquired.

'That was no ordinary sword my friend. I thought it must have belonged to a great warrior. The lady tried to wield it like her own, but she had trouble with its weight.'

'Did she use it against anyone?'

'She tried, but as I said it was too heavy. Still her companion wielded it about, though I thought it did not belong to him either.'

'It belongs to me,' stated Gawain. 'The three troublemakers are thieves and I mean to bring them to justice.'

The old man shook Gawain's hands and wished him luck.

'Which way did they go? And how long ago did they leave?'

The old man told him that they left before nightfall heading north towards the region known as Rheged.

This was a blow, for a vast amount of land now lay between him and his quarry. This information however had saved the man losing valuable time in hunting in the towns to the east. He was keen to go in chase but the landlord came over to give him additional information that was to prove most useful.

'On their arrival one of the maidens asked me about a legend from these parts.'

Gawain listened intently.

'She had heard that two infamous giants stalked the hills nearby. They were brothers and had, so legend says, been given a prize to look after. That prize was so precious that in the time of King Uther many a brave soldier came looking for it. Stories continued, many becoming outlandish, but all centred around the mountains of Rheged.'

Gawain thanked the man and asked precise directions to the range of mountains. The landlord drew him a rough and ready map, which he studied before putting it into a pocket in his breeches. He had been warned not to venture there at night, but Gawain failed to listen to good reason. His impetuous nature was such that action even at night was better than brooding alone in some room or other. He realised that it was not revenge or even justice that drove him on, but a strange fascination with the unnatural woman called Ragnell.

Finding his way through the narrow passages and the craggy mountain cliffs proved dangerous and twice Gawain slipped and fell; the first time he hurt his hand when he lost hold of a piece of rock and fell down a gully, the second time he fell, he lost his footing and dropped down several feet onto a ledge. Quite by accident he had stumbled upon a cave and after checking his faculties he decided to rest up there until such time as he could see where he was going. The shelter was most welcome as he stretched himself out and made repairs to his hands which were torn. The wind seem to howl and make all kind of threatening and sinister sounds as it bellowed throughout the valleys below him. The night air had gotten colder and so the man set about building a fire to stay warm. Once the fire was lit the scenery became less menacing, allowing the man to ponder over the recent strange events. It was imperative he retrieved Arthur's great sword but he was aware something else was driving him on. Even if he was appalled by the antics of the undisciplined woman, he still saw something of his own character in her. She was daring and free spirited, but such uncontrolled aggression led to disaster. It was his great mentor King Arthur who had forced him to control his emotions. This had probably saved his life more times than he cared to remember. Perhaps he could become the lady's saviour and stop her from some catastrophe.

*

Yvain had regretted his temper and his argument with his lovely Nemue, so when a message arrived from her requesting a rendezvous he immediately abandoned his post.

He left no word for his mistress, Lady Morgan, but hurried away from Lothian towards the great wall and Corbenic. It never occurred to him that Corbenic was probably the last place the lady was likely to be. He took one of Lot's best horses just as night turned to day. The meeting place was the small village called Wedale, just Pelles's side of the wall.

Activity in the village was drawing to a close for the day when the young man wandered into the blacksmith's to ask for directions. Although there was barely any light, the blacksmith was hard at work at his kiln. Yvain was immediately hit by the heat and felt the flames almost cinder his eyes by their ferocity. The blacksmith had in one hand a sword and in the other his bellows. He forged the weapon in the blistering heat, by manipulating his right arm back and forth allowing the bellows to intensify the heat he needed. Yvain waited until the man lifted the sword out of the kiln to hammer it into shape with his hammer and anvil. He looked old and frail, but the strength of the blows confounded that observation. After the man had struck many blows and managed to straighten the sword somewhat, he thrust it down into a barrel of water by his side. The air was quickly transformed by smoke and a sizzling sound that pierced the ear. It was only after the sizzling eased that the man became aware that someone was standing nearby.

'I'm sorry,' the man exclaimed as he turned to look on Yvain.

Without blinking an eye Yvain stood motionless as he saw before him a man with barely any face. His cheeks were sunk so deep into his face that the viewer could see his skeletal bones protruding from his facade. To add to his deformity the man had a stoop which made him look old as did his grey skin, but his eyes were strong and striking. Yvain thought something about the man was familiar, but he doubted he had ever seen him before.

'Forgive me for intruding,' Yvain stated. 'I was looking for the way to the old church at Torsonce.'

The man stared for quite some time at Yvain, before answering. 'You do not want to go there my friend, trust me on that.'

Yvain smiled. 'I have urgent business there and I would appreciate your assistance...'

Again the man repeated a warning. 'If you care for your young maiden you will leave this place and return from whence you came.'

'My young maiden?' questioned Yvain. 'You speak as if you know me sir, but I can not recall ever meeting you...'

'I have seen you many times although to my shame I never conversed with you properly.'

'Pray tell me when we met?'

'You are in the service of Lady Morgan, are you not?'

'How in the devil can you know this?'

'The lady is most dear to me and needs your assistance, so return to her my friend.'

'But I have a rendezvous...'

'Yes with your sweetheart, the lady called Nemue.'

'You seem to know all about me, but how can that be?'

The old man touched his neck with his right hand and seemed concerned for a moment. 'You do not wear it anymore?' he asked.

In a reflex movement Yvain touched his own neck. Somehow he knew what the man meant. The necklace given to him by Nemue was no longer where it should have been. In fit of anger he had torn it from his nape and had broken it. 'Are you the devil?'

'Ah, I can not tell you who I am. Believe in your sweetheart, she is still the same girl you fell in love with. '

Feeling a little irate, Yvain began to question the man's statement. 'Even my mistress, Lady Morgan has fallen out with her. She no longer is concerned with justice and seeks only power and self-glory.'

'No, she works for good and loves you greatly. If you choose to abandon the lady, then go to your rendezvous, but be warned you will put the lady's life in great danger if you do.'

'She is the one who has asked for this meeting.'

The blacksmith shook his head. 'Your enemies have arranged this assignation with the intention of causing her great pain and suffering.'

Yvain gulped in mouthfuls of air and stood perplexed and confused. 'Why would anyone want to hurt Nemue?'

'The Queen has warrants out for her arrest and seeks ways to damage and weaken your mistress, Lady Morgan.'

'If Nemue is in trouble then I must go to her.'

'She is not. Only if you continue on your course will she be in danger.'

'You speak in riddles. Just tell me where the church is if you please.'

The man came towards Yvain and put his hand on his shoulder. 'One last piece of advice my friend, never trust correspondence that does not come through Lady Morgan's couriers.'

Yvain's eyes saw the man's hand and blinked, for he was sure the hand on his shoulder was fully skeletal in appearance. Several blinks later Yvain turned to look upon the man's face to find he had vanished into thin air. He remained in a daze for several moments before leaving the blacksmith's and heading west along a dirt road. He couldn't be sure where he was going, and in truth his senses were so shook that he cared little at that moment, but after awhile he met two maidens on the road and asked them how to find the church of Torsonce. They told him he was heading in the right direction, to keep on the road and he should see its spire soon. He thanked them and continued on his way, but as he spied the said spire, the blacksmiths' words of warning sounded in his ear.

Chapter 13

'I can't believe what I am hearing. You're telling me I became...'

'All for the good of our cause,' Guinevere announced.

Polyxena's hands went up to her face as she shook her head. 'Do you mean to say I've killed people?'

Guinevere took hold of her friend's hand and gently squeezed it in hers. 'You did it for me and for the good of our country.'

'A killer...I don't believe I could hurt another...'

'Once your memory returns you'll remember how people treated you and how easy it is to despise them.'

Polyxena's face was white from shock, but somehow she knew there was another revelation to come. The lady's intuition told her that the woman sitting next to her was more than just a friend.

Guinevere knew it was time to reveal her other big secret. 'We break all known conventions, because we have something unique...something special...'

'When you touch me it makes me feel strange...'

Guinevere's face exuberated joy as she lent forward to whisper something in her friend's ear. 'I wish you could remember our first embrace...'

Polyxena pulled back from Guinevere's mouth and let go of her hand. 'We...were lovers?' she muttered.

The Queen's heart almost stopped for a moment, as she feared her sweetheart's rejection. She took hold of the lady's hand again and sought to clarify the position. 'We are still lovers, but more than that we are kindred spirits. I will explain how this all came about, but first we must eat for it is getting late...'

*

Lancelot still had a look of a sullen boy as he approached his wife who was sitting on the High Throne. The room was crowded with dignitaries. They all waited to see what reception Guinevere would give to her errant husband. If they expected a confrontation, they were to be disappointed for the Queen was heartily relieved to see the man. Many in the crowd whispered in disbelief as she opened her arms to welcome his embrace.

The sullen look dissipated as Guinevere set about rebuilding their relationship. She whispered in Lancelot's ear informing him that the young woman was no longer in her employ. She begged him to forgive her and swore that things from now on would be quite different.

Lancelot although surprised, accepted the Queen's apology and said the matter was forgotten. Guinevere's cheerful mood had confounded the man, making him almost speechless. He had never seen his wife so happy and wondered whether her good mood was down to his sudden return or some other event.

The lady's good spirits was entirely due to the fact the Lady Polyxena had returned to her safe, if not entirely in one piece. She managed to sooth the lady's concerns, regarding their unconventional love, but she still feared an unfavourable reaction. Their situation was made more complicated with Lancelot's return to Caerleon. The Queen would have play act in front of everyone, including the lady she loved and that would be uncomfortable.

For the remainder of the day she was forced to smile, be pleasant, and impart her news to her husband. The married couple spent the rest of the day in each other's company talking of possible futures and promising renewed effects to make their union work. It all sounded sincere, but both parties had strategies and plans that did not include each other.

It was late before Guinevere could leave her duty and track down Polyxena. She found her in the servant's quarters, well away from her own dwelling. The Queen could not spend the time she wanted with her lover, which was upsetting for her. Politics meant she would have to continue with her pretence for awhile.

Polyxena looked the same and yet, because of a stupid blow to the head, she no longer seemed the woman she knew. Something about her had changed and yet Guinevere did not for one moment suspect that their relationship would change.

In entering the room the Queen was almost set upon by the eager young woman. 'You must tell me more of my past,' insisted Polyxena.

'I will relate to you, a little more of our story.'

As Guinevere's sat opposite she reached forward and touched her friend's neck. 'As I have said, you were found guilty of murdering your father.' Guinevere hand then began to loosen the tresses of her lover's hair. The hair fell down around Polyxena's shoulders as Guinevere used her fingers to smooth the lady's locks to make her look beautiful.

It was an act of love and one that had a strange effect on the lady with amnesia. She felt safe knowing she was part of someone's life. 'How could you see my potential as an assassin?' she asked.

'I saw how you behaved and how you poured derision on the High Council.'

'I showed no fear?'

'No, instead you showed strength...it was that strength that convinced me to put you to good use.'

'I do not remember, but I suspect I killed my father in a passionate rage.'

'That is what I found interesting. You took your time and planned his murder will due care.'

A shiver went through Polyxena's body. 'You make me seem cold and callous.'

Guinevere smiled. 'You are the most passionate person I have ever met, but like me you are forced to put on a mask.'

*

The God Gwawl emerged through the dark and the mists of Avalon, to appear on the shore of Foaine. His boyish face was contorted with rage; the lines across his forehead spoke of his anger, his high protruding cheekbones spoke of his anxiety, and his lightly blooded lips spoken of his resolve. He had come to threaten Vivienne and to ask her some forthright questions.

The lady of the lake knew of his coming and was prepared for his barrage of abuse. She swam towards the shore and slowly emerged from her pool. She looked indignantly at her compatriot and his scornful face.

Gwawl stood on the sandy beach with his arms outstretched and his temper barely under control. 'You did this, didn't you?' he shouted.

Vivienne did not move and did not attempt to answer his question. She looked mildly annoyed and somewhat contemptuous.

'Do you deny it?' cried Gwawl.

With a sigh, Vivienne annoyance grew more pronounced. 'Of course I deny it. You don't really think I would harm my own kind.'

Gwawl studied the lady of the lake with his eyes and found the lady's resolve as great as his own. 'I don't know what you did...'

Vivienne raised her voice. 'How dare you accuse me? Did I not warn all of you of the dangers?'

'It is someone's fault.'

'I see you too, feared this outcome or you would not be here.'

Gwawl almost stuttered his reply. 'I...changed my mind at the last moment.'

'Why? I'll tell you shall I. It was madness to try and repair the ship in this underdeveloped land, sheer madness.'

'Pwyll was so sure we had found everything we needed, he convinced the others...'

'The others believed what they wanted to.'

Gwawl looked desolate. 'I can hardly believe they are all truly gone.'

Vivienne frowned. 'Don't get sentimental; I don't think I could stand that.'

Gwawl's eyes opened wider. 'Humans,' he announced suddenly.

The lady of the lake suppressed the desire to scream and asked him to explain his interjection.

'It was on your suggestion that we employ the troublesome giant.'

'Yes. It made good sense with his height and his strength.'

'He did it on your instructions no doubt.'

'Now you are talking nonsense. The giant, as you probably know, is as gentle as any lamb.'

'Human terms again. You are obsessed with them and their troublesome world.'

Vivienne looked angry now, her nose twitched and her ears moved back and forth. These tiny actions, her fairies knew well, were a sure sign that the lady was about to explode with rage. 'This is my world now and these pitiful creatures and their mundane problems are all I have to keep from despondency.'

With an air of disgust Gwawl groaned his disapproval. 'It would seem this world is now, also mine.'

Vivienne sighed in relief. 'You must come to terms with this place, just as I have been forced to.'

Gwawl's face darkened. 'That is the real reason I am here. I want one of the cylinders.'

'We are not going go over this again.'

'I know you possess them. You only need one, so give me the other.'

Vivienne was slow to answer. The last thing she needed was a war with the last of her kind. If a bargain could be reached, perhaps it would make sense to give into Gwawl's demand. She wondered what the God would offer her in return for the magic of the cylinder.

'They were designed to give us life in strange lands, how can you deny me that right now.'

Without the cylinders and the air that came from them, the Gods would have succumbed to the harshness of the human air. The magic of their own atmosphere somehow intermixed with the air of the humans, allowed them to breathe and live in the alien world. Distance was the only problem, for the air could only reach so far before it began to dissipate and grow weaker. This had meant that the Gods were forced to stay in an area not well occupied and not too large. Avalon suited their purpose and for many years they lived there and tried to rebuild their damaged rocket. Only Vivienne thought of Avalon as her home and only she had made plans to stay. Now, Gwawl was forced to think of his future amongst the humans.

'What do I get for my generosity?' asked Vivienne.

A smile came over Gwawl's lips. 'What you want I suspect is for me to leave here and not to come back.'

Vivienne knew her compatriot could see into her mind and although he was harder to penetrate she could see his thought process enough to know that he feared her as much as she feared him. 'We do not communicate with each other again? We go our separate ways?'

Gwawl agreed. 'The warmth of the east beckons to me. I have grown tired of this bleak landscape and its perpetual wetness.'

'How will you get there?' asked Vivienne.

'I was hoping you could lend me a few of your tiny creatures.'

'They're not mine…'

'They are only obedient to you.'

'You want them to suspend time…'

'Only until I find a place that I like.'

'I'm sure that will be no problem, however I need some sort of guarantee you will not return one day.'

Gwawl seemed weary of the lady's suspicion. 'How can I give you that when I do not know how long the air in the cylinder will last?'

'You must choose an isolated place. A place where there are few humans.'

'Since I hate the vile creatures I don't think that shall be an issue.'

'Very well, I shall provide you with one of the cylinders, but, Gwawl, do not try to trick me.'

'I do not wish any harm to come to you. We will rule over our own lands in the understanding that neither of us will interfere with the other's dominion.'

This situation suited both Gods. Needless to say neither of them trusted the other.

'I will send the cylinder to you soon, but first I want you to do something for me. Call it an act of good faith if you wish.'

Gwawl took a long and reflective look at Vivienne. He feared his powers were already weakening for she had managed to block out her hiding place from his mind. He bowed his head in compliance.

'You have a ring that once belonged to Rhiannon, I wish to possess it.'

The ring the lady spoke of was simple in design and beautiful in construction. Its silver was woven around a stone of sparkling blue intensity.

Gwawl was mystified why the lady would want such a thing, but for him it had a strong significance. It was the only item he possessed of his one and only love. To give up the ring would bring him much sadness, but he had no choice. 'I will bring the ring when we meet again. When will this be?' he asked the lady.

'You are not welcome to stay here, you must wait on Annwn.'

'What's left of it you mean?'

Gwawl was not happy at being dismissed in such a way, but he felt he had no choice but to go along with Vivienne's wishes.

'It won't be for long,' assured the lady.

Chapter 14

Yvain stood outside the church for quite some time before deciding to enter. Making hard decisions was not something that came easy to the man. As he entered by the front door, he felt a stinging sensation around his neck which forced him to hesitate for a moment. Again as if by some force of magic, the blacksmith's words of warning came into his head. Yet he still entered, despite his foreboding, and began to walk down the aisle. As the light from the sun pierced through the narrow windows, it bathed him in a glorious light. This lightened his mood and his anxiety eased further when a jovial priest came forward to embrace him as a brother.

The priest welcomed his new visitor with a broad smile and began to chat away to him on mundane things. The priest called himself Mathew and was keen to engage with Yvain on the subject of religion. Yvain was anxious to broach the subject of Nemue, but feared the priest would be ignorant of their rendezvous, so he said nothing. Mathew was clothed in a dark monk's habit and wore a cross around his neck and worn out sandals. His whole appearance gave the impression of poverty and selflessness. Yvain feared that the man would not have any information that would be of any use to him, but he was wrong on that assumption.

'You have travelled some distance I see,' the priest declared.

'How can you tell?'

The priest pouted his lips and smiled. 'You have much dust and dirt on your clothes and your cheeks are still red from exertion.'

'You have a keen eye, father.'

'Oh, I wasn't always a priest you know. I served as a soldier in foreign lands in my youth.'

'You must have killed many people as a soldier? Does not that make your new position rather difficult?'

'On the contrary, I think it gives me a unique perspective into the minds of men.'

'I see. I hate to intrude on you further, but I don't suppose you have seen a young woman in you church this morning. She would be small in height and have a pretty face.'

'The young woman wouldn't happen to be called Nemue, would she?'

'Yes she would. Is she here now?'

'No she could not wait, but she gave me instructions to bring you to her.'

Nemue followed the old religion, so the chances that she would have confided in a priest of the new religion were somewhat remote. However the innocent Yvain swallowed the lie.

'Will you not be missed here?'

'I have plenty of time on my hands, you needn't worry about me.'

The two men left the church to ride further into Corbenic and into the heart of the stronghold of the Queen. The jovial priest who escorted Lady Morgan's servant on the journey was none other than Germanus himself.

Nemue was on route to her rendezvous with Vivienne on Avalon, when she became diverted. She had received a note, which appeared to been written in the hand of Yvain, asking her to meet him at the abandoned castle of Listinoise.

The castle was a well known place for lovers so the meeting place itself did not arouse suspicion, however the timing and the fact that most of her friends were aware of her current business did make her fearful.

She approached the castle on her white horse with caution and did not dismount. She listened for the sound of people walking or talking but not a sound was heard. This intensified her fear. She shouted Yvain's name but got no response. She was about to turn her horse around when two men appeared from behind a crumbling wall. They brought with them Yvain, who was tied with a rope that went from his legs, up to his hands and further up to his neck. The burly men laughed as they turned the rope by small degrees, tightening the noose around Yvain's neck and increasing the poor man's pain.

'Two more turns and he will choke, my lady. You do not want to see that now, do you?'

The voice came from the lady's right hand side and she glanced to where she thought the man must be. She saw a darkened shape move slowly towards her. She could not see the man's face, but his garb was strange in design for it flowed from his head down to his ankles. It became clear that the man was a Christian cleric or a bishop. In fact the lady thought she recognised him as the bishop called Germanus.

Nemue had fallen for the trap and was awaiting the bishop to make his demands. The thought entered her mind that the plan to kill the Queen had been discovered, but she waited for confirmation before saying a word.

Germanus seemed in no hurry either. After all it was not his neck that was feeling the pain and discomfort of the rope. 'I'm afraid my men enjoy hurting people, they believe they can drive out the devil by such actions. I, on the other hand feel that pain should be avoided whenever possible. Don't you agree, my lady?'

Nemue did agree as she pleaded for Yvain to be released.

'I wish no harm to come to him...'

'Just me I suppose?' Nemue quipped.

'Not at all, I wish you both to live to a ripe old age. I need your help and I reckoned this was the only way to get your attention.'

'You have my attention now, but I beg of you to loosen the rope so that my friend can at least speak.'

Germanus gave the order to loosen the rope around Yvain's neck. The man coughed several times after the deed was done, and managed to squawk a defiant curse at his captors.

The bishop turned again to look at Nemue. 'I have done what you asked. Now you must do something for me.'

'Just what is it you want?'

Germanus came a few paces closer and invited the lady to dismount from her horse. When the lady refused Germanus gave the order to tighten the rope again, but Nemue gave in and dismounted. Now on the ground the lady felt less safe but Germanus surprised her by pulling from a pouch a piece of parchment which he handed to her. The language written on the animal skin was that by the man's own hands. He had copied the inscription on the God's chalice exactly and was hoping for a translation from the young lady.

'Tell me what it says and what it means and you have my word you can both go free.'

Taking the parchment from the man, Nemue studied it.

'It is not a language I recognise and I thought I knew them all,' boasted Germanus.

'What makes you think I know what you do not?'

'You have powers, given to you by your friend the Lady of the Lake that makes you the only human capable of unravelling these words.'

The young woman studied the parchment but complained she could not see the words in the poor light. A third man came from within the rubble of the castle carrying a fire torch and descended down the slight decline towards Nemue. With the light from the torch both Nemue and Germanus could study the scroll more closely.

Nemue knew what the inscription was, for her lady had informed her of the chalice's importance. She knew better than to give the man the message it carried, so she procrastinated and declared the inscription must be incomplete.

'I wrote down the letters myself, I missed nothing...'

'Their language is different. Perhaps you missed a symbol, for they use symbols and not just letters.'

'I am not some fool. I missed nothing.'

'I would need to see the object to be sure.'

'Any tricks and I will give the word to kill your friend.'

'I find it hard to trust a Christian. I have always found them to be liars and hypocrites.'

Germanus dismissed the lady's remark and told her they had a journey to go on. Nemue glanced over to Yvain and tried to offer him the warmth of her smile, but the man failed to acknowledge her gesture. He could not move, for one turn from his tormenters and he might choke to death.

Although Nemue didn't know it, Germanus was taking her to his inner sanctuary. This was a place that no one knew about except his most trusted servants. Not even Queen Guinevere knew of its existence.

Germanus was a careful man and took the precaution of blindfolding his captives on their journey. It was an awkward and uncomfortable journey for Yvain, but Nemue had such powers that allowed her to see through the blindfold. She now knew her enemy's secret lair and was sure that the information would one day be put to good use. She had already pledged to take her revenge on the sanctimonious bishop for the anguish he had caused her.

Germanus called a halt to the journey and his men had bundled Nemue and Yvain into a cold dark room. The air was harsh as Yvain struggled to speak after having to endure his bondage for so long. Nemue complained about their treatment but a door closed and the young couple found themselves alone.

Nemue lost no time in helping her friend loosen his bounds and before long all the rope that had been tied so tight was lying on the floor beside them. Yvain gasped for breath and the young woman told him to breathe deeply. Still upset Yvain was not easily placated, but after an awkward silence the man took the girl in his arms and whispered his thanks.

'Don't thank me too soon,' Nemue replied. 'We are still in a lot of trouble.'

'I'm sure you will think of something.'

Nemue smiled. 'I'm glad you think I am some kind of miracle worker.'

'You have magic, you surely can't deny that,' queried Yvain.

'And magic can cure every problem?'

'Well can't it?'

'We shall see. The main thing is that you are alright?'

The young man studied his young love and saw the worry on her face. Truly the ghost of King Arthur was right, the girl still loved him. He brought his stiff fingers up close to Nemue's face and caressed her cheek. 'How could we allow anything to stand in the way of our love?' he asked. Nemue answered his question with a passionate kiss. In each other's arm the young couple forgot their troubles for a moment.

Their idyllic moment was cut short by the arrival of Germanus and two of his guards. After putting two fire torches on the wall the guards left, leaving their master alone with the two young people. Wearing a falcon's glove, Germanus carefully produced from a pouch the chalice that once belonged to the Gods.

Nemue went to take the object from the man, but he issued her with a warning. 'Careful, it has a strange power. I dare not hold it for more than a moment.'

Nemue only smiled and using her two hands took the object from Germanus without fear. The bishop looked on in amazement as the girl suffered no ill effects at all. Nemue studied the object and in particular the inscription upon the base. She knew the words and its meaning but she was not going to divulge the chalice's secret. Instead she lied, and what a lie. She told the Christian dignitary exactly what he most wanted to believe. 'I feel honoured,' she stated. Thank you for allowing me to touch your most sacred object.'

Germanus stood mystified. 'What do you mean?'

'I hold in my hand the vessel that once your Lord, the one you call Jesus passed around his disciples.'

Open mouthed, the bishop shook his head. 'You lie. This is a pagan object that carries pagan power...'

'You judge too fast holy man. The Gods on Avalon are no different from the man you call Jesus.'

Germanus was becoming quite agitated. 'Why do you lie? I don't understand...'

'I have no cause to lie.'

'Do you not feel its strange power go through your body?' asked Germanus.

'Only the pure in heart can hold this object without ill effects.'

Germanus looked curiously at the maiden. 'I don't mean to imply anything, but are you pure...'

Yvain came to the lady's defence. 'Nemue is pure in heart,' he passionately assured the man.

Feeling warmed by her young man's statement, Nemue continued with her deception. 'I am guessing the Queen is behind this?'

Germanus neither confirmed nor denied this.

'If she is, then she will never be able to control the sacred object's power.'

'So you admit it has power?'

'Oh yes, it has great power.'

'Power to destroy armies?' asked the bishop.

'Yes, but that is not what it is for.'

Germanus was tired of standing, so he and his two companions squatted down on the dungeon floor and continued to chat. The bishop was fascinated to hear more and pleaded with the maiden to tell him everything she knew about the object. This she proceeded to do.

'Only the Gods know of its true power but the lady of the lake has told me a tale that will chill your blood.'

Both men listened intently. Nemue loved to tell stories and loved to embellish them so as to fascinate her audience.

'In the hands of the righteous the chalice can heal the sick and bring great joy to mankind, but in the wrong hands it can destroy whole communities, bringing famine and pestilence.

Germanus wanted to believe the young woman, but his logic told him to be cautious. 'Can a man change? I mean can the chalice make a man change for good?'

'If you wish to do good deeds, heal the sick, help the poor then yes I believe the chalice will help you become a good man.'

'This tale you speak about...tell me of it?'

'The lady of the lake told me about a series of plagues that struck down the Egyptians in the reign of a Pharaoh by the name of Rameses. It was all due, according to the lady, to the theft of this chalice. The Egyptians craved great wealth and continued to plunder their neighbours, sacking them of their goods, including gold, silver and precious jewels. Their greed led to a catastrophe that nearly wiped out their entire population. Like King Arthur, the Pharaoh learnt of this sacred object and coveted it. He commanded his soldiers to steal the object and bring it to him. They did just that, but the Gods took their revenge by laying waste to the Pharaoh's lands. When his people starved, Rameses summoned a man known to be a friend to the Gods to broker a deal. He promised to give back the chalice if the Gods would make his crops grow again.'

'You speak of a man that is known to me,' Germanus interrupted. 'You speak of a man called Moses.'

'Yes, that is the name the lady told to me.'

'Then I can not believe this story of plagues...'

'Do you want me to continue?' asked an irritable Nemue.

Germanus although a little wary, was still fascinated to hear the rest of the tale.

'With all their crops destroyed the Egyptians faced death, only a miracle could save them. This miracle came in the form of this man called Moses. He promised to feed everyone in the land and all from one small sized ark. This he agreed to do if Rameses would in return set free all his people. The Pharaoh agreed and work started away from prying eyes on the wooden and gold casing needed to house the sacred object.'

'No one has ever proven that such an ark ever existed,' claimed Germanus.

'I can tell you that it did, for the lady of the lake claims she has seen it.'

Germanus although still engrossed, thought the tale was for him becoming too fantastical.

The young woman continued as before. 'The people who designed the outer case worked away from prying eyes and were fed by the Gods a strange white substance. They found their strength and abilities enhanced by this strange food. It took four men a matter of days to create the safe housing for the magical ark. The Gods themselves then attached the safety encasement to the object. At the end of the construction the chosen men were rewarded for their endeavour by having both their eyes and their tongues torn out from their bodies.'

Although neither Nemue nor Germanus reacted to this cruelty, Yvain shrieked in horror.

'What happened to the ark?' inquired Germanus.

Not wishing to dull the end of her tale the young maiden ignored the bishop's question for now. 'The ark was small but heavy and took about four to six men to carry. The Pharaoh was presented with it and given precise instructions in its use. Being a man of bad faith Rameses did not set Moses and his people free, and as a punishment the Gods struck down his son and many in his court with a terrible disease. The Pharaoh blamed the death of his son upon the ark and so he had it transported back to Moses and the Israelites. Moses took his people and the ark and headed for the desert. Rameses, sick with grief, was persuaded to go after them by his wife Nefertiti, to exact revenge. He followed Moses and all his people into the desert...'

'Yes, and Moses parted the red sea and the Israelites made their escape,' imparted Germanus becoming impatient.

Nemue smiled. 'Going by the Roman calendar, Moses and his people survived in the harsh desert for nearly forty years.'

'You are telling me that this ark fed all his people for forty years?' questioned Yvain.

'I am stating only what was told to me.' Nemue quietly said.

'This ark, where is it now?' asked Germanus.

It was a question Nemue had asked the lady of the lake too, but that great lady refused to tell her its exact position. 'According to the lady it languishes in a far off place, buried deep in the ground.'

'If she is a God, why does she not send a party to rescue it?' asked the bishop.

'She told me it was better to let it rot in the earth, rather to have humans abuse its power.'

'Surely by now it will have lost its power?' Yvain asked.

'The lady believes its power remains.'

'A fine tale, but what does it have to do with the chalice?' asked Germanus.

'The chalice has a similar power and I fear our lands will suffer a similar fate if your Queen does not hand it back to the lady of the lake.'

A smiling Germanus thought to ridicule the young woman. 'This God, she could use the vessel to destroy all of us if she wished?

Nemue did not answer.

'I will make sure Guinevere does not abuse the chalice's power, but I can not be parted from it.'

'If I thought for one moment you could control the woman I would gladly tell you what the inscription says and how to unlock the power within.'

Germanus got to his feet in a rage. 'I will not let anyone use it for evil purposes...'

Yvain and Nemue got to their feet also. The girl remained calm and addressed the bishop in a soft tone of voice. 'Abandon your vile Queen and help to us to establish order and unity in our land by supporting Lady Morgan. You could be the most powerful figure in the religious world. I could teach you how to control the power of the vessel and we could do such amazing things together. '

The man pondered a moment. 'You mean to trick me,' he stated.

'I mean to open your eyes to the chance of immortality, your grace.'

Yvain wanted to clarify what would happen if Nemue did not help the man, but remained silent. Germanus was surprised by the maiden's use of reverence and wondered if her offer was sincere. Nemue thought she had convinced the bishop to become a turncoat. An eerie silence hung heavy around the dungeon as all parties thought over the situation they were in.

The bishop broke the spell by producing a dagger from beneath his cloak and holding it up close to Yvain's throat. 'Now,' he said, 'tell me how to invoke the chalice's power?'

Nemue to the men's surprise smiled. 'You have chosen evil over good and that makes it impossible for you to control the power of the vessel. Slit my love's throat if you will, but if you do I promise you will burn in hell. I'll even come down there myself and stoke the flames.'

Germanus found that his attention was being disrupted by the powerful stare of the lady's bright blue eyes. He felt his will leaving him and a burning sensation overwhelmed his right hand. He could not hold on to the dagger for it felt like it had just come from a blacksmith's furnace. His head felt like it was going to burst as a great pain shot through it. The man dropped his weapon and suddenly found it impossible to speak. The power of the lady's will was overcoming his whole body.

Nemue's eyes seemed to burrow into the man's brain. Yvain said something to his lady but the maiden could not hear his words. It took a passionate plea from him to stop the girl from killing the bishop by her sheer willpower. To the young man's relief Germanus collapsed slowly into his arms unconscious, but not dead.

'What about the guards?' he whispered to Nemue.

'Oh, they are like their master fast asleep.

Chapter 15

With the witness statements under lock and key, Mador felt a lot more at ease concerning his treacherous Queen. If he was arrested then he vowed that her secrets would come out and they might both swing from the gallows. Only Penelope knew where the documents were and if anything happened to him, she was empowered to release them to Lady Morgan.

He was becoming paranoid for he suspected spies everywhere he went. He felt like some hunted animal always afraid to look forward for fear of being cut down from behind. His only consolation was to be found in the company of Penelope, but even here his instincts told him something wasn't right. The lady behaved the same, but something about his touch seemed to make her nervous. Or at least that's how it seemed to him.

It appeared to him recently that the lady was spending more time with his daughter, than with him. The two women had become close and to his relief his child's erratic behaviour had ceased. It was a struggle to get the object of his desire alone and this made him terribly frustrated. Sometimes during the day he managed a few snippets of pleasure where he managed a kiss or two from the lady. To his surprise even in those fleeting moments she would bring up the subject of wives. His first wife was dead and, for all he cared, his second wife might as well be. Yet the woman was interested in their fate. It suddenly occurred to him that perhaps she wanted to become wife number three. Either that or she suspected him of murdering them.

This terrible thought had made him determined to confront the lady and set her mind at ease. He would calm the situation and turn it to his advantage. A promise here, a present there and the lady would once more adorn his bed. With the key to Penelope's bedchamber in his hand the man felt like a thief in the night as he tiptoed down the corridors of his own castle. What he wasn't aware of, was that he was not the only one making furtive wanderings around the corridors.

Mador, candle in hand, came to the lady's door, unlocked it and entered. He peered in the semi-darkness in the direction of the bed and approached. Penelope was asleep and was facing away from the door as Mador descended upon her. Putting his right knee on the bed he reached forward and gently shook the lady. This had little effect as Penelope only groaned a little and continued to sleep. The man put down the candle on the side table, before climbing onto the bed. He took off his clothes in a hurry and slipped under the covers and began to touch the lady with his hands. This had the effect of awakening Penelope but in a dazed state she screamed and lashed out at her intruder.

A figure crept into the bedchamber just as the lady screamed. This figure ran forward into the darkened room to assault Mador with a weapon, probably a dagger. The blows rained down upon him quick and fast, despite his efforts to protect himself with his hands, the blood began to squirt everywhere. The attacker seemed to be in a rage as they lashed out in frenzy, striking blow after blow. Penelope screamed and threw herself off the bed onto the floor where she continued to witness the assault. Finally the blows became less frequent as the perpetrator tired from the exertion. Penelope looked up at the figure, now resting on the bed and feared she was next.

It had all happened so quickly, that the shock of it all still hadn't registered with the lady. She cowered on the floor unawares that the top half of her body was covered in blood.

The eyes of the figure on the bed stared at Penelope but the person did not come any closer. The lady put up her hands to cover her face fearing that an attack was imminent, but none came. She heard the rustling of sheets then the sound of someone running away. After a moment, she took her hands away from her face to peer around the room looking for any trace of the assailant. The lady slowly got to her feet and although still shaking, walked around the room in her bare feet. Despite stumbling over a few things the lady got to the door where she exited into the corridor. She was convinced she knew who the perpetrator was and for that reason she did not immediately raise the alarm.

Megan's bedchamber lay a good distance from her own, but it was imperative she checked it out, to see if the lady was there. If Megan had carried out this terrible deed Penelope rightly or wrongly wanted to protect her. The thought of the poor child rotten in a cold cell in chains, or still worse hanging from a rope made the woman sweat with anxiety.

The lady should have thought of her own situation for it was rather desperate; for Mador's dead body lay on her bed, the act of brutality was enacted in her bedchamber and still worse, her white bedclothes were covered in the man's blood. All it would take for her to be accused of the act was for her to stumble across some of the man's guards. Scurrying along the castle corridor leading to Megan's room, the lady kept her eyes peeled and prayed that no one would see her.

She had gotten within a few steps of the room when the alarm was raised. She heard shouts and cries coming from her own room, followed footsteps of guards running. Megan came out of her room to complain about the noise, to be met by several guards surrounding Penelope. She had fresh clean bedclothes on and yawned. 'What is going on here?' she demanded to know.

The guards did not answer immediately, but once they had moved a little to one side the blooded figure of Penelope came into Megan's view.

'My God, sister what has happened?' she cried.
Still shaking, the lady babbled for a moment, before two guards ran towards the small group to announce the Lord Mador was dead. All eyes turned towards the blood soaked woman. The two guards nearest to Penelope began to manhandle her, but Megan shouted at them to stop. They

did, but asked the lady to accompany them to the dungeons.

'She will do nothing of the kind,' commanded Megan. The guards looked at one and other, but none were brave enough to contradict their young mistress. 'You must send for the local prefect to come here without delay. I will take care of this lady and make sure she is cleaned up...'

'Should you not leave her as she is, until the authorities arrive?'

'You dare to question me?' thundered the girl.

The guard shook his head, while two others ran away to fetch the prefect. Megan ushered her friend into her room where she set about removing the blood from her body and giving her a new set of clothes to wear.

*

Leogran and Cadfan were walking up and down the bedchamber perplexed by this sudden change of events. With each glance over at the naked body which was still slouched over the bed, riddled with dagger wounds, they sweated.

The blood had turned the white bedcovers red. Neither man had said a word for quite some time, but their eyes spoke to each other. At last Leogran made his thoughts known. 'It doesn't look good,' he observed. 'All alone in the room with the man, his blood all over her body...it seems clear to me what happened.'

Cadfan wasn't so quick to judge. 'Perhaps it isn't how it seems? Perhaps there was an intruder?'

'The guards saw no one. I'm afraid at best it looks like a crime of passion.'

'Nonsense, the lady had no passion for the man.'

'She sleeps with him, what would you call that?'

'Are you forgetting the role we gave the lady to play in this matter?'

'I don't remember us forcing her to do anything she didn't want to.'

This was true, but Cadfan wanted someone else to blame for the mess that was before them. 'We must cover this up,' he suggested. 'Dispose of the body somewhere so that no one will ever find it.'

Leogran stood looking at the man, his face a picture of indignation. 'I have sworn an oath, as have you, to carry out our duty without prejudice and without interference. I cannot cover up a murder.'

'Not even if it means saving you own skin?'

'How are we responsible for a crime of passion?'

'Our masters might think differently, especially the Queen...'

'I don't see her caring, not now that someone else has taken care of her little problem.'

'Mador wasn't just anyone. He was a man of great power and influence, even the Queen daren't just have him killed.'

Leogran moved closer to his deputy. He stood over Cadfan and with his commanding presence made the smaller man feel intimidated. 'No one knows of the Queen's involvement and it must remain so,' he commanded. Cadfan agreed. 'What of our problem though? We surely can't let our colleague take the blame.'

'If she's guilty, we shouldn't protect her.'

Cadfan's sullenness worried his superior. He thought by removing him from the case he might be doing his friend a favour, but when he suggested such a thing Cadfan threw into a rage. 'This is my case and my responsibility. I refuse to abandon the lady...'

'Since it is your responsibility I will hear no more of a cover up. You do your duty and if the evidence proves the lady is guilty then she will receive the same treatment as any one else.'

Cadfan agreed and brought up the subject of questioning. 'We should leave the questioning until morning,' he suggested.

An angry Leogran disagreed. 'No different than anyone else,' he shouted.

'The ladies are upset and with it being so late I thought...'

With a sigh, Leogran showed no compassion. 'I will question them now, before they have time to concoct a story.'

Raising his voice Cadfan protested. 'No, if it is my case I will question them and not you.'

This was not the first time his deputy had shown him petulance, but due to the circumstances he was prepared to let it go this time.

'Are they still in Lady Megan's room?' asked Leogran.

'Yes, I have two of my men watching them.'

'Then let's get it over with.'

'You will not interfere?'

'No, I will be an observer only.'

The questioning started well mannered enough with Cadfan taking the lead. The two women clung to each other as they clasped each other's hands as the men began their interrogation.

Cadfan addressed Penelope. 'This intruder, did you get a chance to see his face at all?'

'No, it was too dark see anything, besides it happened so quickly.'

'But you thought it was a man?'

The lady hesitated. 'I can't be sure, but it was done with such force.'

Leogran whispered something in Cadfan's ear.

'You have said that you were not Mador's lover, but he was found in your bed. Can you explain this?'

Megan's eyes glanced at her friend. 'You do not understand what my father was like,' she announced.

Cadfan rebuked the interruption.

'It would be foolish for me to deny it. I was the man's lover.'

An excited Megan rose to her feet. 'No, you don't understand she is his wife...'

Both men knew this was not so, but the young woman sounded so sincere that they accepted she believed what she said. Penelope managed to calm young Megan down before the questioning continued.

'Let's stop pretending that you do not know who I am,' stated a petulant Penelope.

Leogran agreed and began to take over the questioning.

'Why did you kill him? Did he try and rape you?'

'I didn't kill him. I had no reason too.'

'What about the knife, what did you do with that?' queried Leogran.

'I had no knife.'

Megan was getting excited and lunged forward towards the inquisitor. The man stepped back to defend himself, as the young woman raised her arms as if to strike him with her fists. She didn't get the chance for Cadfan stopped her and forced her back onto a chair.

'Maybe we're questioning the wrong person,' stated a ruffled Leogran.

Penelope came to her charge's defence. 'You have no right to question us at all,' she complained. 'Haven't we been through quite enough for one night.'

'Perhaps it could wait until tomorrow?' Cadfan suggested.

'No it can't. A murder has been committed and we have before us a well known criminal.'

Looking confused the young women waited for an explanation.

'You were not aware that we had found you out,' stated Leogran.

Penelope looked bewildered. 'What do you mean?'

'I do not buy your story of a loss of memory. I think you took this assignment so as to rob the Duke. Perhaps you had reason to believe he had treasure hidden in the castle. In any case you argued and you ended up stabbing him to death.'

Cadfan had to restrain Megan again as she tried to get up from her chair. 'I did it. I killed him and I'm glad I did.'

'Do not listen to her,' screamed Penelope. 'She doesn't know what she is saying...'

'Perhaps you both did it?' suggested the prefect.

'Don't be ridiculous we didn't do anything,' stated Penelope.

Cadfan sought to dampen down the idea that the women were the perpetrators. 'We have no proof against these ladies...'

'I have three witnesses to the fact that our colleague was covered in the man's blood. She must have been on that bed when the attack took place.'

'She could have been trying to save him,' suggested Cadfan.

'The blood was nor smeared, but splashed over her. She was definitely present when the attack took place. One of our men found her sodden bed shirt lying hidden behind a cabinet in this room.'

Cadfan looked first at one woman and then at the other. He realised his superior was not going to let this go. 'Do you want to arrest both of them?' he asked. 'If so I would suggest we make sure we have enough evidence to make the charges hold.'

Penelope knew there was no real proof against Megan, but if the prefect started questioning everyone in the house then the girl's madness would soon become apparent. They would charge her with the crime and her life would be as good as over. So without thinking she decided to take the blame. She was as sure as she could be that the girl did it, but she was just as sure that the poor child was out of her mind when she did.

Chapter 16

Morning brought a fresh wind and a torrent of rain, as the heavens opened to batter the craggy rocks and green valleys that had become Gawain's new vista. He was quite content to stay in the shelter and not brave the elements, but a bellow of a cry from a woman drifted upwards to where he lay.

Jumping to his feet he peered out over the vast panorama to try and pinpoint the sound. He shouted in the direction to where he thought the cry came from. 'Hello, where are you? Are you in some danger?'

The young man had no way of knowing if the woman who cried out was Ragnell or Rosalinda, but chances were it was one or the other. Gawain waited for a reply but this time it was a man's voice he heard. 'Down here, by the large gully to your left,' the man cried.

Gawain felt sure it was his quarry and that Morholt was the one who had answered his call. Wasting no time the unarmed man left his shelter, to climb down several dangerous ridges in the direction of the large gully. It was the same slippery gully, that the night before, he had fallen down and hurt his hand. He was soon on the scene and there he spied two of his adversaries, Morholt and Rosalinda. The man was standing over the lady, with his arm outstretched holding her weight in mid-air. She was dangling over a precipice that dropped down about fifty feet.

'Quickly,' shouted Morholt, 'help me pull her up.'

Without thinking Gawain came to his robbers' help. He reached down, holding onto a small rock, and with one hand helped Morholt to pull up the damsel to safety.

Out of breath the young woman praised her rescuers unreservedly. Morholt glanced over to Gawain and waited for some reproach or some act of violence that did not come. Instead Gawain stared back at the man.

It was Rosalinda's quick reaction to her saviour that went some way to ease the tension. She quickly embraced Lot's son. 'Oh sir, we are pleased to see you, truly we are.'

Gawain said he did not doubt it.

'You will help us, won't you?'

Gawain was rather dumbstruck by the question. 'I hate to remind you, but there is the question of my belongings...'

Morholt quickly emptied out his possessions before the man. There wasn't much left of his money, but two, out of the three pieces of jewellery was set before him. 'Ragnell has the other piece,' said the man.

Only Gawain's ring was missing. As he scooped up his belongings from the ground, he addressed the lady with an air of sarcasm. 'And where is the lovely Ragnell?'

'Oh sir, I can see you are angry with us, but do not blame my poor sister she has no control over what she does.'

Sounding less than compassionate, Gawain asked his question again this time with more vigour. Morholt explained she went off on her own during the night despite their efforts to persuade her to wait until daylight.

Rosalinda explained. 'She waited until we were asleep before leaving our camp in the middle of the night.'

'We knew she was headed this way for she is obsessed with some legend...'

'I too have heard something of this legend,' Gawain interrupted. 'What could be so valuable to risk climbing mountains in the dark?'

Morholt glanced at Rosalinda. The lady grimaced. 'For goodness sake tell him,' she cried.

'Tell me what? Gawain queried.

'Are you a religious man?' inquired Morholt.

The question was somewhat unexpected and Gawain admitted he wasn't.

Morholt continued. 'You have heard of Moses no doubt and his journey with his people in the desert?'

Gawain said he knew a little of the story, stating that as a boy his mother had told him about Moses and the Ten Commandments.

With the torrent still in full flow it was not surprising Rosalinda spoke of finding cover. Gawain thought the climb to his cave was too dangerous for the lady, so he suggested a smaller inlet closer to where they were.

Once inside the three young people tried their best to dry themselves. A small fire was lit and they all huddled round it to recover from the cold and the rain. It wasn't long before Gawain demanded answers.

It was Rosalinda who did most of the talking as she began with a revelation. Looking Gawain square in the eye, she pleaded for his understanding. 'You see I am Ragnell's elder sister and guardian. She has always been the headstrong one, but I fear lately she has begun to lose her mind.'

'How so?' asked Gawain.

'You saw for yourself, she has a great capacity for violence...'

'I too have a similar capacity.'

'Yes, but you are a man. Aren't men supposed to be warriors?'

'I have known one or two women who could hold their own in a man's fight.'

'That describes Ragnell perfectly. She is just like a man, but she has a body of a woman.'

'That could be a useful combination.'

'You seem to admire her strength and resolve, but you have seen for yourself how impossible she can be.'

Gawain pondered and seemed to agree.

'It was Ragnell who struck you from behind and stole your possessions.'

Gawain did not challenge the statement.

'She will get herself killed or hung for sure,' stated her sister.

'I will help you find her. For one thing I want my sword back and I must admit to being a little intrigued by all this.'

'Oh, thank you kind sir, but remember she is dangerous.'

'I too can be dangerous. Tell me more of this legend and what it has to do with Moses?'

'I do not know that much, Ragnell is the one who has studied the manuscripts and has listened to the teachings. She is convinced that an object belonging to the one true God is somewhere buried in these mountains.'

'I am ignorant of the story so tell me all that you can,' Gawain pleaded.

'It is said that the Christian God ordered Moses to build an ark. It was said to be made of wood and gold and was to be housed inside another object of much great value. That inner object has been the cause of much debate, by learned people and of priests for a long time.'

'What do you think is inside the ark?' asked Gawain.

'I truly have no idea, but my sister has many theories.'

'Go on, tell me some of them.'

'As I have said she has studied this more than I. She has told me different things at different times; once she told that she thought the God lived inside, but then she told me that two sacred tablets given to Moses were housed within. Truth be told, I'm sure she has no real idea either.'

Morholt contributed his thoughts on the matter. 'I know a little of its history. The ark changed hands several times; the Israelites lost a great war and it was said the ark fell into the hands of the Philistines, who were a Hebrew tribe from the west. Frightening stories began to be spread concerning horrible deaths to anyone who came into contact with the ark. The story goes that the Philistines couldn't wait to get rid of the object, so they put the chest on a cart and harnessed two cows to it and whipped the poor beasts towards the borders of Bethshemesh. In the morning when the people of Bethshemesh came into the valley to harvest the wheat, they saw the cart with the ark on it. Ignorant of its danger, many touched it and others stood too close, and many died a horrible death soon after. The elders of their people summoned the Levites, who alone seemed to know how to handle the ark.'

'This all happened a great distance from here, how could this religious relic have found its way here?' Gawain queried.

'I asked Ragnell that same question,' stated Rosalinda. 'She told me a little more of its history saying that the object was safely housed in King Solomon's great temple, but that it changed hands once again this time to a great Queen called Sheba. Given as a present perhaps, the ark was brought to the capital of Sheba's kingdom, Axum. Many think it is still there, but others think that the Babylonians were tricked and that the ark they took was a fake.'

The rain had eased outside but Gawain was so enthralled by the tale that even when Morholt suggested venturing back out onto the mountain, he refused. 'Go on, tell me more.'

Rosalinda continued. 'With the spread of Christianity many different stories flourished concerning the ark. Thanks to a manuscript that Ragnell managed to get her hands on, an unlikely lead led to this part of the world.'

'Does she still have this manuscript?' asked Lot's son.

'Yes, it never leaves her person. All she would say on the matter was that much later the safety of the ark was given to a friend of Jesus of Nazareth's by the name of Joseph of Arimathea.'

Gawain waited for more clarification.

Morholt helped his companion out. 'It is documented that this Joseph of Arimathea visited our lands shortly before he died.'

'And you think he left the ark or cart, somewhere in this area?'

Rosalinda shook her head. 'We do not, but my obsessed sister has got it into her head that it is here.'

'Perhaps she has more information that we do?' suggested Morholt.

'That might be so, but I fear she will get herself killed if we do not put an end this madness.'

Gawain should not have felt admiration for the woman who had tried to kill him, but somehow he did. She had such a determination and was so fearless that he longed to see her again. Madness or not, he hoped there was something to her quest. With the tale told, the three young people ventured out onto the mountains to try and track the lonely adventurer.

*

News of a great catastrophe on Avalon and its surrounding area, reached the Kings and Queens of the land. Guinevere took the opportunity to dispense with Lancelot's services by sending him there to gather the facts. She had no idea that the fires were caused by the Gods and she certainly had no idea that nearly all of them had died.

Lancelot must have suspected the Queen wanted him out of the way, for the errand seemed better suited to a junior officer of her guards than to the King of Caerleon. Still he accepted and was grateful, for the task of assassin had suddenly become a terrible burden to him. Two drops of poison in Guinevere's evening drink and he would have all that he had ever wanted. Yet he hesitated. Something, call it a conscience maybe, was making him doubt his resolve. The departure would give the man time to think and perhaps come up with a different scenario.

Guinevere was relieved to see Lancelot leave. This allowed her to further implant her memories onto Polyxena's consciousness, but the lady's memory continued to be stubborn.

It was strange to be told things about one's self that you could not recall, even more strange, to hear deeds that you were supposed to have done that seemed alien to you. The person that Guinevere was revealing to her somehow seemed outlandish and exotic, not the person she thought she should be.

After spending the morning with Guinevere, Polyxena retired to her new bedroom to rest and to contemplate the newest adventure she had been told about. It sounded exciting being a spy and risking capture, but it also a little preposterous. As she stretched herself out on the divan, the lady laid her head on a pillow and closed her eyes.

She was in a meadow surrounded by grass and wild flowers. She was not alone for two other young women were by her side. They were alike, they could even have passed for twins; one had long dark hair that flowed down her back, brown eyes, a engaging smile and a habit of using her hand to sweep away her hair from her face, the other was a little taller, blonde haired, with piercing green eyes, and a mischievous sounding laugh.

The blonde young woman was laughing now and directing her merriment in her direction. 'You cannot deny it, sister? Not that I blame you I too would like to see the young man without his clothes on.'

The other young woman laughed too, but not so heartily. 'You must not tease Elaine, it is not lady like.'

The blonde woman laughed even louder. 'Who wants to be a lady?'

She could not see her own face, but when she spoke it was not in the voice she recognised. 'I was only passing the river; it wasn't as if I was following the man.'

'That would make a change,' suggested the blonde woman.

The dark haired woman directed a frown at her near twin.

'Did you see everything?' asked the blonde.

'I don't know what you mean?'

'When he came out of the river...was he?'

'He was naked...and I saw quite enough.'

'Don't be bashful. You must talk to him. Make him see how beautiful you are.'

The blonde woman turned to her dark haired companion to plead for a little assistance.

'Morgause is right, you should talk with him. I shall arrange it, but first we must do something with your appearance.'

'What is wrong with my appearance?'

Morgause smiled and came towards her, but addressed the other woman. 'We must do something with her hair?'

'I have something that will untangle her unruly tresses.'

'Perhaps I don't want them untangled.'

'Listen to your sister,' suggested Morgause. 'With her help she'll make you the most beautiful maiden in all Britannia.'

'I like myself just the way I am.'

'Don't you want to capture Lancelot's heart?' asked Morgause.

She continued to complain to her two companions, but as time went by she allowed them to redo her hair, put sweet smelling oils on her body and change her appearance with the use of rouge. 'I must look terrible,' she complained.

'You look beautiful. Doesn't she Morgan?'

Morgan smiled. 'She does, but now to arrange a little rendezvous.'

As by magic the deed was done for there he was, the handsome young Lancelot standing looking out to sea. In his hand he held a note. She moved slowly towards him and just before she came up close, he turned and addressed her. 'It was you who sent me the note?' he inquired.

She was aware of her head moving up and down in answer.

'I have read it twenty times or more...it is full of fine sentiment...'

'You would not make fun of me, my lord?'

Lancelot shook his head. 'Oh no, kind lady I speak the truth. Never has a man been more fortunate to receive such a token.'

'I have seen you many times and yet we have never spoken.'

Lancelot looked into her eyes. 'I know who you are of course. I guess it was only a matter of time before we conversed...'

'What shall we converse about?'

Lancelot took hold of her right hand and held it up to his lips. As he kissed it, he bent forward to continue with his adulation.

'I see you mistake me for someone else.'

Lancelot tried to disguise a smile.

'I see you are as many say you are...'

'Pray tell me what you mean?'

'They tell tales of your amorous encounters. I thought, perhaps wrongly, that the myth and reality were two different things.'

Lancelot's smile was replaced with a frown. 'You reproach me for what others say. Surely that can not be fair.'

'It is not right that you should make light of my feelings...'

Lancelot took a step forward. 'I am a man and a warrior and not used to the finer aspects of court etiquette but you were the one who arranged our meeting.'

'I regret that now...'

She turned to go, but Lancelot took hold of her arm and made a plea. 'I leave tomorrow to fight with the King. I might never return.'

She waited a moment to see what the man would do next, but she did not have to wait long. He took her in his arms and kissed her on the lips.

Polyxena opened her eyes and stared up to see the friendly face of Guinevere standing over her. Her first instinct was to relate to the Queen her visions, but something stopped her. She wondered if what she saw was in fact a memory. If it was then something was wrong. She could not be two people; she could not be both worldly and innocent. Another complication came into her thoughts. The handsome young man who kissed her with such passion was the same man that was now the King and married to Guinevere.

Chapter 17

Sybil quietened her brood and began to explain the disaster to Nemue, but the concept was too great for the maiden to comprehend. The small travelling party quickly left the main road, thanks to the advice from the fairies, and were now travelling unseen along an old dirt path.

The Queen of the fairies was more excitable than usual for the news of the death of the Gods had shaken her and her fellow creatures to the core. 'You must come back with me to Avalon,' the fairy insisted.

'I was on my way there when you came upon us,' replied Nemue.

'Our lady is in need of your assistance,' Sybil stipulated.

Nemue could see how upset the Queen of the fairies was, but little did she know of the full extent of the creature's troubles. 'I take it this was not something that the lady had planned?' she asked.

Sybil shook her tiny head.

Yvain had been told to go on ahead, but he knew something was wrong for although he could not see the creatures he heard their high pitch wail. To the man it sound like a wounded animal ensnared in some devilish trap and it made him grimace.

Nemue asked more questions, but Sybil seemed unable to clarify the details.

'All I know is their contraption blew up and the lady thinks they must all have perished. All except one. That one is a creature so devious and evil that even our mistress fears him. She needs your help in making sure that he does not trick her.'

Nemue asked for more details about the other God that had survived.

Sybil said she knew little but him, except he was untrustworthy.

Nemue thought the Queen of the fairies was hiding something from her. 'There's something else troubling you?'

The fairy admitted there was. 'I can not bother my lady with it now, but I am so upset that I do not know where to go to seek assistance.'

'Perhaps I can help you.'

'Oh it's my silly King. He has done the most stupid thing imaginable.'

The young lady asked Sybil what that was.

'You wouldn't believe it, but he has housed himself in a human body and now can not escape for the human, the woman called Elaine, has gone missing.'

'Vivienne, can surely see her in her pool?'

'I did not want to burden our lady further with this...'

'Perhaps her sister, Lady Morgan can help?'

'I feel it is too late. He can not leave the human's body, or it will turn to dust. He will be forever trapped inside it now. Likewise, Elaine will be trapped forever in her new body.'

Nemue shook her head and said she was confused. 'Is there nothing that we can do?'

'I fear only our great lady...but she has her own troubles to deal with...'

'We shall solve Vivienne's problems first. Then we shall tackle Eros's predicament,' stated a confident Nemue.

*

Gawain and his two companions travelled slowly, thanks to the conditions and the strength of the lady. The young people were all fit, but nonetheless before long all three were tiring as they came upon the Rheged Mountains.

These were if anything steeper, more rugged and uninhabitable than the mountains they had just negotiated. The two men glanced at each other, but never spoke.

Rosalinda knew what was on their minds. 'If my sister can climb these mountains then so can I.'

It was Gawain who thought up the idea. 'I have come to this place unprepared, but I see you have brought with you some rope. We must fasten this rope around each other, so that if one falls the others can help them.'

The others all agreed and a short time afterwards the rope was secure and the three adventurers set forth towards the largest of the three mountains. The uphill climb was tough and not just for Rosalinda. As their spirits began to ebb away with their tiredness, they stopped for a rest. Rosalinda looked up and cried out. 'There! Look a figure up ahead.'

Staring into the cloudy misty, the men hunted with their eyes. Sure enough several furloughs ahead, they saw a moving figure.

'That must be her,' stated the young lady.

The men agreed and the three tried to increase their pace up the mountain in pursuit.

'Should we not shout up to her?' asked Gawain.

'If she sees us coming she might try to hide,' answered Rosalinda.

'Why would she do that?' queried Gawain.

Out of breath from increasing their pace, the young woman stopped for a moment. The others did so too. 'You do not know what she can be like. I fear she no longer thinks rationally. Some times I wonder if I am even safe in her company.'

'Surely not,' the men protested.

'She can be unpredictable and violent, but she would never hurt you,' offered Morholt.

The lady, after some thought, agreed as they set off again with their climb. Gawain at this point decided to break his ties with his companions. Turning to Morholt he set out his reasoning. 'She might get away, if we stay as a group. Let me go on and you take care of Rosalinda...'

'We will lose you,' Morholt speculated.

'I will shout down to you, as soon as I catch up with her.'

Morholt agreed and Rosalinda did not complain. So Gawain untied the rope around his waist and trudged forward at the quickest pace he could muster. His companions watched as he attacked the mountain with renewed vigour. They glanced at each other and Rosalinda smiled. 'He's almost as mad as she is.'

*

With a spray of angel dust upon her, Nemue ventured down deep into the burrows of the lake. She was a good swimmer and was assured she could stay underwater for a long time thanks to the pixies' magic.

Diving down as far as she could, the young woman was dazzled by the splendour of the underwater world she saw before her. This was no ordinary world but a world made up of great palaces and sea creatures different from any seen by any human. Nemue swam unhindered, for no guards stood in her way, as she swam through the open gates of a great palace. Looking about her she saw a variety of sea urchins, dolphins, and beasts of indescribable beauty swim beside her. She thought they all knew who she was and were pleased to see her. They seemed to be guiding her to where she should be going. Eventually they changed their course and moved back to where they had come from. The water was so clean and blue that it almost blinded the girl with its radiance. Finally she saw the lady of the lake come out from a room and approach her. The bubbles flouted up past young Nemue as the lady opened her mouth to speak. 'I am glad you are here.'

Nemue's own words sounded peculiar in the water as she answered Vivienne. 'The fairies are worried. I believe you have an enemy that you might need my help with.'

'Sybil shouldn't talk so much.'

'All the fairies are concerned that you will abandon them.'

The lady shook her head and a host of bubbles generated upwards again. 'Tell them all will be well, but I needed some time to be on my own.'

'I understand, but I fear they do not.'

The lady agreed that was quite possible. 'You might need to use all your powers to protect me when we rendezvous with Gwawl.'

'This Gwawl, is he that dangerous?'

'We have made a bargain, but I do not trust him.'

'You want me to?'

'Have a spell ready to stop him in his tracks if he proves deceitful.'

Nemue nodded. 'I have brought with me a present,' the girl said. She unravelled a cloth that housed the chalice and saw it float slowly forward towards the lady. The sea Goddess caught the chalice in her right hand and peered at it almost as it wasn't real.

'You are a good human and I will reward you with anything you wish.'

To the God's surprise young Nemue stated the most humble of wishes. 'I have reconsidered and find that I do not want power or great wealth, but only to spend the rest of my life in the company of my true love.'

Still admiring the chalice, the lady of the lake was slow to react. When she did look away from the object her expression was one of hurt. 'You would turn victory into defeat...'

Nemue said she would do everything in her power to see Lady Morgan crowned Queen of the five kingdoms.

'Five kingdoms,' shouted the Goddess. 'I can offer you and her so much more.'

'Just a little while ago I would have jumped for joy at being offered great power, but now I have learnt a valuable lesson.'

'Human love again?' queried the Goddess.

'Yes, I find my life empty without it.'

'Yvain, if I recall was not the most forgiving of humans...'

'He has forgiven me and has promised to wait until Lady Morgan is safe before agreeing to be my husband.'

'I am happy for you, although I can not pretend I agree with your choice. The world of the humans needs a lot of care. I can not do it all on my own.'

'I will carry out this last task for you but then I crave my release from my obligations.'

'Tell those silly creatures not to worry I will soon reappear before them,' stated a tetchy Vivienne.

Nemue said she would. 'Eros has done something stupid...'

'Yes I know. He finds himself in quite a predicament...'

'Is there nothing you can do for him?'

'I should let him rot in the human's body, but I guess after this other matter is dealt with I shall forgive him and think of something.'

Chapter 18

Ragnell had seen the party below her on the mountain and feared they were members of the law. She frantically looked for a place to hide, but caves were scarce on the Rheged Mountains. It took the lady awhile to find an inlet big enough for her to squeeze through and disappear from sight. The opening was just large enough for one individual to negotiate. She expected once inside that she would be trapped and unable to move, but she was wrong. The opening hid a secret that nearly cost the lady dear.

Having squeezed her way into the crevice the lady heard what she thought was a waterfall. Forcing her way further into the recess she found herself pitted against a great darkness. Feeling her way downward her hands lost grip of the rock and she felt the space below her empty.

The horrible sensation of falling made the lady cross herself and pray to her one true God. She asked forgiveness for all her past wrongs and awaited judgement. Either she would end up in heaven or she would be dragged down to hell, either way she was ready to announce her arrival.

To her amazement she did not die, but landed safely on her backside in a dusty ditch inside a large cavern. She cried out in pain, but soon forgot her aches when she saw that the cave was lit by a series of lanterns that miraculously shone upon the cave walls illuminating the exquisite beauty of many great carvings.

Skilled craftsmen must have spent years carving out these motifs from the stone. The lady saw before her; figures of flying men with wings, large standing figures covered in a form of armour that encased them from head to toe, and creatures that appeared to be half human and half animal.

Ragnell rose to her feet, rubbed her sore bottom, and studied the beautiful carvings in more detail. She found them bizarre and enchanting, and much too wonderful not to touch. She caressed the smooth rock around the winged figure and saw that two smaller figures rode on its back. These figures were human, and they looked rather pleased with themselves, as they looked downwards perhaps to the earth below. The winged creature resembled a bird more than a man, for it had a beak like that of a large hawk.

The young woman moved on, further into the cave to explore more. She heard more clearly the sound of water falling and was guided by it until she came to a second chamber. This grotto was much larger in size and equally bright, but its walls had been corroded by the water that trickled down them. The rocks perhaps had once housed equally fine works of art but had now been washed clean, all except one. Straight ahead of Ragnell appeared what looked like an entrance, and on the wall next to that entrance she saw a series of depictions. These depictions appeared to tell a story, a language not that different from the Egyptian hieroglyphics that she had once witnessed.

However there was a problem facing the lady, in getting to the entrance, and that was the fact that the ground had given way. A large chasm lay between where she stood and the entrance. At first she thought about attempting a jump, but without a running start, it was too far and too dangerous. Staring defeat in the face the lady turned and thought about returning the way she had come, but something in her nature forbad her from giving up so easily. She turned back again and peered across the divide at the pictograms that were sketched crudely but effectively in many different colour dyes. How long they had been there the lady could not tell, but she felt privileged to be able to witness them.

As she considered her situation, she remembered the rope tied around her person and wondered if she could somehow fasten it to the other side and climb across. She looked for some rock that would hold her weight, but there was only a ledge. Even if by some miracle she found a way across, the ledge was so small that she could not be sure it would be big enough to stand on. As she was still studying the entrance, and the scant ground around it, she thought she heard a voice cry out.

The cavern allowed the noise to ricochet around its walls making the sound seem distorted and not human. Most women would have been frightened but not Ragnell. She tried to follow the sound to see where it was coming from. She retraced her steps until she stood back where she had made her entrance. The sound vibrated again and this time it sounded more human and clearer.

'Ragnell,' shouted Gawain. 'Where are you? Do you need any help?'

So it was the rather good-looking soldier who was after her thought the lady. He was after his sword no doubt. The thing was big and cumbersome and had weighed her down, but it was the finest sword she had ever seen so she was reluctant to be parted from it. Should she call out to the man and share her find or should she keep quiet? While she was considering this she heard a grunt and saw a few pieces of earth trickle down towards her feet. A moment later, Gawain dropped down the crevice, just like the lady had, and landed not too far from her feet.

Gawain's blasphemous oratory echoed around the cave as he cursed his companion. Ragnell reacted quicker than the man and pulled out Excalibur before he could get to his feet. Sitting, dirty and full of pain the young man was not in a good frame of mind. He looked up at the young woman and dared her to run him through. 'Cut me down good lady and put me out of my misery,' he declared. 'I am tired, wet and cold...as for my bottom it hurts as if a swarm of bees have stung me...so do me a favour and pierce me through the heart.'

Ragnell's laugh echoed around the cave, bouncing off the walls and sounding comical and grotesque at the same time. Looking up at the lady, Gawain saw the funny side of his predicament and laughed too. After the laughter died down, the man sought to get to his feet, but the lady still had Excalibur in her hand and poked it into Gawain's chest. 'Ah, that hurt,' the man cried. 'Put the damn sword down and help me up.'

Ragnell shook her head. 'Not until I know what you are doing here?'

'You must have known I would come looking for you,' Gawain suggested.

'No, I do not know why you should follow me?'

Gawain eyed the sword.

'This? Is this why you tracked me down and nearly got yourself killed?'

'It's my sword and I want it back,' the man complained.

The lady smiled. 'Is it really your sword, or did you steal it from some great lord?'

'I am a great lord,' thundered Gawain.

'You brawl in cheap taverns, but yet you say you're a great lord.'

Gawain began to get to his feet, but again the point of his sword forced him back to his knees.

'You're beginning to annoy me. I told you the sword belongs to me, now give it back.'

'Your real name first. The one you gave at the tavern was obviously a false one, so astound me with your fame.'

'One thing is for sure, you're no lady.'

'Don't think of me as such. Think of me as soldier, a warrior just like yourself.'

'You have a high opinion of yourself,' grumbled Gawain.

Ragnell smiled. 'You can handle yourself in a fight, so I do believe some of your story.'

'Now that we have established my honesty, can I please get to my feet?'

'Yes, but slowly...I don't want to cut you with this.'

Gawain got to his feet, brushed himself down and for the first time took a look around the cave. To his astonishment he found himself transfixed by the beauty in the cave sculptures. 'Oh my,' he gasped. 'What is this place?'

The lady was perhaps the only human alive that had any idea what the place was, but she hesitated to impart her knowledge to the young man. She did not trust him and was still concerned as to his reasons for following her.

'Your name if you please.'

'Gawain,' the young man bellowed.

Ragnell stared at him. 'Ah...I do believe I have heard the name. You have made wars in foreign climes under King Arthur's banner and have boasted of your many conquests. I have heard that you are a man of many words but of few deeds.'

'No one insults me like that,' shouted the man.

'You mean no one dare tells you the truth,' corrected the lady.

The man frowned while the lady smiled. 'Tell me Gawain, why do you find me so interesting?

'Huh, you are conceited?'

'You complain of coldness, tiredness and of an aching body, yet you go to all this trouble for a mere sword.'

Sounding gruff and tired, the man mumbled that it wasn't just any sword.

The lady glanced at the object she held in both her hands and gently nodded her head. 'It feels different. Why does it feel so different?'

'It once belonged to our great King.'

'King Arthur's special sword,' the lady enthused, 'just what I need to accomplish my quest.'

'It's my sword now...'

'It belongs to whoever has possession of it.'

Gawain thought to change the subject. 'Your sister is worried about you. She can not be far behind...'

'My poor sister how she worries, but she must not find this place, no one must.'

'What's so special about this cave?'

Ragnell did not answer.

Gawain smiled, looked past the woman to the sculptures. 'This is no ordinary place is it?'

There was a strange silence between the two beings as the lady pondered her situation, and the young man wondered if he dare lunge for his sword. The silence was broken when the lady lowered Excalibur to sink into the dirt and rested upon it. 'You could rush me and probably take the sword from me, but we might both get injured. In any case I feel I must trust someone, so it might as well be you. I wish to call a truce because I have a proposition to set before you.'

*

When Elaine did not appear at King Lot's castle, Lady Morgan knew something was wrong. She and Morgause talked over the situation and confronted Eros who was back to complaining about his human ailments.

The three were locked safely in one the towers of the great castle, as Lady Morgan began to interrogate the fairy.

Eros coughed. 'This human body is so weak…How can you survive?'

Morgan took hold of both the arms of the body of Elaine and castigated Eros. 'How could you do such a foolish thing?' she complained.

'It just happened,' the fairy admitted. 'We thought it would be fun…'

'My sister has gone through enough traumas for one lifetime. She needed a period of quietness.'

'The lady did not feel that way. She was frustrated at being imprisoned…'

'What are we to do?' pleaded Morgan angrily.

'I do not know…even the Lady of the Lake has abandoned me.'

Morgause addressed her sister. 'Someone must get access to Caerleon to find out what has happened to Elaine.'

Morgan nodded her head. 'I must find my way in…'

'You can't go. You must make preparations for your wedding…'

'That can go to the devil…'

'No I can't.'

'Oh, you suddenly agree with my decision now?'

Morgause shook her head. 'If we are to defeat that evil woman we must all make sacrifices.'

'It's not you who will have to lie with the swine.'

'I don't envy you that, but it won't be forever.'

Morgan agreed finally that she had to stay, but when Morgause put herself forward she objected. 'I cannot have two sisters ensnared in the enemy camp.

'I could go,' suggested Eros.

Both women thundered their disapproval. 'You have done enough damage,' complained Morgan.

'How can we trust you after your stupidity,' suggested Morgause.

A downcast Eros offered a further suggestion. 'I could summon Sybil and she could help protect Lady Morgause. She can even make her look quite different…'

'No more magic,' yelled Lady Morgan.

The sisters finally agreed to allow Morgause to go and investigate. Before long Sybil had arrived and without the use of magic had transformed the lady's face completely. The fairy used materials that had the effect of making Morgause look much older; she now processed wrinkles around the eyes, her skin was dull and grey in colour, while her eyes, thanks to two covers, took on a totally different colour.

Morgause was handed a mirror and almost collapsed at the sight of what she saw. 'Good God, to think I might actually look like this one day.'

'You look wonderfully old,' admitted Morgan.

Sybil finished putting the final touches and declared that even her own mother would not recognise her.

'She must not know about this,' declared Morgan.

Everyone agreed.

'You will think of something to tell her?' queried Morgause to her sister.

'Don't worry. I'll say I have sent you on some errand.'

There was no place for privacy so Sybil and Eros conferred in a corner. 'Tell me dear one, does Vivienne know of my predicament?'

Sybil stuck her tiny nose in the air and scolded her husband. 'Of course she does, but she has other business to attend to…'

'But she will not leave me like this?' he queried.

'As a punishment she just might.'

'I have changed my mind concerning these humans and their awful bodies. I think their shells are poor vessels for living.'

'You have learnt your lesson, then?'

Eros admitted he had. 'Do you forgive me yet?'

'You do not get off so likely. I will think of a good punishment if ever you return to your true form.'

'I will gladly submit to whatever punishment you deem necessary my dear.'

'Stop this dear business...I am not some pitiful human who needs to be told nonsense.'

Chapter 19

Using a trick that he had seen King Arthur do, Gawain had managed to fasten a rope around a rock on the other side of the cavern. The only problem was that the rope was not long enough to wrap around their bodies. This meant that they would have to swing across on the rope using their bare hands. The force of the swing alone might see their bodies smashed against the rocks. Even if the force did not kill them, it might well make them lose their grip and see then fall into the chasm.

After talking awhile with Ragnell, the young warrior suspected she was not insane at all but only obsessed. Her selfish attitude even extended to her sister. It didn't seem to bother her that Rosalinda would be worried out of her mind.

Ragnell still didn't trust the young man, so her attitude to him remained the same. The lady snatched the rope away from his hands. 'You think me a fool,' she cried.

Gawain tried to snatch it back, but the lady held on. 'I should go first,' explained the man, 'so if it doesn't work at least you would still be alive...'

'You could also just leave me here and go after the treasure on your own.'

Gawain once more challenged the lady to explain what the treasure really was.

'You know too much already, thanks to my over talkative sister. I'm only allowing you to trail along in case your strength is needed.'

'Oh, I'm glad to be of some use,' declared the man.

'Enough of your senseless chatter, I am going first so stand back.'

Gawain refused to budge. 'Can I trust you to throw the rope back?'

Muttering to herself, the lady slapped the man across the face with her right hand. Caught by surprise, Gawain blinked before returning the compliment by slapping the lady back.

'I refuse to fight a lady.'

'I've told you before I am not a lady.'

Gawain saw Excalibur from the corner of his eye. It was still standing to attention in the dirt near the opening. He was marginally closer to it than his opponent and thought about making a dash for it. Ragnell saw him glance to the right and smiled. 'I once killed a man by throwing my dagger into his back,' she announced.

The statement was made with such venom that Gawain wondered who the identity of the man was. Could he be the reason Ragnell was the way she was. Did he rape her or kill someone she knew? He wanted to know more about her, but conversing with the lady was a dangerous business. The absurdness of the situation suddenly hit him, so he decided calmly to reclaim Excalibur. Waiting slowly he advanced towards the sword.

'Don't move,' cried the woman.

Gawain glanced at the lady but continued.

'I said stop.'

'Stab me in the back if you wish, but don't you think we might need the sword.'

Gawain reached the sword and pulled it out of the ground. The lady took the tip of the dagger in her hand and put it up close to her shoulder as if to throw it. She hesitated and at the last moment threw the knife onto the ground at the man's feet. Gawain picked the dagger up and casually handed it back to the lady. 'You might need this soon my lady,' he stated.

'God knows how you've survived to the present day,' remarked the lady. 'You do like to take chances with your life.'

'Don't you?'

'I hope you're not suggesting we're alike?'

'Only in our recklessness,' suggested the man.

'Talking of recklessness, shall we take the plunge?'

'Together?'

'Our combined weight might slow our pace across.'

'But will the rope hold us both?'

'There is only one way to find out.'

It was at this moment that a connection was forged between the two young people. They both managed a smile and although it was cumbersome they both agreed that the sword had to come with them. 'I will fasten it around my shoulders,' declared Gawain.

Ragnell reluctantly agreed. 'Is there anyway to protect ourselves from the impact, when our bodies crash into the rocks,' she queried.

'I fear there is nothing we can do, but pray for a little luck.'

'We can not hold onto the rope for long, so I will venture to find a foothold while you help me to climb onto it.'

Gawain refused to argue the point, but did offer the girl a reminder of their true position. 'You do realise we will more than likely plunge to our deaths.'

'Yes, so if you want to bow out?'

'I never back down in anything.'

The young woman smiled. 'Admit it; you're after the treasure just like I am?'

'Some old cart that is probably rotten with worms...of course I must be.'

The man helped the lady to grip the rope as tight as she could, and then grabbed it himself.

They leaped onto the rope and swung from one side of the gorge to the other. As they travelled through the air a strange thing happened for the light in the cave went out leaving them in almost total darkness.

Their bodies crashed against the rocks, with Gawain's body taking the brunt of the impact. They swung back and forth for awhile and did not speak, until Gawain uttered some swear words and cursed the lady hanging next to him. 'You and your bright ideas...now look what you've done.'

'Take one of your hands and hold onto my belt...I'm going to swing across and see if I can find a hand hold of any kind.'

'No,' shouted the man. 'You'll get us both killed.'
'We've got to do something.'
'We must climb up the rope. I'll go first.'
The lady agreed.
Climbing a rope in the darkness was an eerie thing and several times Gawain's boots would stand on the lady's fingers and she would shout abuse at him. Several times her fingers wrapped around the man's legs almost pulling him over and he would curse the lady for her impatience.
'You climb like a pitiful girl,' Ragnell complained. 'I should have gone first, we'd be at the entrance by now...'
'If you had gone first we'd be spattered to a thousand pieces at the bottom of the gorge.'
'Do hurry up, my arms are getting sore.'
'I'm resting...like you my arms are aching...'
'You can rest when we reach the entrance,' Ragnell informed him.
Gawain started climbing again and like his companion he had no idea if they were near their goal or not.
'It can't be much further?' complained the girl.
'Wait, I think we're here,'
The man reached forth with his right hand, into the darkness, and felt around. The palm of his hand touched the smoothness of the rock. It seemed to his touch that it was a platform, tiny perhaps but big enough to hold two human beings he suspected.
'The rope will move about as I swing myself up onto the platform, so just make sure you have a steady grip,' Gawain instructed.
The lady braced herself and readjusted her grip. Sure enough the rope swung about and at one point the lady's body crashed against the rocks, but she held tight.
Gawain used all his power from his shoulders to lift himself up onto the ledge and with his legs kicking managed to get the top part of his body secure onto the platform. He breathed one last gulp and heaved the rest of his body upwards. The stone was smooth but uneven as Gawain made the mistake of relaxing too soon. His left leg began to lose its grip and he began to slide backwards.

*

This was Helena's first visit to the eastern part of the world and to the place that all Romans now called their capital, Constantinople. The city was the greatest trading capital of the known world and with all its magic and wonder it beguiled the diminutive figure of Helena, into silence.

Lucius, a guide in the lady's employ, was proud to be seen walking by the side of his lovely companion, as they strolled down the Mese (Middle Street) towards the Milion Monument.

The Roman showed the lady the formidable cathedral of Hagia Sophia (Holy Wisdom) as they travelled westwards towards the impressive palaces of Lausos and Antiochus. They entered the oval-shaped Forum (Market) of Constantine where many an Emperor had been welcomed home in triumph. They continued along the Imperial road past more palaces until they reached the Forum of the Bull.

It wasn't just the quality and beauty of the goods on offer that left the lady dazed, but the variety of sweet aromas. She stopped and bargained for many goods, but always Lucius informed her that the dealer was charging too much. She listened to a variety of languages, including Greek and Latin but for the most part was understood well enough to make her own decisions.

The Mese was lined with colonnaded porticoes which housed many shops with every conceivable kind of food; there were rare meats such as gazelle, wild ass, and exotic seafood such as botago (salted mullet roe) and fruits that she had never witnessed before, like aubergines, lemons and oranges. Lucius took great pleasure in showing the lady all the different delicates and spices that saturated the human senses.

The lady was intrigued about her companion, but was afraid to pry into his past life. After all she was here to find another man, a man she had every intention of marrying. Their time together crossing the narrow sea and their journey over land had fermented into a nice friendship.

The lady found the man not only generous, but witty and forthright too. She was surprised by his understanding of her situation and wondered why he found it so hard to forget his past.

Lucius stopped at a shop and bought a few lemons for the lady. He used his teeth to peel away the top of one and then using his fingers, he revealed its bright yellow texture and offered it to Helena. 'Take a bite,' he suggested.

With the lemon still in his hand Helena bent forward and sunk her teeth into it. She giggled as splashes of the fruit ran up her nose and across her face. The remaining juice and substance went into her mouth. It was a unique taste and one that surprised the lady with its sharp tang. It was curious how the taste remained strong long time after the contents had been consumed.

A smiling Lucius inquired if the lady enjoyed the taste.

'Indeed, but why do we never see these fruits in Britannia.'

'If I had more ambition then I would trade in such things and bring them to our shores, but I am a lazy man...'

The lady shook her head. 'How can you say such a thing? We have travelled many leagues together and without your help I would never have made this far. It is only through your great kindness and strength that I have at last reached my journey's end.'

The man felt the blood in his face catch fire just like his heart had done many days previous. The lady was so luminous to look upon and so generous in her manner that the thought of never seeing her again after the morrow wrenched at his heart.

Helena saw for the first time the man's embarrassment but for some reason she was not cross with him. It was a curious situation, but thanks to Lucius's good work they had at last tracked Titius down.

'I have managed to arrange an appointment with the Magister Militum (Master of Soldiers) for early tomorrow.'

'Will we be able to see Titius too?' asked the lady.

The man shook his head. 'For some reason the secretary to the Magister implied he was not able to attend.'

Helena was disappointed, but tried her best to look happy. 'It would appear I will have to wait a little longer to see my friend again.'

Lucius remained optimistic and tried to tempt the lady with more delicious food. This time he showed her a stall that sold an assortment of sweet desserts and drinks. He persuaded her to try Constantinople's famous quince marmalade.

*

Castor had done the impossible. Using every contact from his past that he could find, somehow he had managed to track down the man called Merlin. Through months of piecing together small clues, the man had found the sorcerer hiding in the caves along the coast of Cornubia (Cornwell).

The man from Gaul was aware that Penelope wished never to return to her past life, but he also knew that without help he could not prevent the lady from being hanged.

By describing Penelope to local people and food sellers around the eastern part of Lundonia he was lucky to stumble upon a couple who claimed to have known her. The old couple sold fruit and vegetables at the market in Candlewick and boasted to him that the lady was once a regular customer. He could still hear the man eulogize about the woman, calling her a real lady, sweet in nature and always generous. It was his wife who told the tragic tale that opened Castor's eyes to the lady's true identity. She described in some detail the awful events of that early October day at the place called Cardinal.

'The story goes that the man known as Merlin was so drunk that he tripped and spilled his candle onto a drape by accident. This started a fire so bad that every piece of timber was burnt and every person, bar one perished. In all, four charred bodies were discovered, two men and two women; the lady of the house, her father and their two servants, but miraculously Merlin survived. The local people hounded him from the area and the last we heard of him he had gone back to his old ways of rambling about the countryside.'

It was a tragic tale, but a tale that opened Castor's eyes to the fact that the lady he knew as Penelope was in fact a lady by the name of Gallia. He found out that she entered into a marriage with the infamous Merlin only recently, but that their lives together had been beset by arguments.

The entrance to the tunnel appeared large as Castor walked towards it. He could see the last remnants of fire as he approached, but he was unprepared to witness the sight he saw standing at the entrance. The man he saw had long grey hair and a grey beard and looked more like some wild animal than a human. His hands and face were dirty, as were his bare arms. It was these Castor stared at, for the dirt was intermingled with blood. In his right hand Merlin had a long knife which was also covered in red and black. It appeared to Castor that the man was cutting himself repeatedly as if to play some kind of bizarre ritual or game.

Merlin looked up from his mutilation to see a bald headed man in a smart fur rimmed cloak approach him. 'Get away. Get away or I'll cut you,' he shouted to Castor. He outstretched his arm threateningly showing the rugged contours of the knife.

Castor stopped and began to explain the reason for his visit.

No sooner had his wife's name been mentioned, that Merlin screeched in pain. 'I killed her,' he sobbed. 'I killed her...I killed her.'

Castor did the best he could to explain to the deranged man that his wife wasn't dead, but it was all in vain. Nothing he could say could convince the man that his beloved Gallia was still alive.

'Have you come to arrest me?' queried Merlin.

'No, I have come to take you to your wife,'

The man laughed, but it was a chilling sound that sent shivers down Castor's back. 'At last my deliverer,' Merlin murmured. 'I'm glad the Gods have seen fit to punish me. Will you make it quick, or I'm I to die a slow painful death worthy of my crimes.'

Castor shook his head. 'No, I have come to restore you to your beloved.'

Merlin smarted and berated his visitor. 'You have no cause to inflict unnecessary pain by your cruel jests. My wife is dead so leave her in peace.'

Castor dared to take a few steps closer. 'Your nightmare is over now my friend, come journey with me to a new life...'

'Journey,' Merlin scoffed. 'The only journey left for me is the one along the river Styx to the Underworld.'

'No, it is imperative that you come with me back to Lundonia.'

'So that is my punishment. I must revisit the scene of my crime...'

'It was not a crime, only an accident...'

'Leave me in peace,' screamed Merlin.

Feeling exhausted and near the end of his tether, Castor tried to find another way to reach the dissolute man. 'Lady Morgan is most worried,' he suddenly announced.

'The lady has my mother to help her, she doesn't need me. Even my own mother has abandoned me,' Merlin whispered to himself.

'There is a woman who claims to be your wife, Gallia. She is accused of murder and is to stand trial in a few days. You must not let this criminal besmirch your wife's good name and tarnish it forever.'

Merlin lowered his knife and let it fall to the ground beside him. He studied the man before him and for the first time looked interested in what he had to say. 'Say that again,' he requested.

Castor did so. He emphasized the seriousness of the allegations facing the woman claiming to be his wife. 'There are many other charges against this lady...including robbery, conspiracy and even treason.'

Merlin flopped down onto his knees and invited the man to do the same. Castor did so.

'Look at me,' Merlin ordered. 'Do I look like a man who can help you or anyone else?'

It was true. Castor did not doubt that he was sitting beside the most pitiful man he had ever witnessed, but he also did not doubt that he was the only man capable of rescuing the lady.

Chapter 20

Between the quick thinking of Ragnell and his own bravery, Gawain's life was saved. She felt the man above her slide back and perceived that if she did not do something immediately the man would fall to his death. She grabbed the man's right leg and tried to hold on to it, but she endangered herself for the rope moved so rapidly that she almost lost her own hold.

Gawain thought his time had come, but in one last defiant gesture he threw his hands backwards in a desperate effort to find the rope. A combination of Ragnell's quick thinking and the man's instinct for survival saved the day. The weight of Gawain's body almost catapulted his saviour from the rope, but despite her body crashing against the rocks, Ragnell managed to hold on. She grabbed hold of Gawain's shirt and pulled him to her. They hung perilously together, for a good while, almost fearful to breathe in case their movement would tip them into the abyss.

While all this near death excitement was going on, neither adventurer dared to speak. Finally Ragnell broke the silence. 'Tell me are all Celtic men such weaklings?' Still breathing heavily Gawain issued a challenge. 'If you think you can do better, go ahead.'

The lady proposed to do just that. 'You have good strong shoulders, have you not? I wish to use them to stand on.'

Ragnell was keen to put in motion her plan, but Gawain was still unsure how dangerous it was. 'It surely doesn't matter,' complained the lady. 'We must make another attempt quickly or we must die.'

Gawain agreed and the two beings exchanged places, with Ragnell climbing up the rope and Gawain moving in the opposite direction. The lady was now in a place to attempt to climb onto the shelf, but Gawain had one last word of warning. 'Move a little to your right and aim there. That seems to be the only place the rock is even.'

Ragnell moved her body as far to her right as she could and leaped into the darkness. Her hands hit the rock face with a thud, but because her legs were higher than Gawain's had been she could use her upper body strength to pull herself onto the ledge. With her heart almost bursting from her body and her arms yelping from the effort, the lady's joy could not be curtailed. She screeched into the chasm allowing that place to echo her joy for many encores.

Still hanging onto the rope awaiting assistance was an impatient Gawain. He climbed up to the top of it and searched in the darkness for his companion. 'Hurry up, give me your hand,' he requested.

For a moment the lady hesitated. Kneeling down she peered down at the shadowy figure of Gawain, but offered no assistance. 'Can you be trusted not to betray me one day?' she queried.

'I am a man of honour,' the man cried.

Ragnell was fearful of falling so she managed to slide her left hand in between a crack in the rock immediately above Gawain. Still unsure as to how heavy the man was she stretched forth her right hand rather tentatively.

Even in the darkness of the cave somehow Gawain was guided to the lady's hand. He gripped it tight and began to hoist himself up, but the lady seemed unable to pull him any distance. 'You must use both your hands,' explained Gawain.

'I cannot, I will be pulled over.'

'Please try. If you feel yourself moving forward too quickly by all means let go of my hand.'

Just a few moments earlier the lady had doubted the man, but now because of his surprising statement she was convinced his heart was true. She stretched forth her other hand to allow Gawain to grab hold of it. His legs scratched against the rocks in a frantic effort to gain any help he could, but it was the strength of the lady's arms alone that pulled the man up onto the ledge. The lady screamed in agony when finally she could let go of her companion's arms.

In the darkness both sat on the ledge and stared at one another. One blue eyed creature stared across at another as one of them began to praise the other unreservedly. 'Few men could have done what you just did,' Gawain announced.

'Few men would be so bold to attempt such madness,' replied the lady.

Gawain laughed. 'I have never met anyone quite like you,' he declared.

The lady rubbed one arm then the other in an effort to ease the pain still shooting through her limbs. Gawain took over the job of masseur and was diligently gentle. The light that had bathed the cavern before their attempt to reach the other side suddenly sprung up again. The couple looked at each other in amazement but said nothing.

Gawain in an effort to understand the strange happenings tried to get the lady to reveal more of her secrets. 'You are not surprised at this strange place, why is that?'

At first the lady was loathe to give up her knowledge, but perhaps because she feared they might never see the light of the day again she imparted a little of what she had learnt. 'It is hard to distinguish truth from myth, but I believe we have stumbled upon the most secret place in the Christian world.'

Gawain's face looked blank and the lady saw his scepticism but she continued nonetheless. 'I can see your pagan mistrust,' the lady stated. 'But can you explain the lights in this place, or the carved figures or the paintings?'

Gawain admitted he couldn't.

'I believe as we progress further in this place we will encounter two ferocious giants.'

A smiling Gawain commented that the lady must possess some form of prophecy, but the young lady only laughed. 'You must think me mad, but I have proof of what I say.'

'The manuscript that never leaves your person?' queried the man.

'So she has told you about that,' said the lady with a mournful sigh.

Ragnell rolled up her pants to reveal the top part of her right leg. Tied tightly around it, with fine silk was a yellow parchment. It was torn and thin, ragged around its corners and clearly quite old. 'It is in Hebrew, so unless you read that language you will have to take my word for what it says.'

The man was pleased to accept the lady's explanation. Ragnell opened the folded document with great care. She briefly retold the tale of Joseph of Arimathea and his journey to find a home for the sacred objects that were said to belong to the one called Jesus of Nazareth. She looked up from the document for a moment to catch a watchful Gawain staring at her. It was clear the young man was attracted to the young woman. 'I have seen that look before my friend. It is not wise to think of me in that way...'

'I do not know what you mean,' answered Gawain innocently.

'I am not capable of loving you. If you persist it will only lead to you misery at my hand.'

'You make it sound rather attractive.'

'Do not joke, I am serious.'

'Now that sounds like a challenge to me...'

'In my quieter moments I wish to harm no one, but when my blood boils I wish to inflict as much pain on any man I come across...'

'Some man has wronged you and so you seek revenge on all men.'

'What has Rosalinda been saying to you?' asked Ragnell.

'She did not mention anyone, but remember I have been following you for days.'

'Ah, the tavern fight, did the young man die?'

'I never found out, but I guess you do not care.'

'Now you prejudge me.'

An unpleasant taste formed in the young man's mouth. He found his companion's matter of fact attitude to life and death repellent. 'So these giants, I don't suppose you know their names?'

Returning to look over the manuscript, the lady studied in some detail the bottom of the document. 'It does not mention their names. All it says is that two great walls of flesh will stand guard over the treasure until such time as the chosen one will return to take possession.'

'Until recently I would have decried the mere suggestion of giants, but now I know better.'

'You have met one?' asked the lady.

'No, but my brother has in the place forbidden...'

'You speak of the realm of the Gods, sometime referred to as Avalon.'

'Yes. Have you visited the place?'

Ragnell grinned. 'Where do you think I discovered this parchment?'

Gawain grinned back at the lady.

'We have rested enough, we must go on...'

After the lady put the parchment back onto her leg, she made to get to her feet. However Gawain placed his hand on her shoulder forcing her to stay on her knees. The lady gave the young man a look of displeasure. 'You seem determined to provoke me.'

'No, my lady I only wish to ask you a question.'

'Then un-touch me and ask.'

Gawain let go of the lady's shoulder. 'The document, does it mention gold, silver and other such treasures?'

'So that is what you think of me. You think me a robber, only interested in treasure and personal gain.'

'I think the obsession is filled with intrigue, but nonetheless I still think you are nothing more that a treasure hunter.'

The lady turned sharply and suggested the man keep hold of her belt. They left the entrance that was no bigger than the size of four men to shimmy along a narrow ledge clinging onto each other as they went. By some miracle a source of light, hidden from view, highlighted their path.

The source could not be seen but without it their journey would have been impossible. With their backs to the wall of the inner mountain, they painstakingly edged their way forward. They had not gone far before they started to hear strange noises and cries.

'It would appear we are not alone,' whispered Gawain.

'From another source I think I have found the names of the giants.'

'Tell me again, why do we want to meet these giants?'

'I'm sure that with that mighty sword of yours, you can dispense with them without much trouble.'

'Suddenly I have a worth,' the man joked.

The couple slowed their pace to a near halt as they tried to negotiate a tight corner. They feared falling, for the drop seemed endless. Gawain looked down and saw nothing but ragged rocks on all sides to him. He went to warn the lady, but the lady beat him to it. 'Don't look down,' she stated, 'for there's nothing to see.'

They both took a rest just before they turned the corner to the look upon their new terrain. Gawain whispered again. 'The names, my lady?' he inquired.

'Why are you whispering?'

'I don't know. Maybe the giants have good hearing.'

'My father spoke to me of two dangerous beasts, brothers called Gog and Magog. No one knows how old they are or if they can be destroyed, only that they are large in size and most fierce.'

'If you're trying to reassure me, it's not working.'

'I just thought I should warn you, that's all.'

'It's not as if I could turn around and go back is it?'

'You could, but I would insist upon you giving me your sword.'

'The sword is never going to leave my side again.'

'Now I see what you truly love.'

*

In a day or two Lancelot would return and Elaine would see the man in a new light. Because of the change in her appearance the man did not recognise her. Going by her recollections so far, she must have known Lancelot quite well. Maybe fifteen years ago they had been close, but something must have happened.

Guinevere continued with her stories of Polyxena the spy, telling her how brilliant she had been on this mission or that. It all sounded wrong and unbelievable.

The young woman's instinct told her that the person described could not be her and began to pay little attention to the stories.

As for Guinevere, she was worried. She could tell that her companion was uninterested in her past and was more than a little confused as to what might happen in the near future. Thinking it might clear the air she decided to divulge some of her plans to her friend. 'Are you worried about Lancelot by any chance?' she asked.

Elaine blinked several times before answering. 'I don't know what you mean,' she stammered.

Guinevere came over to her and sat on the edge of the chair. 'He will not come between us. I need his army for now, but once my enemies are defeated I will dispense with him.'

The coldness of these words shook the lady. 'What will you do to him?'

'I'm sure I'll think of something,' joked the Queen.

Guinevere expected a chuckle or at least a smile from her companion, but when this did not happen she became pensive. 'You look worried. Don't be, I will take care of you.'

'I feel I don't belong here…'

'That is natural. You are confused because of the blow to your head, but you'll start to remember soon…and then it will all make sense.'

Elaine managed a smile. 'I suspect you are right.'

'Once I have all the power at my disposal, we shall live our lives the way we want.'

Elaine knew what the Queen meant and the idea appeared repugnant to her. 'We can never do that.'

Guinevere tried to smile. 'Who is this timid woman I see before me, surely not the same one who spat in my eye the moment she was sentenced to death.'

'You miss her I can tell...but I cannot be that woman...'

'In time you will be...'

Tip toeing along a corridor, an old looking Morgause spied Sybil ahead beckoning for her to hurry her pace. The tiny fairy was showing the lady the way to Elaine's room when she suddenly flew upwards in a panic. Luckily only Morgause heard the noise she made. 'Go back,' she screeched to the human.

Morgause acknowledged the command by retreating back along the corridor in a hurry. She waited for what seemed an age before Sybil, who had entered the room unnoticed, came back to inform her it was now safe to approach.

'The guards?' queried Morgause.

'Sleeping like babies,' the fairy declared.

'You have seen Elaine?'

'Yes, but remember she will look...'

'Yes I know...Morgan told me what she looks like...'

Morgause walked towards the bedchamber, with Sybil perched on her shoulder.

'There is something else,' revealed the fairy.

'What do you mean?'

'Your sister has lost her memory...'

'What!? How do you know this?'

'I overhead enough of her confession with the Queen to comprehend it, but fear not, I'm sure the bonds of sisterhood...'

'We have never really been that close.'

Sybil hummed an old tune. One that was vaguely familiar to the lady. This carefree attitude surprised Morgause. 'Someone will hear you.'

Shaking her tiny head, Sybil reminded her human companion that only she could see and hear her.

'Still we have a problem, one that needs our attention.'

'That is why I am humming. It helps me to think.'

The time for thinking was over as Morgause entered the bedchamber and approached her sister who was sitting near the narrow window looking out across the ramparts.

The two sisters turned their heads to look upon each other only to witness mistrust and bewilderment upon each other's faces. Neither of the women looked the way they should, but despite that there was a sort of recognition between them nonetheless.

Elaine rose from her chair and came towards Morgause. Morgause hurriedly tried to peel away her disguise, but even before she had really started, Elaine muttered her name. 'You are called Morgause aren't you?'

A smiling Morgause opened her arms. The two women embraced and cried.

'You are my sister, Elaine,' stipulated Morgause.

With their arms stretched out, together they studied each other's strange faces.

'You look so much older,' announced Elaine.

Morgause started to laugh. 'And you look so much younger,' she replied.

'Are we really sisters?' asked Elaine.

'Don't you know? Can't you remember?'

'Well, I am recalling pieces of my past. I remember you and my other sister Morgan, but...

Morgause could see her sister struggle to comprehend her predicament.

'Guinevere believes me to be this other person, a woman by the name of Polyxena. It is all rather confusing.'

Morgause glanced at Sybil and saw that Elaine saw her too. Elaine walked up close to the tiny creature and put forth her hand.

Sybil moved back a little, but smiled at the human. 'You have the magic,' she suggested.

Looking bewildered Elaine went to touch the tiny creature. 'You are so beautiful...but can you be real?'

'I am real to you and to a few chosen ones.'

'Magic? You said I have the magic, what do you mean by that?'

Morgause interrupted. 'We have come to take you away from this place.'

For someone being offered their freedom Elaine's reaction was surprising. 'I am in no danger here. For reasons I can't explain, I wish to remain here a little longer.'

Morgause took hold of her sister's arm and made Elaine look in her eyes. 'What nonsense is this? We have risked a great deal to free you and yet you wish to remain.'

Elaine offered scant explanation to her sister, but it was Sybil who sensed a reason. She flew close to Morgause and whispered something in her ear.

Morgause walked with her sister around the room and reproached her with a question. 'You have formed some kind of attachment? Please tell me it isn't this evil woman.'

A flushed looking Elaine told her it wasn't.

'Then who? What possible reason could you have for remaining here?'

'Love,' whispered Elaine. 'I remember a little of my past and a man that I once loved.'

Morgause's facial expression told Elaine that she knew the identity of this man. She wasn't sure though, but assumed that her sister had no idea that this person was also accused of several murders, including her own.

Chapter 21

'It must be late, don't you think?' suggested Gawain.

'It must be dark outside by now,' Ragnell replied. 'Are you thinking about my sister by any chance?'

Gawain admitted to being a little concerned. 'It is very cold out on the mountain.'

'Morholt will look after her.'

Gawain stifled a laugh. 'The Gods never make it easy do they?' he pronounced.

The lady failed to comment. Her body, especially her face and hands, were dripping with sweat. She turned her head to look at Gawain who looked equally wet and weary.

'What do we do now?' the young man asked.

'Find some other route.'

Gawain's eyes opened wider. 'Ragnell you must give up.'

Ragnell shook her head. 'There must be another way,' she pleaded.

'There is only this way...unless you can somehow fly.'

The ledge that had given them such hope had only led them around in a circle back to where they had started. The ledge itself was becoming crumbly and weak and could give way at any time which Gawain pointed out to the lady.

Ragnell, with the help of the unknown light source, began to study the pictorials at the entrance to the gate of the chasm. They were small in form, drawn with some black substance probably a dye or maybe soot from a stone. Each portrayed a single entity; the first one looked like a man with a large bowl on his head, while the next depicted a man with spike like objects jutting from his head, the third had three parts to it, the largest being the middle and was separate from the rest as it was set at an angle. Looking further down the lady came upon two peculiar rows of figures that did not appear to be human. There were two rows of four, all depicted beings with tails, long bodies and snake like heads. This seemed like a revelation to the young lady who knelt down to see the figures more closely.

The man held onto her belt. 'Careful,' he warned, 'one gust of wind and you could go over into the abyss.'

'It's too dangerous for us to both to look at the same time, but once I get up you must change places with me.'

The man did what the lady had advised and examined the figures on the cave wall while she held onto the breach of his pants. He looked puzzled. 'What I can't understand is the light source,' he queried.

'It is peculiar isn't it, but then again everything about this place is strange.'

'Is someone toying with us?' suggested Gawain.

'I take it you don't mean the giants?'

'I mean the Gods.'

'There is only one God and he doesn't play games just to amuse himself.'

The couple discussed their situation and began to row. No matter what Gawain suggested, the lady refused to listen. Finally he told her he was leaving.

'You can't leave,' she told him. 'Not unless you are prepared to leave without your sword.'

Gawain grumbled and groaned and even swore into the hollow cavern, but found he could not abandon the lady. A thought occurred to him. 'These last pictorials, they remind me a little of Gaheris's description of the lady of the lake.'

'This lady, you say she has a beak like a bird and a body of a snake?' inquired Ragnell.

To the lady's surprise the young man did not laugh, but implied that she was indeed different.

'A tail?' the lady queried again.

'Yes, although she does not possess a beak…at least no one has told me that she does.'

'This lady, she can not be human…so are you saying she is a God?

'I cannot say, although she lives in the place that is forbidden to humans…'

'The treasure is not on Avalon,' an irritable Ragnell pronounced. 'I would have found it, if it was.'

'My aunt, Lady Morgan has returned some treasure to the Gods only recently...'

'Yes, but not the ark, nor the grail.'

'These things mean nothing to me. This grail what is that?'

'It is the sacred cup that Jesus passed around his disciples at the last supper. Are you telling me you have never heard of this tale?'

'No. I leave all the scholarly matters to my learned brothers.'

'It's a pity this Gaheris is not with us now.'

The young man was offended, but tried to laugh off the insult. 'Even he cannot fly,' he pointed out to the lady.

'You have never learnt to read nor write?' Ragnell asked.

Looking a little embarrassed the man told her that such things were not that important.

The lady disagreed. 'Do you not want to improve your mind?'

'I'm perfectly happy with my life.' A shiver went through the man as he looked at the lady. 'Is it my imagination,' he said, 'or is it getting colder?'

Ragnell agreed. 'The light is also beginning to fade.'

'We must pull up the rope and try to swing back across before the light goes out again.'

'No, we can't give up.'

'Who said we were giving up? We will come back with more rope and better provisions.'

'Only us, no one else must know.'

'What about your sister?'

'No, not even her.'

The man agreed.

'But how will we ever find the inlet again?' wondered Ragnell.

'Let's deal with one problem at a time,' Gawain suggested.

*

The night was drawing to a close, but Morgause still had not convinced her sister to leave with her.

'If you do not come with me now, I'll knock you out and carry you away...'

Elaine laid her hand on her sister's shoulder. 'Don't be angry at me,' she whispered. 'I am different now, I'm sure of that. What little I do remember of my past, I seemed a weak, timid creature, wholly dependant upon you, Morgan and my mother. I can't explain it, but I no longer feel weak or timid, in fact I feel strong...a new person.'

'Come with me, please. We have so much to discuss, including Lancelot.'

'What about Lancelot?'

'He is not the man he was...he has changed. A terrible evil has seeped into his heart...'

'You mean Guinevere?'

'You have no idea how wicked she truly is.'

'Strange I know, but she is kind to me. It must be because of this Polyxena.'

'You are not this woman, and in time she will find this out.'

'Maybe, but in the meantime I can be of use to Morgan. I will pass on any information that is helpful. If Guinevere is about to attack my sister she will know about it in plenty of time.'

Morgause sighed. 'Eros, the King of the fairies is housed in your body, what is he to do?'

Sybil came into view and spoke softly to the sisters. 'We must leave now, before the castle inhabitants awaken.'

'You say that we had seven days and now our time is up. If that is true then it is already too late...'

Sybil interrupted the human. 'I could compel you to leave with us.'

Elaine pondered the Sybil's words, before making an astonishing announcement. 'He can leave my feeble body...it has always been prone to sickness and maladies if my scant memory is correct.'

'You're talking nonsense,' an animated Morgause announced.

'You cannot mean that,' Sybil also conjectured.

Elaine smiled. 'I do mean it. I will never again be afraid. Something of strength has entered my being and I feel loathe to lose it.'

Sybil seemed pleased enough. It was good to think that her husband, fool though he may be, would be free again. She did not concern herself with the humans, with Morgause and Morgan. Their problems were not her problems.

Morgause would not leave it like that and showered a tirade of disparaging remarks at her sister. This did not have any effect and Morgause was just about to resort to violence when Sybil announced that someone was coming.

They all listened as the sound of footsteps came nearer. Sybil quickly disappeared, while Elaine helped Morgause to hide behind a screen. The footsteps stopped and the heavy handle of the door turned with a squeak. The figure of Guinevere entered the room.

The Queen was convinced she had heard voices so when she entered she was surprised to find her friend alone. 'I thought you had company,' suggested Guinevere.

Elaine shook her head. 'I was talking to myself.'

'I thought I heard more than one voice.'

'No it was only me. I couldn't jolt my thoughts so I was berating my stubborn memory.'

'Don't try and force it, it will come in time.'

Guinevere sat down and ushered Elaine to do the same. Once seated, the Queen announced she would have to leave immediately.

'Is it news from Lancelot?' inquired Elaine.

'Yes, it appears the stories were not exaggerated, the devastation is quite bad. More interestingly, Lancelot states that there is no sign of the Gods.'

'Have they destroyed themselves perhaps?' questioned Elaine.

Guinevere could not be sure, but had thought the same thing. 'I hate to leave you, but I will return as soon as I can...'

'Let me come too.'

'You must rest and get strong; your ambush caused you much anguish...'

'Please, my body is strong and I no longer suffer from any headache. Let me come with you, we can converse some more of our past. I feel my memory just needs a little prodding and only you can do that.'

Guinevere was pleased to hear her friend's plea and gave into her request easily enough. She had high hopes of the journey. She suspected the old Polyxena was soon to reappear and their happiness was close at hand.

The Queen left her friend to prepare for the journey. Riding through the Dee Forest at night was dangerous, even with fire torches, but Guinevere planned to take plenty of men with her.

Morguase made one final plea to Elaine, but her sister was adamant and would not budge. She was left with no choice but to blurt out her secret. 'Lancelot is the last person you should have feelings for.'

Elaine smiled, as she began to get dress for her departure. 'Do you not remember how we all wished to get to know him?'

'What you cannot recall is that fateful day he...'

Morgause had gone red in the face. Elaine noticed and wrongly concluded that her sister had feelings for the man too. 'You care for him also?' she remarked.

Morgause shook her head and swore angrily. You need to know the truth. Morgan with the help of the Gods brought you back to life. You were dead, killed by Lancelot...or at least it appears to have been by him.'

'Are you saying I was dead...that is ludicrous. You'll say anything to get me to change my mind.'

'It is the truth. Come with me now and ask Morgan if you do not believe me.'

'I've made my decision. I need to see him again and look into his eyes. I want to know if he remembers me or not.'

'He won't because you look different. You look like this Polyxena...not like your true self.'

'You're confusing me. I need to see him again and talk with him. I can get him to remember our days together.'

Morgause took hold of her sister's arm and forced her down on to the chair. 'Were they so wonderful sister dear, all I remember were the many nights you cried?'

'You do not remember such a thing.'

Sybil started to flutter her wings and become animated at the sight of the two women fighting and arguing. 'I am leaving now. If you want me to get you safely away from this place you must leave now.'

Morgause said she was ready. 'I've got a good mind to beat you like I used to.'

'One word from me and I could have you in irons. Leave while you still can.'

Morgause indicated to Sybil she was ready. She moved quietly to the door, but turned one last time. 'Be careful,' she whispered. 'Do not trust anyone.'

*

Pulling the rope up posed no problem, but finding a rock on the other side of the crevice that could be used to tie it against was. There simply wasn't one. Gawain looked at Ragnell. 'Do you feel as stupid as I do?' he asked.

Ragnell did not answer, but scoured both sides of the crevice for a solution. There seemed to be no way out. Suddenly she dropped to her knees and peered downwards into the abyss. All she saw were ragged rocks, jutting out from either side of the mountain and in the middle, nothing but a dark hole. 'I wonder what lies down there?' she said.

'Death, what else,' suggested the man.

Glancing upwards the lady suggested they use the rope to climb down and see.

Gawain seemed unimpressed with the idea.

'What have we got to lose?'

'You might want to kill yourself, but I do not.'

The lady got to her feet and pushed the rope over the edge again. She then turned her back and took hold of the rope before starting to climb downwards. Gawain watched for a moment and then followed. The rope was not that long, about the length of four humans so it only took a short time before Ragnell reached its end. To add to their problems the light in the cavern continued to fade until it was little more than a pale flicker.

'Now what?' asked Gawain.

Again without answering, the young woman forced her two feet into slits in the rock and sought handholds. She managed to climb down the rock face, foot by foot and hand by hand. One false move, one slip and she would go down into the unknown probably to her death. Careful though she was, several times her foot came loose and the lady almost slipped. Thanks to her strong arms and hands she managed to hold on, until such time as she managed to get her feet back into position.

Gawain followed Ragnell and found the climb equally arduous, not least because his attention was on the girl more than on his own descent. After climbing down another ten feet the lady stopped. She kicked out at the rock with her right leg to find that the boot did not touch the rock at all. There was a space. How big it was remained to be seen, for the light had all but gone out. She called to Gawain. 'I think I've found a cleft,' she announced.

'Can you see anything?' he asked.

Ragnell said she couldn't but thought she could go down one more rung with her hands.

'Slowly then,' advised the man.

Her first hand caught hold of a rung in the rock, them her second hand before finally she tried to touch the rock with her feet. Again her feet and legs touched nothing indicating there was no more rock. One more suggested the lady. Gawain cried out for her to stop.

Ragnell's right hand felt for a rung but found none, luckily Ragnell's other hand was well enwrapped around a rung and her balance remained steady. Without stopping to think the lady did a reckless thing. Feeling sure that the gap was neither too large nor too small she decided to jump at an angle into what she hoped was a cleft. She swung to her left and let go of her handhold into the space.

All Gawain heard was a thud as Ragnell's body struck stone. He could not be sure how far she had fallen, but in a panic he cried out her name.

The lady was close by and had landed as she had hoped onto a good size cleft. Feeling her legs with her hand, the lady moaned out in pain.

'Are you all right?' yelled Gawain.

'Yes, I think so. One more hold down then check with your feet.'

Gawain followed the lady's instructions and landed beside her on the cleft. So far so good he told her. Looking into the cleft the two young people saw nothing but blackness. As they helped each other to their feet, they realised the hole in the rock was bigger than they might have thought. There was only one way to go, so again Ragnell led the way. Their pace had to be slow because of the lack of light and again it was the lady who suggested that Gawain keep a hold of her belt. He did so and began to curse his misfortune. 'Of all the dumb places in the world to die this must be dumbest.'

'You do whine a lot,' complained the lady. 'We're not dead yet, are we?'

'No,' grumbled the young man. 'All we need now are your damn mythical giants.'

'If we are close to the treasure then they will be not be far away.'

A sound resembling a slaughtered boar howled somewhere ahead of them. The lady stopped and Gawain whispered to her. 'I think they have just smelt their supper.'

The cries got louder as they continued their journey on foot into the core of the cave. A narrow tunnel weaved from side to side until at last the couple turned a corner to find themselves on a plateau. Four large fire torches illuminated the scene that they saw. The large piece of ground they had found was flat and had two stone objects on it; one was a decorative man size statue or memorial, the other was an Egyptian style sarcophagus.

The lady could not withhold her joy. 'We've found it! We've found it! We have found the Ark of the Covenant!' Gawain was less enthusiastic and tried to hold Ragnell from racing forward towards the objects. He tried to hold onto her belt, but she wriggled free from his grip. As she approached the sarcophagus, the lady felt the ground beneath her feet begin to open up and swallow her. Luckily Gawain rushed forward to her assistance and pulled her back wrenching the maiden through the air, back onto the safe ground on which he stood. The ground continued to give way leaving a large gap between them and the object they so desired to see.

Ragnell and Gawain stood locked in each others' arms and transfixed to the spot. It was then that the roar became ear splitting and they witnessed for the first time the giants. They were alike in appearance, tall, twelve feet in height perhaps, covered in black hair, with huge arms and legs and relatively small heads. Their eyes were big, allowing them great vision, while their mouths had large canine looking teeth over lapping their lips. They moved from behind the sarcophagus to stand guard over it. They growled at the humans and showed them their sharp looking incisors that still had traces of blood on them.

'You are cowards,' shouted Gawain across to the giants, in his most contemptuous voice.

Neither human expected the giants to communicate, so it came as a surprise when Magog the larger of the two giants replied. 'Come over here and we will see who the cowards are,' he cried.

'That is the point. You take away the ground to keep you both safe. I think you are scared in case we cut you into small pieces and throw you down the rocks into the abyss.

Both giants howled with laughter. 'We will feed on you throughout the whole winter, Magog stated.

Gog elaborated. 'Human flesh is so tasty.'

Instead of frightening the humans the giant saw both the man and woman were smiling back at them.

Ragnell continued the goading. She turned her head to address Gawain. 'They say the giants became extinct because they were so stupid.'

'Yes they do say that. People would often laugh and hurl abuse at them when they passed.'

'I always wanted to spit in the eye of giant. It's supposed to bring you good luck.'

'These creatures are too terrified to let you anywhere near them.'

'Enough of your stupid talk,' thundered Magog.

His brother moved behind the sarcophagus and the floor of ground between the humans and giants was restored. Looking rather pleased with their efforts the young humans ventured forward to take on the giants. With the help of Ragnell, Gawain pulled Excalibur from his back and stood resolutely ready to do battle. Despite telling the lady to leave the fighting to him, Ragnell had her own sword out ready to take on the much larger beasts.

Chapter 22

At first the giants merely toyed with the tiny humans, but then they realised the sting of their swords were real. Magog took a liking to the lady and went to pick her up with one hand but the lady slashed her sword across his arm, making him drop her onto the ground again. Gritting his teeth he began to utter a mouthful of obscenities which the woman took offense to. 'If you have nothing nice to say you should keep your big fat mouth shut,' yelled the lady.

Ragnell's goading had the desired effect, for Magog went into an angry rage and swung his right leg at the lady. Thanks to the quickness of Ragnell's reactions, the blow missed and struck the ground with an almighty thud. The creature yelled in pain, and continued to mouth more obscenities. The lady took her chance to inflict a further blow on her opponent by quickly getting to her feet and aiming a blow from her sword at his sore foot. Her blow was so effective that Magog fell to his knees. With his squealing still echoing around the cave Magog somehow got to his feet and stared at the puny female before him. As she moved forward to strike again, the giant, either from fear or wisdom, stepped back from the lady's approach.

Gog was fairing no better either. His arrogance was equal to his brother's as he thought he could just squat the man with his huge hands. After six or seven goes at this he realised the man was too quick, so he stopped to think. While he rested Gawain took advantage of his inactivity to lash Excalibur around his legs and feet. The large beast started to jump and hop about in an effort to avoid being seriously injured. It was a comical sight to see Gog jump about like a man jumping on hot coals.

The giants realised that their role of protector of the sarcophagus was a privileged one and that the Gods had rewarded them well by giving them as much food as they could possibly eat. Their tenure was for an indefinite period so they must have thought they were immortal, but their blood flowed and their mortality suddenly became a concern. Gog and Magog regrouped and while keeping an eye on the quicksilver humans communicated their concerns to one and other.

'Listen brother,' whispered Gog. 'I don't fancy wasting any more time on these creatures.'

Magog agreed. 'With one big blow we will catapult them into oblivion.'

The giants bent down and blew from their mouths as much air out of their lungs as they could muster. Gawain saw the torrent coming and grabbed Ragnell around the waist forcing her to the ground. It all happened so quickly that even Gawain's actions had little effect. The wind caused the man and woman to be lifted and flung against a range of rocks. The force of the impact caused them both to be knocked unconscious.

After congratulating each other, Magog picked up the prize that was Excalibur and studied it. 'No ordinary sword,' he muttered.

'No, it looks to have been made by them.'

'That's impossible. Why would a human possess such an item?'

Gog had no answer. 'They promised to come back, but I fear they have forgotten us.'

Magog tried to reassure his brother. 'They would not leave their treasure behind.'

'Do you ever wonder what's inside?'

'They made it clear we would die if we tried to look.'

'Aren't you curious?'

'No, good food is all I crave.'

'Not female companionship?'

'The last female giant died a long time ago.'

Gog glanced across to the humans. 'Do you think they're dead?'

'I do hope so, that female was a menace.'

'What about the sword?' asked Gog.

There was a moment's silence. 'It's mine,' announced his brother.

Gog was taken aback with this statement. 'It can't be yours. What have I got...'

Magog indicated with his eyes where Ragnell's sword lay.

'That isn't fair. You can not compare the two.'

Magog smiled. 'I picked up the best one, so I get to keep it.'

Gog wasn't prepared to leave it like that. 'We fight for it,' he announced.

His brother laughed. 'What use is it anyway...'

'Then give it to me.'

Magog shook his head. The two giants stood face to face and argued some more. It wasn't long before they locked horns and began to arm wrestle. It was a slow brutal fight where two giants gorged at each other's eyes and ears, where they tried to break each other's arms and legs, where they head butted one and other and kicked out at one another in a fury.

Gog's injuries, from the sword fight, were less severe than his brother's so it was he who took the initiative. After head butting his opponent Gog jumped on top of him and with his hands tried to break his neck. He pulled Magog's head back, while the giant screamed for him to stop. Magog used his elbow to smash his brother across the face. It took three blows like this before Gog finally let go. Now on their knees they continued to wrestle on the floor of the cave.

Meantime when all this was going on, and Gawain and Ragnell remained unconscious, a spectator appeared unseen by the giants. This spectator stood well back from the carnage and kept out of sight. His features were hidden somewhat by the dark clothes he wore and by his hands that remained in front of his face the whole time the giants fought.

Gog continued to be the aggressor as he forced his brother down on the floor again. This time Gog meant to finish the job for he took Excalibur and was about to place the blade across the throat of Magog when a strange thing happened. The sword floated up out of Gog's hands and remained suspended in mid-air. The fight stopped as both giants stared at the object. Whether they thought magic was at work or whether they thought the Gods were displeased, they immediately cowed their heads in shame.

The mysterious figure came out from the shadows and appeared before the terrified giants. His features became clearer; his face was half-eaten away and showed a skeletal fragment protruding from his left eye, the rest of his body appeared to be more bone than skin, while his mouth showed blackened teeth and his lips were thin. In truth the man looked more like an erect skeleton than a man. Still he walked forward to stand before the giants who remained on their knees with their heads bowed.

'Oh please,' pleaded Gog. 'We are sorry we have angered the Gods, it will not happen again.'

The man spoke slowly as if every syllable that he uttered was being torn from his body. His voice was that of a Celtic man, a man of authority who was used to giving orders. 'You have abused your duty and have allowed two humans to come in contact with our treasure.'

Magog pleaded for forgiveness and assured the figure that they had done their duty by preventing the humans from getting any further. Gog rearticulated his brother's sentiments. The figure, by the power of his will, turned Excalibur around so it pointed in the direction of the giants. Fearing that the magic sword was about to cut them down the giants pleaded even harder in an effort to save their skins.

'Enough of your complaining,' scolded the skeletal figure. 'The Gods you fear so much are gone. They can not harm you anymore, but I can.'

Looking confused the giants thought the danger was past and began to get to their feet. Excalibur raced forward towards them and forced them by its point to get back on their knees.

Again the giants sought forgiveness. 'Oh, great one, forgive us we are just stupid beasts...'

The figure agreed and even chuckled a little. 'I could kill you but there are so few of your kind left. Besides you have done your duty to the best of your ability. You did not look inside the tomb and for that reason I will give you your freedom.'

The giants looked at each other, but found words hard to come by.

Excalibur flew through the air and was caught by the skeletal hand of the figure. There it stayed by his side as if somehow it had always been there.

Gog and Magog looked for instructions but the figure only pointed to the only way out.

Gog addressed the figure. 'We can never climb our way out of this place, we will surely die trying.'

'You managed to enter the cavern.'

'Yes, but only with the help of the Gods,' Magog replied.

A small crow suddenly appeared on the shoulder of the strange figure. 'Take this bird with you, it will show you the way and if you still struggle you can always call out my name.'

Looking more relieved Magog asked the figure what his name was. The figure replied that it was King Arthur. The giants bowed again and began to praise the creature that announced that he was the King of the Celts, but the figure became impatient and scolded them for their hypocrisy.

The giants moved towards the narrow tunnels that Gawain and Ragnell had appeared from. The ghost of Arthur saw them disappear from his sight before turning his attention the two young people lying on the ground. A stunned Gawain moaned, put his hand on his head and complained of his aching skull. He looked at Ragnell, who was still unconscious, and tried to revive her by gently nudging her arm. The lady did not move. Fearing that she might be dead he listened to her heart and was relieved that it still had a beat. Turning his head he studied his immediate area expecting to see the giants but they were nowhere to be seen. From the corner of his eye he thought he saw a tall figure standing near the sarcophagus with his arms folded.

Gawain got to his feet and slowly moved over to where the man stood. The man's appearance shocked him for he looked more like a ghost than a living person. Through the hazy mist left over from the blow to his head, he couldn't quite be sure of what he saw. As he ambled forward to take a closer look, the man took on a recognisable face and Gawain stopped. 'My God is it you? Can it really be you, my King?'

The man's face resembled that of King Arthur's, but his shape did not remain constant. When Gawain raised his head again, after a short bow, he saw more of a skeletal figure than a man of flesh. Still the figure or phantom before him had the appearance of his uncle and when he looked closer he saw Excalibur was attached to his side. The phantom smiled grotesquely and yet at the same time gracefully back at the young man. 'You really should take better care of my possessions,' he stated.

Not a man usually lost for words, Gawain found it hard to express his excitement, joy, fear, and sheer surprise. Still here he was standing next to a man he knew to be dead. He was in the presence of spirit, a phantom, yet he felt no fear only wonderment. 'Tell me, why are you here?' he asked.

The figure of Arthur glanced in the direction of the sarcophagus. 'I'm here to stop you and your friend from making a big mistake.'

'Is my friend going to be all right?'

'Yes, I just wanted a word with my favourite nephew before awakening her.'

'She believes this tomb holds the treasure of the Christ, the one the Christians believe was the son of God.'

'Do you believe in this one true God?'

Gawain said that he did.

'So tell me what do you think lies beneath the stone lid?'

'I can only tell you what Ragnell believes. She believes it holds such treasures as the Holy Grail and the Ark of the Covenant.'

The figure's thin mouth managed a crooked smile. 'If it does, does she not also know that it is dangerous to touch these objects?'

'Perhaps she does, but she is a wilful creature and will not be put off by such stories.'

'Can she be more wilful than you?'

'She is strong in character as she in body strength.'

'Don't tell me my nephew has met his match?'

'I have never met a woman quite like her.'

'I will leave now, but for my sake do not try to open the sarcophagus.'

'Don't go, stay and tell me how you come to be the way you are.'

'Great misery will come if you allow the woman to open the tomb.'

'Then stay and stop her yourself.'

The figure of Arthur shook his head and told Gawain that it was his destiny and no one else's.

A groan from Ragnell made the young man turn his head for a moment, when he turned it back again the phantom figure of Arthur was gone. A clatter of steel hit the ground and Excalibur lay at the young man's feet.

*

The area was scorched, the usual green was replaced with black and the whole area reeked of smoke and yet it was the place that two Gods decided to meet.

The eerie atmosphere of Annwn made for a strange rendezvous place, but for once no phantom or spirit was anywhere to be seen. Instead Gwawl was sitting crossed legged by the shore, in full Trojan armour, dangling his sword in and out of the water in a movement that suggested restlessness.

He did not look up from his labours despite hearing the whish of water and a mini eruption from the sea. 'You do like to be dramatic,' suggested Gwawl.

'At least I am punctual,' remarked The Lady of the Lake.

Gwawl looked straight ahead and saw Vivienne step across the water, as if she was walking on dry land. 'You have brought the cylinder?' he inquired.

'Have you brought Rhiannon's ring?'

Gwawl smiled. 'I have it.'

Vivienne did not produce the cylinder at first and indicated to Gwawl to look into the water around her feet. He did this and saw deep down on the sea floor a silver looking object sparkle.

'Is it safe?' Gwawl asked, sounding a little concerned.

'It will remain intact until I release it from the sea bed.'

Gwawl held up the ring with his hand. It glittered with the morning sun. 'What a careful being, you are,' he pronounced.

'Give me the ring,' commanded Vivienne.

Gwawl threw the ring into the air towards the lady. Vivienne caught the item with her right hand and immediately examined it.

'You have me puzzled, why do you want such a thing?'

Without taking her eyes off the ring, Vivienne answered. 'Pwyll had no right to give it to another.'

'I think I understand,' stated the God. 'I've kept my part of the deal...'

With her slight movement of her head the cylinder rose up from the sea bed into Vivienne's hand.

Gwawl got to his feet and moved forward into the water towards the Lady of the Lake. His enthusiasm nearly scuppered the deal, for the lady took immediate precipitate action. Using her eyes Vivienne's power evoked a powerful light that nearly blinded the God.

Only after Gwawl had been halted did the Lady of the Lake cease her powerful ray.

'You mean to break your promise?' suggested Gwawl.

'No, but your sudden movement alarmed me. I worry that you will stay here and compete with me for this land.'

'I do not wish to stay here a moment longer than I have to.'

'Have you found your special place then?'

'I have picked it out, but I might need to address a few issues.'

'Please do not tell me anything. No doubt I will hear about your exploits in due course.'

'It is far from here, so you do not have to worry.'

Vivienne let go of the cylinder. It moved through the air and stopped immediately in front of Gwawl. The God touched it and smiled. 'Life is precious,' he pronounced.

'Yes, that particular drum should give you another hundred years of human life.'

Gwawl sighed in exultation. 'I look forward to every moment...'

'My pixies await your pleasure.'

Gwawl nodded. 'This is goodbye then?'

'Please don't pretend you will be sad to never see me again.'

'I am glad to have a future, thanks to your kindness.'

'Kindness had nothing to do with it I can assure you. Just remember if you take a human for your mate the consequences can be difficult.'

'How did you know I was thinking of such a thing?'

'You've made yourself beautiful for a reason and that must be to mate.'

'I guess I am hoping to find my Helen...just like the real life Paris.'

'Remember how that turned out my lord. Do be careful...'

'I will choose wisely.'

A noise suddenly surrounded Gwawl, as several fairies encircled him and spoke in their quick high octane voices.

Vivienne watched as both the God and the fairies disappeared from her sight. From the corner of her eye, she witnessed Nemue emerge from the sea.

'That went without incident,' suggested the young woman.

'We must keep an eye on his progress...'

Nemue wondered if the we, meant that the Lady of the Lake had forgotten to set her free. 'My role in your world must diminish, you did promise...'

'Yes in due course you will marry your young man, but first we must secure the throne for Lady Morgan. No word from Lancelot?'

Nemue frowned. 'He is weak and I fear has lost any nerve he once had.'

'He must be compelled to act.'

'I will do whatever you suggest.'

'If power is not a sufficient stimulant then perhaps love will be.'

Chapter 23

'I see you have slain the giants,' Ragnell acknowledged.
Gawain tried to explain.
'You're saying some phantom killed them?'
'No, he let them go free?'
'Why?'
Gawain shook his head. 'I don't understand it. He told me not to open the sarcophagus and yet he forced its protectors from this place.'
Ragnell smiled. 'It would seem your phantom is something of a contradiction.'
Gawain looked confused and after helping the lady to her feet tried to persuade her not to try and open the tomb.
'This phantom, are you sure he is not a figment of your imagination? After the blow on your head you might have imagined him.'
'Maybe you're right, but it seemed so real. In any case where are the giants?
Ragnell could not answer that. She was in a hurry to open the tomb and look inside, but Gawain barred her way.
The young lady laughed. 'After all we've been through you can't honestly expect me to walk away without looking inside.'
In the short time that the man had known her, he knew that nothing but brute force would stop her from her goal. The lady tried to force her way past him, but he moved along side her and blocked her path again.
Ragnell's eyes seemed like they were on fire, or maybe it was just the light from the fire torch. Either way he could see the lady's resolve as she put her hand on the hilt of her sword.
'I will not fight you my lady,' imparted Gawain.
'Let me pass then.'
Gawain shook his head.

Ragnell pulled out her sword but held it down by her side in a non aggressive manner. Still Gawain refused to budge. So the lady pointed her sword at him. 'Let me pass,' she shouted. The man shook his head. The lady lunged with her sword and caught Gawain on his arm. As the blood began to flow the lady almost cried in frustration. 'Now look what you made me do.' She tore away apart of her cloth shirt and offered to help Gawain stop the bleeding. He allowed her to use the cloth as a tourniquet and stood staring at the lady's anguished face.

'Please let's not quarrel,' she pleaded.

After his wound was tied and the bleeding stopped the man agreed to help the woman to open the sarcophagus only if she explained to him some more about her obsession.

Ragnell was reluctant to comply, but when she saw that Gawain would not budge on the issue, she seemed to give in.

'You want to know my whole story, all about my parents, all about my past lovers, all the boring stuff that makes up who this creature is before you?'

'I might not find it boring?'

'It's all romantic rubbish. I am like this because my father beat me up, my mother ignored me when I was a child and hate all men because a man raped me when I was twelve. Are you satisfied? Can we open the tomb now, I don't know about you but I'm tired and hungry.'

'Is it impossible for you to tell the truth?' Gawain asked.

'Why don't you ask my sister, she seems keen to impart all my secrets?'

'I want to hear it from you.'

'You act like we are close, blood relatives or something. You mean nothing to me. I can do without your help...'

'You need my help to lift the sarcophagus.'

Dropping his voice a little, Gawain asked the most pertinent of question he could. 'Were you raped as a child?'

He was surprised to see a smile begin to appear on Ragnell's lips. 'That would make things easier for you to understand, wouldn't it?'

'What does that mean?'

'I don't hate men, although I do find most of them pretty useless. There is only room for one thing in my life and that is finding the holy relics.'

'But you are not the most holy of people...'

'Thank you very much. Just because I'm not a priest, doesn't mean I can't feel the essence of religion.'

'I still think you are hiding something?'

'Of course I'm hiding something, doesn't everyone? You have secrets. I am sure you wouldn't want everyone to know about some of them.'

'So you're saying, leave me alone. I'm cold blooded, heartless and not in need of anybody's love.'

'I'm not in need of your love. Now you know everything about me you need to know. Let's open this tomb and get the hell out of here.'

Finally Gawain gave up and agreed to help lift the sarcophagus. They put their hands gently on the tomb and were relieved to find that the stone was only cold and not filled with a fire of any prophecy. The lid was heavy and it took them awhile even to move it a little, but evidently it budged and they removed it completely.

Gawain had no idea what to expect, but Ragnell expected certain things; such as a chalice, (Holy Grail) an ark, or other treasures like gold, silver and sacred parchments. At first they thought the tomb was empty, for all they saw was some white powder substance. Ragnell ignored her own advice and put her hands inside to move away the substance to see if anything was underneath. She felt no pain and no irritation, only the smooth feel of a substance that resembled sand. As she removed some of the powder she felt two objects caked within the white sand. She quickly put her two hands around one and lifted it up. It was heavy and in the shape of a large egg. Looking at her companion the lady seemed lost for words. Gawain then pulled the second egg out of the tomb and both humans stood looking at something they found curious. They felt a force or an entity within the eggs, something that appeared to move. As they studied them in more detail they saw a glow of light emanate around the middle of each egg.

'What in the name of God have we found?' asked Gawain.

Ragnell had as much idea as her companion, 'Could they be giant's eggs?' she inquired.

'I know giants do not produce eggs...'

'Then you make a guess, for I have no idea why someone would go to all this trouble for two overgrown chicken eggs.'

Gawain pondered and thought he might have come up with an answer, but was reluctant to offer his conclusions for fear of ridicule. The lady's mind thought similarly but she too waited before offering up her opinion.

Almost as if the lady needed a little reassuring, she asked a question. 'When did the last dragons die out?'

*

The Magister Militum welcomed Lucius and Helena into his spacious room and offered them some wine. He was an old stern looking soldier, with grey hair and an enlarged stomach. It was clear that his days of fighting were over and that his role of supreme commander was an administrative one. He looked at the lady curiously as the couple sat down at his desk.

Lucius began to explain the purpose of their inquiry, but he did not get a chance to finish for the Magister interrupted. He glanced at Helena again. 'I know your purpose and have the particulars before me.'

The lady was feeling uncomfortable and believed the man had some bad news to impart so she asked him straight out. 'You seem displeased with my presence here, why is that?'

The Magister apologised and said that he would rather have the conversation with the man alone. Helena hid her anger but refused to leave the room.

'I have something to impart to you, but it is best understood between men,' the Roman commander advised.

'We believe that a Legion Commander by the name of Titius Scipio is being held captive in this fortress,' stated Lucius.

The Magister frowned but did not answer.

'We would like permission to see him,' continued Lucius.

The Roman official put his hand up to his face and muttered something to the man. Helena was losing her patience and demanded that the man answer their questions. He continued to ignore the lady and tried to converse exclusively with the man. He offered no reason for his behaviour but insisted that the lady should leave the room. When he could not convince the lady to do what he asked he heaved a huge sigh. He informed them that this was a military matter and did not concern them.

'This lady has travelled over land and sea to find this man. You can not be cruel as to let her go home without even seeing him.'

The old Roman soldier seem to mellow at the story of their perilous journey and the lady's resolve. Eventually he bowed his head a little and agreed to tell them what they wanted to know. 'He was like a brother to me, but he broke his oath of allegiance to his Emperor. It is a terrible thing when a commander decides to desert his post. It sets a bad example throughout the whole Empire.'

Lucius was beginning to fear the worst, but Helena still asked to see the man.

The Magister continued with his tale. 'No one was more surprised when he arrived here unannounced. I could not understand his logic when he pleaded to be given his old command again. This was impossible and I'm sure in his heart he must have known this. I had no choice but to put him in a prison and await my orders concerning his fate. It did not take long for the High Command to make their decision. For them it was not a difficult decision. He was court-marshalled and I was one of the three Tribunus who decided his fate.'

Lady Helena felt a sudden shiver as she began to comprehend what the man was saying. 'This court, has it taken place?' she asked.

'It wasn't necessary.'

'I don't understand?' Helena queried.

Helena continued to press the man.

There was a pause before the man answered. 'It might be hard for you to understand.' He was referring to Helena, but looking in the direction of Lucius. 'I'm sure you will appreciate the man's dilemma?' he said.

Helena had no idea what Magister was hinting at.

'What would you do in his place?' he asked of Lucius.

The lady turned her head to look upon her companion. 'What is he talking about?'

Lucius realised that he would have inform the lady of her lover's fate. It was not easy for him to inflict such pain on someone he had become fond of, but the Roman official was not going to reveal it so he had no choice. He turned his body to face Helena and in a voice that was both soft and kind he related how Titius had met his end.

The lady refused to believe it. 'He wouldn't! You don't know him...he wouldn't do such a thing.'

Lucius tried to explain, but the lady didn't want explanations.

The Magister intervened in an effort to soften the blow. 'It was the honourable thing to do,' he stated.

Helena rounded on the man and blasted him with abuse. The man was shocked to hear the lady speak so. With the help of Lucius the lady regained her self control and asked for more information. 'Where is he buried?' she inquired.

The man described the place and gave directions how to get there. In a manner both abrupt and discourteous the lady left the room in a temper. Lucius went after her, but she announced that she wanted to be left on her own.

The ground was flat and green and had an assortment of crosses, stones, and flowers covering it. It was a peaceful place, a place away from the hustle of the everyday and a place that Lady Helena now found herself. After being given directions to the exact spot the lady finally came upon the man's grave and she became overcome with sadness. It was impoverished compared to most, for it had no cross or flowers, only a collection of stones standing haphazardly upon the soil.

Try as she could to control her emotions the lady could not find the self-restraint to remain dignified. She dropped to her knees and threw herself full length on top of the dirt in an act of inconsolable emotion. It wouldn't have mattered to the lady if anyone witnessed her hysteria, although only one person did and that person was her friend.

Lucius had followed her to the grave side and was standing close by. His instinct told him to remain quiet and to allow the maiden some time alone. The lady tried to hold back her sobs as she whispered her regrets and her frustration at the man's decision. 'You should have stayed with me. How could you doubt my true feelings for you? Didn't I always smile in your company? Didn't I always listen to everything you had to say with such wonderment? Why didn't you kiss me upon the lips my love, not even once, I know you wanted to, I could see it in your eyes. You could never know how much I dreamt of that moment.' The lady sobbed again and gave one last plea. 'How could you be so selfish and leave me all alone?'

The man standing witnessing the woman's pain took a few steps forward and whispered her name. 'Helena...I have something for you.'

It took the lady a moment to appreciate she was not alone and to rise to her feet. With her dirt covered hands she tried to wipe away her tears and regain some composure. 'Why are you here?' she asked.

A mournful Lucius, handed the lady a piece of fine parchment. The lady stared at the scroll before taking it off the man and asking him what it was.

'After you left the commander gave this to me. He said it was the last wish of Titius that you should have it. '

The lady looked at the scroll before breaking the seal and opening the note. Lucius turned his body to one side away from the lady's view. Unaware of his actions the lady studied her note and read it to herself. What she read was the man's attempt to explain his actions to her and a kind of eulogy to her honour. *'Do not grieve for me. I am an old soldier, used to death and always ready to meet my maker. I came home to my true mistress, for she has stood steadfastly by me for near forty of our Justinian years. A true soldier cannot run away from his duty, but neither can a man run away from his own destiny. It was my destiny to save you and to give you back your life. Make good use of it, for your life means more to me than all the promises made to me by the virgins on Elysium. Our love could never have worked my dear one, for our ages and our experience were so different. Marry the young Celt. He can give you children and happiness, things that I can not possibly give to you. Remember me as a man that was enriched by your presence and your kind words. Name your first male child after me if you like, providing your husband is amenable of course. I leave you all my worldly possessions of which there is precious little. I had two pieces of fine jewellery made, one of which is a brooch with your inscription. It is a token of my love and affection for you. My death was an honourable one, just like my life and my love for you. Do not see it as anything else. A soldier should either die on the battlefield or by his own sword.'*

The words were meant to ease the lady's pain, but it did not. Somehow it made the lady even more angry and keen to lash out at someone. The only person present was Lucius and so she buried her fists into the strong man's chest in an effort to expunge her frustration. The man was happy to soak up the lady's blows and be her shoulder to cry on.

Chapter 24

A clean-shaven Merlin looked back at his own image in the mirror and saw tears begin to flow down his face. His transformation in looks was due to the kindness of the man who had provided him with his new accommodation. Castor had made him feel he had some worth by offering him his friendship. The reason he witnessed his own tears was not because the task before him seemed impossible, but because he felt that he had lost his wife for a second time. Not only did she not recognise him but her questions of their past left him feeling uneasy.

Merlin's new friend had managed to gain two passes to visit the woman who claimed to be his wife in jail. The sorcerer was convinced that the lady was a fraud, so he entered the cell with his anger at its height. He stepped forward to address the lady, but he was confounded by what he saw. Her appearance even in the dismal light was unmistakable. Her proud face hadn't changed, despite her hardship, while her powerful eyes still managed to take his breathe away. He was about to call out her name when he felt his legs go beneath him and the blood in his face drain away. His eyes closed and he fell to the ground face first. Only the quickness of the lady's reactions saved him from a serious inquiry.

Still staring back at his image in the mirror, the man remembered the moment he re-opened his eyes and stared up at his wife. Standing over him the lady offered him some words of comfort. 'The awful smell in this place is enough to make anyone feel ill,' she commented.

It was her voice, it was her kind words, yet there was something wrong. There was no recognition in her face at all. Castor made the polite introductions and almost as if he was dreaming he heard the lady answer to the name of Penelope. Although he heard it, it did not register with him for he blurted out his wife's real name. 'Gallia my darling,' he cried. 'I thought you were dead.'

The lady looked at Castor for an explanation, before looking at the man still kneeling on the cell floor. 'What is the meaning of all this?' she inquired. Castor tried to explain, but Merlin kept interrupting his address making it impossible for the lady to comprehend. Finally Castor managed to keep Merlin quiet long enough to offer the lady an explanation of sorts. The lady listened without commenting. She was aware that the man who claimed to be her husband was staring at her, but she remained passive throughout the telling of the tale.

'So I am this woman you say, this Gallia and this man is my husband?

There was a silent pause as husband and wife stared back at one and another.

'You expect me to take your word for that?' asked the lady of her friend.

Castor said he could provide enough evidence to convince the lady that it was so. Merlin got to his feet and shook his head. 'No, Gallia I have no rights over you, I hand them back to you and only offer my assistance in freeing you from your present predicament.'

The offer seemed to surprise the lady as she put her hand up to her head and sighed. 'You bring me false hope sir, for no one can help me.'

Castor strenuously disagreed. 'This man has friends in high places...'

'Only the Queen can offer me any kind of mercy, so I've been told,' Gallia insisted.

'You are no friend to the Queen,' announced Merlin.

The lady pressed the man to tell her what he meant by the statement.

'In the past you have helped others to thwart the lady.'

'That sounds rather mysterious.'

Merlin smiled. 'Your actions saved a lady from the gallows and made the Queen look foolish.'

It was Gallia's turn to smile. 'Perhaps my past life is more memorable than I thought. Go on, tell me more.'

'You remember nothing at all of your past?' questioned Merlin.

'No, nothing...vaguely places...'

'Lady Morgan, do you remember her?'

With a rather blank expression Gallia said the name was familiar. 'Have I met her?'

'You cannot recall her face?'

'No. Then again I cannot recall your face either. You're a complete stranger to me.'

Merlin started to tell the lady a little of her past, but Castor interrupted his tale. 'We haven't much time. We must plan a strategy, before the guards come back.'

They both agreed. The three moved to the slit in the prison wall that offered a little light and began to discuss their options. Merlin was forceful and promised to approach Lady Morgan whom Gallia learnt was a lady of great power, to ask for her assistance.

'That's fine and good, but can she offer me a reprieve.'

'I will not let anything happen to you,' promised her husband.

'In two days time the trial will take place and I see little chance of an acquittal,' admitted the lady.

'Time is against us,' Merlin admitted. 'I must find a way to have the trial put back for a few days.'

'The lady's health is a matter of concern,' offered Castor.

'Yes indeed, that might work.'

The lady shook her head. 'I'm accused of murder. They'll never let me just walk out of here.'

'Do as I say and they just might. When we leave you must pretend to be ill and complain of a pain in your stomach.'

'If I eat the evening meal I won't have to pretend.'

Merlin came up close to Gallia. 'I will see if I can find a physician to come and examine you. Remember, complain like your life depended on it.'

'Everything must go through that pig of a prefect called Leogran,' informed Castor.

Turning his head to look upon his friend, Merlin jested that the man was of no consequence.

Castor never asked for an explanation and none was forthcoming. A short time later the two men left to return to Castor's nephew's home.

Merlin continued to stare into the mirror, but as he stared at himself a vision began to distort and transform. His face began to deform its shape; the man's eyes changed, his nose, his ears, even his old skin began to repair itself. Merlin was changing into another being. Not content in changing into a man, the sorcerer had transformed into a lady, but not just any lady.

Gallia was contemplating what had just occurred and wondering who the devil this Merlin was. She was about to put his instructions into force, for the meal of a sickly looking broth lay on the ground next to her straw bed. Before her play acting began she considered the attributes of the man who claimed to be her husband; he was older than her, skinny in frame, haggard in looks, not good-looking, at least not anymore and yet his eyes were kind. His stare was powerful, intense, leaving the viewer in no doubt that he was a man of strong resolve, yet his eyes also told of great loss, and of great pain. There was something about the man that rather frightened the lady. She suspected he held some dark secret that was eating away at his insides.

So this was the man I married, thought the lady. How strange to feel nothing for one's husband, neither love nor hate. His reaction in seeing her was strange also, suggesting perhaps of some conflict between them. Yes, didn't he say something about her being dead? Yes, because of her situation she had been as good as dead, but he meant really dead, as in buried or cremated. He thought she had died, but why? What catastrophe had struck her down and left her without a memory?

The questions kept coming leaving the lady troubled and for the first time since her reincarnation, curious. What little the man had told her suggested she was well respected and a lady used to getting her own way. She had taken part in some great adventure that defeated the Queen no less. She was intrigued to know more, but that would have to wait until she saw the man again. First she had to eat her foul meal and fain being ill. Just what would happen then she had no idea. She was sure that this Merlin was no ordinary man, so she was prepared for anything.

Gallia acted out her role to perfection and before long both a physician and the prefect Leogran were present in her cell. Leogran asked the apothecary his opinion in the condition of the lady. The man scowled at the prefect. 'How can you keep people in this filth,' he complained.

'She is a prisoner charged with murder...'

'Nonetheless she deserves to eat better than the rats that infest this place.'

The two men continued to quarrel about the conditions in the jail while the lady continued to complain about the pain in her stomach.

'She needs a place to rest that is not filthy and food that is fit to eat,' announced the apothecary.

'She also needs to be watched over by guards at all time.'

'Then I suggest the guards come along with us.'

'I cannot allow her to be moved.'

The two men argued some more before their discussion came to an abrupt end by the presence of a third party in the cell. That third party had the men bow before her and offer their apologies for all the noise they were making. Standing in a gown worthy of her status, stood the Queen. How she came to be there the men couldn't possibly comprehend. It was Leogran who spoke first. 'Your grace, I did not expect such an honour...'

'No I'm sure you didn't. Now tell me why this important prisoner is kept in such foul conditions?'

'Your grace, must remember the trial is due in two days...'

'Yes but the lady is in no fit state to be present.'

The apothecary agreed.

'Then we might postpone the proceedings a day or two,' suggested Leogran.

The Queen implied it might be postponed a great deal longer.

'Whatever you think,' said the prefect feebly.

'I will take the woman into my own care,' announced Guinevere. She began to wander around the smelly cell turning her nose in the air and shaking her head. She looked at the apothecary and assured him the lady will be in good hands.

'I shall be honoured to attend upon the lady,' he offered.

'That won't be necessary. I have the best physicians and apothecaries in the land.'

'You're not thinking of taking her away from Cirencester?' a panic stricken Leogran asked.

'I will take her to Caerleon. There I can keep an eye on her and maybe ask her some important questions.'

'But the lady has already admitted to committing the murder.'

The disguise was working perfectly and Leogran was none the wiser. 'Perhaps she lies and is protecting another,' suggested the Queen.

'We considered that a possibility,' announced Leogran.

'We?' asked Guinevere.

'My colleagues...and I...'

'And what have you done about it?'

The prefect was becoming excitable and explained that with the confession he had not deemed it necessary to investigate any further.

'I see, your laziness is appalling,' suggested the lady. 'I propose we postpone the case until the spring to allow you sufficient time to investigate the case more.'

This was appalling thought the prefect, but what could he do. His protests soon died down as he quickly agreed to his Queen's wishes.

Guinevere ordered the guards to help the lady out to a carriage that was waiting outside. Leogran watched as his prisoner was spirited away from his gaol without being able to do anything about it.

The man was too frightened to argue against his Queen, so all he could do was wish the ladies a safe journey and watch the coach drive away from the gaol without further comment.

It was only after the coach was a good distance from the gaol that Merlin sighed and returned to his true self. A terrified Gallia moved away from the apparition and screamed for the driver to stop. The driver did not stop for the man driving the horses so relentlessly forward was Castor.

The lady cowered in the corner of the carriage as she witnessed Merlin transformed back into his true self. She stared at the man for an age, but said nothing.

'You used to find my little disguises amusing,' he told his wife.

Finally the lady found her voice. 'Who the devil are you?' she demanded.

The man apologised as he wrestled himself out of the dress to reveal a simple cloth garment underneath. 'Oh, thank goodness,' he said. He offered his wife his hand and reluctantly she took it and was pulled up onto the seat beside him.

'You are not like other men,' the lady acknowledged.

'I cannot explain. My tricks can sometimes be useful, although at other times they can cause great misery.'

The lady sensed the man's self-loathing. 'I know I should be grateful but what happens to me now?'

It was a good question and one that Merlin had no answer for. The man hoped the lady would consent to live with him, but he was reluctant to suggest such a thing in the lady's present condition. After thinking on the matter for awhile the man suggested a new land and a new life. 'There are lands in the east that can give protection from any King or Queen.'

'Do you speak from experience?' asked Gallia.

Merlin admitted he did.

'What place would you suggest?'

Without hesitation the man mentioned a name he hoped the lady's memory might recognise, that of Antioch. Gallia gave no reaction, but suggested other places in the east whose commerce or trade might make for a better destination. Merlin was curious how the lady knew about such places. The lady could not tell him where such information came from. 'Somehow I just know them,' was all she said.

'Name whatever place you like. After all it will be your new home.'

The lady couldn't remember if she had ever visited any of the places abroad she knew about. 'Where are you taking me now?' she queried.

'Not to Caerleon, but to Lundonia. We will take a trip to the coast and hire a boat to sail to Gaul.'

'You have it all worked out,' said the lady. 'I suppose I should go to wherever you tell me.'

'I will not be coming with you,' stated the man.

Gallia's faced relaxed. 'How will I manage?'

'I have money and contacts if you should need them.'

'Was I such a terrible wife that the thought of my company is too awful to contemplate?'

Merlin smiled. 'You were a wonderful wife, but alas I was a not such a wonderful husband.'

'We have a long journey ahead of us, do we not? Why don't you tell me about our past life together?'

The thought of unburdening his crimes was appealing, but he realised that the lady must never know of his role in the tragedy that led to the death of her father. He could live with his own loathing, but not that of his wife's. Their meeting and her exploits in rescuing Lady Helena he did impart, but their more intimate relations he kept to himself. The journey to Lundonia would take several days and no doubt the lady would press him on why their marriage failed, but he would refuse to say anything other than to blame himself.

Chapter 25

It took less than a day for Guinevere, and Elaine to reach Lancelot's camp over looking the islands known as Avalon. The whole area was scorched by flames which even now, were still smouldering. Lancelot had dared to sail a small boat out to the islands and was surprised to find no sign of life. It seemed the Gods no longer frequented their domain. The final island was shrouded in fog but after trying to land his vessel unsuccessfully Lancelot decided to give up and return to the shore.

He had barely stepped off his boat when he saw Guinevere's white charger come towards him. The Queen looked radiant in her white fur jacket, brown breeches and black boots. He saw another lady riding beside her, one that made him more than a little wary. Lancelot knew very little of the Queen's new companion, other than the gossip that circulated around Caerleon. He had been told wild stories concerning her past duties for the Queen. The rumours implied that she was not a woman to be taken lightly. The general consensus was that she was some kind of bodyguard, or even perhaps Guinevere's personal assassin.

Lancelot made his report to the Queen while they sat in his tent and drank hot mull-wine together. He was aware that Polyxena was only a few steps away and was deeply interested in everything that he said.

'Gone you say?' recapitulated Guinevere.

'I believe they might have been killed by the fire.'

Guinevere smiled. 'How intensive was your search?'

'Not terribly, I thought you might want to lead a larger expedition yourself.'

Guinevere seemed interested in the idea.

Lancelot glanced over at Polyxena who continued to stare in his direction. 'That woman, why do I not know more about her?' asked the King.

Guinevere seemed uninterested. 'She is an old friend...'
'She does not seem old...'
'You do not have to worry about her, she is in my employ.'
'As what exactly?' questioned Lancelot.
'Every woman of worth should have a lady in waiting...'
Lancelot knew in his heart, that she was a person of greater worth than the Queen was trying to make out. 'I've heard rumours that the lady is some kind of assassin.'
Guinevere laughed. 'She is a lady, with impeccable taste and good breeding, but if you want to believe she is an assassin that kills for a living, go ahead and indulge in your fantasy.'
'I get the feeling she is going to be around a great deal.'
'I hope that isn't a problem. I have become quite fond of her.'
Lancelot, at that moment, did not suspect anything of an emotional connection between the two women. Because he was plotting against his spouse he conjectured she might be doing likewise. He suspected Polyxena might have plans to do away with him and so the man was on guard concerning her.

Elaine longed for night to come so that she could somehow find time to steal away from Guinevere and see Lancelot for a moment on her own. As the night came and a further tent was erected for the Queen, Elaine found that her admirer never left her side. The Queen was becoming attentive, despite the presence of her husband.

After a brief supper all the dignities retired including the King and Queen. The night air was chilly, but feeling confused Elaine left the Queen's tent to wander around the camp on her own.

There were five tents in all, they housed about twenty people and another twenty or so soldiers slept on the ground nearby. The lady could feel a coldness that went further than the chill in the night air. She could tell that the relationship between the King and Queen was bad, yet they conversed warmly enough. A breeze made her wrap her shawl around her shoulders a little tighter.

Elaine stepped up to Lancelot's tent and stood waiting outside, as a gentle breeze cooled her face and awakened her from her malady. The King slept alone, despite the improvement in his relationship with his wife. No one commented on this, at least not openly. Two guards approached her and one commanded for her to state her business.

'My business is with your master, kindly awake him and tell him Lady Polyxena wishes to speak with him.'

One guard looked at the other, and both looked unsure of what to do. The lady repeated her request and sounded even more determined than before. 'Why do you look at each other, do as I say.'

Finally, after grumbling to his friend, one of the guards entered Lancelot's tent to carry out the lady's command.

A short moment later, a dishevelled looking Lancelot exited his tent and demanded to know what was so important that it interrupted his sleep.

The sight of Lancelot, looking older, greyer, and not so handsome, made the lady further revaluate the position she was in. Happiness was a fleeting thing she thought. There was an old fable concerning looking back and reliving the past, she couldn't remember it all, but enough to appreciate it was a mistake to rekindle what had gone before. Was she about to make a big mistake, she wondered?

Wiping the sleep from his eyes, Lancelot was perturbed at seeing standing a few feet from him, the Queen's would-be-assassin. 'What do you want with me at this time of night?' he complained.

A sudden fear came over Elaine and she stood motionless. If she did not speak soon, she was aware he would re-enter his tent and have his guards escort her back to her own. 'I must speak with you,' she asserted.

The man looked bemused but asked her to state her business.

'It is a private matter, one not for anybody's ears.'

She was aware that the guards frowned, but they kept their discipline and remained silent.

Lancelot was thinking hard. He did not want to allow someone he believed to be dangerous enter his tent, so he suggested an alternative. 'It's a cool night, shall we go for a short walk. I could do with stretching my legs anyway.'

Elaine agreed.

They walked around the many tents before Elaine started to speak. 'Do you know who I am?' she asked.

'I know little, but have been told you know my wife from some years ago.'

'I am a fraud…I am despite my appearance a lady you once knew well.'

The man stared at the woman, his reactions while scrutinizing her face revealed no recollection. 'I have never seen you until recently.'

The lady sighed. 'I am the Lady Elaine, daughter to Lord Gorlois and Lady Ygerne…'

Lancelot grabbed the lady by the arm. 'What trick is this,' he shouted.

Although the man's grip was painful, Elaine did not grimace and stared into his eyes. 'Do you not remember the summer at Tintagol when we first spoke with one another? I sent you a parchment filled with love poems and you told me how honoured you were to receive them.'

Lancelot eased his grip on the lady's arm. 'How do you know this.' the man bellowed.

'Have you calmed down?' asked Elaine.

Lancelot's face remained red in colour, but his breathing was now controlled and perhaps more importantly so was his wits. 'I do not know who you are, but I warn you to stay away from me.'

A sudden coldness came over Elaine and a hardening of her resolve. 'What do you know of the Gods of these islands?'

It seemed a strange question thought Lancelot. 'I know nothing, why?'

'I was brought back to life by the Goddess of these islands. It is the same Goddess that wants you to kill the Queen now.'

This information was so private that only the man and Nemue knew about it. Again the man reiterated the obvious. 'Who are you?'

Elaine smiled. 'I received a blow to my head, in truth I do not know who I am, not really, but I think I am the lady Elaine. I have her memories at least...'

The man shook his head. 'You cannot be the lady you say, for she is dead.'

'Is that so? They're some who say you killed her.'

Lancelot's anger returned. 'I did no such thing...'

'You had just left me when someone held my head down...'

This revelation shook the man. 'Elaine,' he cried. 'I did not know...I promise...'

'You start to believe me now?'

The man scratched his head. 'It can't be you?'

'We played around the pool for what seemed an age and then you told me you had urgent business to attend to and left. A short time later I heard a sound behind me, but I did not become frightened for I assumed it was you. Then you or someone else held my head under the water until everything went dark.'

An almost tearful man began to plead his innocence. 'It was not me...I swear...I met up with the...'

The man stopped what he was saying and looked up to the heavens. He swore under his breath and cursed Guinevere by name. 'She must have...she knew of course...she knew of our secret rendezvous...she knew.

There was a short pause when everything including time seemed to freeze.

It was Elaine who broke the silence. 'You blame Guinevere, but it was not a woman's hands around my throat, that I am quite sure.'

'She must have employed someone to do the deed.'

Elaine complained that her head hurt and asked for some water to drink. Lancelot escorted her to his tent and offered the lady wine instead. She trembled at the touch of the man, just like she remembered from her bouts of recollections. He was the man she had loved. He would be the man she loved again. More importantly this time, she would be sure he loved her back. 'You have a difficult decision to make,' Elaine informed Lancelot.

'How can you know of this?'

'I'm not sure, but Morgause may have mentioned it.'

'But how could she know?'

Elaine shrugged her shoulders. 'I don't know. All I know is there's been too much killing. The Lancelot I remember would not stoop to assassination.'

'I have changed. I am no longer an honourable man, I lost that distinction the moment I became involved with Guinevere.

'It's not too late to change, to revert back.'

Lancelot smiled. 'You are kind, but if others knew what I have done...'

'I'm not concerned with others. I'm only concerned with us.'

'Can you forget the past and all the mistakes I've made?'

'Yes, but let us leave this land and make a life for ourselves away from family and commitments.'

Lancelot thought for awhile and stayed quiet. Finally he agreed. 'My sword has been used for evil deeds for the last time. I shall kill the evil woman but without spilling a drop of her blood.'

*

'What do we do with them?' asked Gawain.

'We take them with us of course,' replied Ragnell.

It was a lot easier said than done, for the two large eggs could easily be broken and the adventurers had no safe way to carry them. Gawain brought up this point to the young lady but she only shrugged off the young man's query by saying they would manage. So with one egg each they returned the way they had entered, weaving from side to side along the narrow path until they came back to the cleft. The light was back and bright enough for them to find the rope without any trouble. Climbing up it was difficult because of the fear of dropping the eggs into the chasm, but they managed it somehow. When they finally pulled themselves on to the ledge they were met by a quite remarkable sight.

They saw before them a bridge made of wood and rope that spanned the whole length of the cavern. 'It is a miracle,' announced Gawain. The lady however was suspicious and thought it might just be a mirage.

'There's only one way to find out,' stated the man.

He took a few steps closer to the bridge and was about to test it when Ragnell pulled him back with her arm. 'Wait. Let us try to comprehend what has happened here.'

Gawain had little doubt that it had to be the work of the phantom. The spirit of Arthur had worked some magic and put this convenience in place to help them to escape.

'If that is so, then it further goes against the warning he gave to you concerning the sarcophagus.'

Gawain had to agree, but then he mentioned how close his uncle was to him. 'He was extremely fond of me...'

'He wants us to bring these eggs into our world,' Ragnell stated. 'He wants us to unleash the dragons again.'

'That doesn't sound like the King I know. Remember it was his father who destroyed the dragons in the first place.'

'Yes, but who was it you really saw. Your King is dead and who knows who this phantom is?'

Gawain was thinking aloud. 'He was most clever in trying to convince us not to touch the tomb.'

The lady nodded. 'Perhaps we should destroy them?' the lady suddenly announced.

'We can't, we have no right.'

'We do not know the destruction the dragons cause, but from the stories I have heard they were truly terrifying.'

'It would just seem wrong...like slaughtering an unborn child.'

Ragnell smiled at her companion. 'You are quite a romantic, aren't you?'

'I don't know what you mean.'

The two young people had no choice but to step on the bridge. So together they put one foot in front of another and began their walk across step by step. To their amazement they continued without the fear of plunging to their deaths for the bridge was solid. They walked briskly from one side to the other without fear of the causeway giving way. On the other side they turned to look back at the object only to see it vanish as it had never been there. They found the inlet thanks to the mark left on the ground by Excalibur and set about escaping through the small passage. It was just as tight as they remembered it to be, but more difficult to negotiate because of the force needed to fight their way upwards.

Now back on the mountain proper, they realised that their adventure had lasted one whole day. It was now dark and without the prospect of shelter nearby they glanced at each to look for inspiration. 'Perhaps we should return from whence we came,' suggested Gawain.

'We're more likely to smash the eggs on our way down,' stated Ragnell.

The young man still proposed the idea, but Ragnell began her trek down the mountain. Gawain followed her and complained of the cold. 'Don't you feel it?' asked the man.

'I don't think about it, but we better find some shelter soon, before we fall down some gully or crevice.'

Chapter 26

Before Lancelot entered Guinevere's tent, another bout of headaches attacked Elaine. They were severe enough for the man to voice his concern. 'Tell me what ails you?'

Elaine pleaded to be left to sit quietly, but Lancelot held her close and spoke softly of their early days.

It was only after Lancelot left to carry out his mission, that Elaine shut her eyes and began to experience a different sort of reminiscence.

The scene was macabre for she was aware that she was extremely dirty and that the place that she was in, was also unclean. There was straw on the floor and the walls were covered in what looked like excrement. She was thankfully unable to sense this, being unable to either smell or touch her surroundings. To add to her woes, she became aware that she was manacled to the wall of what was obviously a prison.

She heard footsteps approach and when she looked up she saw a woman that she recognized. Guinevere instructed the jailer to open the prison gate and in a moment she entered the gaol. The Queen stepped into the dirty cell and looked around before staring at Elaine. 'This is a fine place I must say. Caught? I thought you of all people would have somehow made your escape.'

To her horror and surprise Elaine became aware that she was not the gentile lady she should have been, but a quite different species all together. Her voice sounded the same, but her language was not the language she had been brought up on. This lady was not Lady Ygerne's daughter, for that lady never knew some of the words that came out of her mouth. Some of the words she had heard others speak, but some she had never heard before, but she was sure they were all crude and vile.

Guinevere reacted to her vitriolic outburst by bending her head back and laughing. The Queen quickly assured her that everything was on hand. 'You didn't really think I'd let them hang you, did you?'

The words came out of her mouth.' I failed you...so yes the thought had occurred to me that you might.'

To her surprise Guinevere, who had on a long blue coloured dress, dropped to her knees beside her.' You will be released from here within a day, just as soon as the ransom is paid.'

The Queen was uncomfortably close now and to her surprise reached out her hand to touch her face. It soon became apparent that the Queen held feelings that went beyond mere friendship. Then to her bewilderment the women kissed each other passionately on the mouth.

Elaine could not feel the kiss, but her reaction to it was bewildering, for far from being repelled she gave back the kiss with interest. Finally they pulled apart from each other but continued to look into each other's eyes.

'How much am I worth to you, then?' she heard herself saying.

'Oh, about a cost of Cardinal I suppose.'

'Not the cost of a King?'

'Most Kings aren't worth that much my dear.'

'I am sorry, I let him get away.'

Guinevere shook her head, as if to make light of the statement. 'He will be killed but there is no rush...'

'He is the one man who could reveal your past...'

'Once recovered, with my help you will complete your task, but until then be quiet and tell me just how grateful you are going to be.'

*

Two days had elapsed since Gawain and Ragnell had successfully made their escape from the cavern. They found their companions Morholt and Rosalinda at the nearest inn, many leagues away from the Rheged Mountains. When they arrived they found that Rosalinda was unwell. She had caught a fever and according to the apothecary her life lay in the balance. For the first time Gawain witnessed a different side to Ragnell's character as she stayed at her sister's side night and day. She applied the medicine when it was needed and refused to sleep as long as her sister was in danger.

Gawain entered Rosalinda's room where he witnessed Ragnell outstretched on the bed beside her sister. The young man helped Ragnell back onto the chair so that he could examine the patient. He placed his hand upon her forehead and found that the sweat that had previously been there had gone. He sighed in relief and his sigh awakened Ragnell from her slumber.

'What, what had happened?' she stammered.

'She sleeps peacefully now. There is no more danger.'

Ragnell got up from her chair to examine her sister and was happy to accept Gawain's statement as fact. 'God be praised,' she exclaimed. 'You should have awoken me nonetheless.'

The young man said he would have if her sister's condition had shown any signs of deteriorating. 'You should get some sleep,' he commented.

The young woman shook her head. 'It's time I left here.'

'She might have a relapse,' commented Gawain.

Ragnell sighed. 'Okay, I'll wait until she's awake, but then I must go.'

'Go where?' asked the young man.

'Far away...over the sea and over much land...'

'In search for this mythical treasure...'

'It's not a myth.'

'What about our other treasure, what should we do about that?'

'You know what I think.'

'I can't just destroy them.'

'It's none of my concern, do whatever you wish with them.'

The lady moved passed Gawain towards the door. The young man caught her arm and moved closer to her. 'I wish I could come with you, but I have other commitments.'

'Did I ask you to come with you?'

'I could be useful to you.'

'If you want to be of use, give me Excalibur.'

Gawain did not comment. She glanced at his arm and he felt obliged to let go of it. The lady left the room to wash and to prepare her meagre supplies for a long trip, while the man contemplated what he could do to stop her from leaving.

A short time later Rosalinda was well enough to eat a little soup and sit up to hear her sister's exploits. Gawain was the only one who knew Ragnell was waiting until first light before sneaking out to continue with her adventure.

*

Elaine jumped up with a start and left her tent with a view to stopping Lancelot from carrying out his task. She became aware that she did not want to be responsible for the death of the lady after all. She might be too late though; perhaps the man had carried out his mission already.

She burst forth into Guinevere's tent, despite her guards' protestations to be met by the sight of the Queen about to sip some wine from a goblet. She immediately screamed for her to stop.

Guinevere opened her mouth and stared at her favourite. 'What the devil is wrong with you?'

'Have you drunk any of it?' queried Elaine.

Guinevere looked at the contents of the goblet and shook her head.

'Thank God for that,' Elaine gasped.

Guinevere glanced at Lancelot who had turned his head to look upon the face that beguiled him. He seemed to the Queen different, lost in his own thoughts. He stared at Elaine as if she had betrayed him.

Elaine had to react quickly, for the look on Guinevere's face told her that she wanted an explanation.

'Is someone going to tell me what is going on?' the Queen yelled.

'It is all a mistake...what did he tell you?'

Guinevere put the goblet down on a small table and approached Polyxena. 'I couldn't sleep so Lancelot persuaded me to try this strong wine...it's supposed to be very potent.'

'It is potent, so potent you will never wake up again.'

'Is it poison?' asked Guinevere.

'Yes, but Lancelot's not to blame...'

Elaine's explanation was drummed out by the Queen shouting for her guards. The two men, who had heard every word, quickly grabbed hold of Lancelot and tied his hands behind his back. They looked at their Queen for their instructions.

'I want six men guarding him at all times. Take him to your commander...'

Lancelot looked lost and complained to Elaine. 'What is happening, why are they doing this to me?'

Elaine tried to explain to the man, but his sad countenance and his fearful pleas were making Guinevere suspicious.

Lancelot declared his love for Elaine in front of Guinevere as the guards escorted him from the tent.

The Queen stared at her favourite and grabbed hold of her arm. 'Love!? He declared his love for you. When did all this happen?'

'It's hard to explain...'

'I think you'd better try.'

How could she explain, she was confused and didn't understand what was happening to her. She was Elaine, the daughter of Lady Ygerne, and sister to the powerful Lady Morgan, yet she was also this other creature, this Polyxena. She was more than just confused; she was beside herself with questions. Guinevere was looking at her expecting answers but she had none to give.

Compassion was not something she expected from the Queen, but Guinevere sighed and offered her own explanation. 'The blow on your head...that and the loss of your memory...it is enough to confuse anyone. You saved me and I am grateful.' The Queen paused. 'This other matter concerning Lancelot...it is clear to me that the man is beguiled by you, but that you do not return his feelings.'

Elaine was aware the Queen wanted her to confirm this was so. It would make everything easier, but it would not be completely true. Even a moment's hesitation would make her more suspicious. 'It is true,' she stated 'Lancelot has, this night, pledged his love for me completely.'

Guinevere sighed in relief and managed to give her favourite a smile. 'It is late. We will talk more of this in the morning...'

Elaine nodded. She was about to leave when Guinevere took hold of her arm and asked her to stay. What could she do? She wanted time to think. She needed time to think. She could not leave Lancelot to take all the blame, but she had to remain free so as to help him escape. What a terrible mess she had created? Her feelings waved from side to side, one moment she was Elaine, young emotional and in love, the next she was more mature concerning herself with a woman she should knew she should hate.

*

'At last our King returns to us,' mocked Vivienne. 'Missing the comforts and pleasures of a human body?' she asked.

'The human body is a weak shell, and full of strange maladies,' replied Eros.

The King of the fairies had now returned to his true form.

'So you are glad to be back?'

'Indeed I am, though the experience will stay with me a long time.'

Vivienne's face relaxed as she related her recent misadventures with her human helpers.

Eros anticipated what was on Vivienne's mind. 'You need things to return to some kind of normality?' he inquired.

'Nemue's future is intertwined with mine. I cannot allow her to go off and play at being a happy wife.'

'We wait your instructions,' said Eros.

Chapter 27

Having taken Gallia to a safe house owned by Castor, Merlin was instructed to rescue the Lady Megan and bring her to his wife. He was reluctant to waste valuable time but the lady was adamant that the girl could not look after herself. It was not as easy as it appeared for the hunt for the escaped prisoner was well under way and extra guards were now secured around Mador's castle.

The problem was easily solved by Merlin, for he became invisible again, breezed past everyone in the castle until he came upon the lady's bedchamber. He entered unseen and found the girl crying beside her bed with a crucifix in her hand. He feared startling her so he whispered softly her name. Megan turned her head and stared into the blackness but saw no one. This was not the first time she had heard voices but this time it was a man's voice and not a woman's. 'Who is there?' the lady cried.

Merlin said he had a message from her stepmother and that she was waiting for her some leagues from here. Megan, in the semi-darkness, reached out her hands to try and find the body that housed the voice, but she could not find it and asked the man to show himself. This Merlin did, but it was a mistake for the fearful young woman then screamed.

A host of guards then burst into her room to find out what the matter was. They searched the place and found no one but the girl in the room. As they left they murmured to themselves that the girl was mad. Indeed their protestations were accurate; the girl was close to losing any sense of reality. Merlin decided to drug her, put her under his invisible cloak and walk out of the castle unseen.

So it was done and before long they galloped towards Dover and a new life. He had thought long and hard about going with his wife on her journey. Until such time as Gallia regained her memory he felt it was wiser to put some distance between them. The day of reckoning would come, but he wanted to put if off for as long as he could.

Dover was busy as always, as Merlin brought Megan to his wife as promised. The women embraced as sisters and were overcome with joy. Castor had brought with him Hamlet which pleased both the ladies equally. Young Megan found the dog irresistible and played with him the whole time the party travelled out to the large coracle. This gave Merlin and Gallia a chance to talk and say their farewells.

Gallia couldn't understand her husband's attitude, even though it made her life a lot easier. It went against nature, she thought, not to want to be by your wife's side. Perhaps he really was acting in her best interests, or perhaps he was trying to hide some dark secret. One day she would remember something from her past and that day she would know whether her husband was a hero or a villain. Until that day she would be content to look after her substitute family and be content to enjoy her freedom.

Sitting together on the small rowing boat, Merlin gave Gallia the last of her instructions. The lady was impressed by his planning skills and his connections. 'You have done a remarkable job under impossible conditions, I am truly amazed,' she said.

The man was not used to being praised and found it hard to conceal his emotion. His love he could not speak of, but his admiration he did. 'You have a compassion that is beyond most humans.'

At first the lady did not know what he was referring to. Then Merlin glanced at the happy Megan and the lady knew that her kindness was being acknowledged. 'All she really needs is someone to love her,' Gallia remarked.

Merlin hoped one day the lady would feel the same for him. 'Your kindness will one day be rewarded,' he pronounced.

Looking a little concerned the lady wondered if they would remain in contact with each other.

'Always,' he replied. 'I will let you know when it's safe for you to return, that is if you care to come back.'

The lady was looking forward to her little adventure, but she also knew that the unanswered questions from her past would draw her back one day. 'I will return and when I do, you must promise me you to reveal everything of our past together.'

Merlin bowed his head in answer.

*

Gawain was awake at first light in a hope of catching Ragnell, but he was too late, the lady had already gone. It left him in a quandary, for he had responsibilities and he had the fate of the dragon eggs to consider. Still the thought of never seeing Ragnell again made him come out in a sweat. He decided to act quickly and awaken Morholt from his bed. He gave the man precise instructions concerning the eggs, telling him to take them to his father's castle in Lothian.

'What will I tell them concerning you?' the bleary eyed Morholt asked.

'Tell them I've gone after my destiny.'

Wiping his eyes free of sleep, the man inquired after Ragnell.

'She's gone,' said Gawain. 'If you have any idea where she would be heading please tell me?'

Forcing himself to get out of his bed the man stopped to yawn. 'Oh that girl, what she puts her poor sister through.'

'You must take care of Rosalinda, at least until such times as we return.'

Still a little dozy the man tried to take in what Gawain was saying. 'I have already promised to marry the lady.'

Gawain smiled and continued to collect his few possessions. 'Give her my love when she wakes and tell her I will look after her sister for her.'

'I wish you luck on that my friend, but I doubt you can tame the untameable.'

Gawain had finished collecting his things, which he put in a leather pouch. 'Do you have any idea where she might have gone?'

With a slight nod of his head the man got to his feet and went searching for his trousers. He found them lying on the floor and began searching them for a hidden pocket. 'I had Rosalinda sew a pouch in these...'

'I don't understand?'

'Ragnell doesn't know but we copied down some of her secret notes.' The man found the pouch, took out a piece of parchment and offered it to Gawain. The young man from Lothian studied it with great care.

'I don't understand,' he said.

Morholt took the parchment from him and tried to explain. 'There are three possible sites of the treasure; one is here in the land of Bran (North Wales), another is in the land of the Israelites and the third is in a land far down the great river of Egypt in a place called Axum. Ragnell has searched to the best of her ability this area and found nothing so either she is heading to the land of Moses or to the land further south, to the land of the black people.'

Gawain tried to recall everything Ragnell had told him and slowly became convinced the lady was heading to the place called Axum. 'She must be mad to try to get there on her own.'

'That one can do anything, my friend. If you go after her she will lead you a merry dance, but at least you will see the world.'

'I presume she will take a ship to Gaul first, but then what?'

'I do not know, but your best chance is to catch her before the lady leaves these shores.'

Gawain agreed and made his farewells. Morholt had one last insight to tell the young man. 'Travel north to the edge of Avalon to a place of wilderness and marshes sometimes referred to as the Blanche launde. There you will find an old man who hires boats. I believe that is where Ragnell has headed. From there she will head to Deisi

(Ireland) where she will get a large vessel to take her further afield.'

The two men hugged and Gawain thanked his friend before hurrying north on his horse as if the devil was on his tail.

The mist of the marshes cast a strange mood over Gawain as he and his faithful horse stumbled and staggered along, towards the coast. The man was cursing Morholt when the disaster occurred. The legs of his faithful horse gave way in the squelchy bog and rider and animal tumbled down into the mud. He managed to pull Excalibur free from it sheath just before his horse succumbed to the mire and vanished. He quickly realised that he was going to be next if he could not somehow pull himself clear. He threw his sword as far as he could in the hope that it would reach a dry piece of ground.

It was the hardest fight of the young man's life as he battled against the elements. He felt his legs get heavier and heavier, but still he kicked and twisted his body in an effort to pull free. Only the top half of his body was clear of the mud and sand for now, but he felt himself sink slowly but surely deeper into the pit. He was in the most dismal of landscapes where the people were few and far between, so he did not expect any help. Many images and thoughts came into his head as he prepared to meet his death. As the last moments of his life dawned, he saw an array of figures from his past; the sweet face of Helena, the wonderful beauty of the area of Lothian, the strong face of his father and the strict face of his mother, the beauty that was Lady Morgan, his brothers' faces, both alive and dead and finally the face of the strong willed Ragnell.

The mud and slime of the ground had done its worst, for only Gawain's head now stood free of the mire. He made his peace with God and cried out to his dead brothers. 'Agravain and Gareth prepare the way for me,' he shouted.

The mud had reached his chin but still the striking face of Ragnell shone down on him, like an image of hope. He thought he heard a voice but his senses told him that was impossible in such a wild place. Then again he heard it, this time more clearly. It was Ragnell and she was shouting something to him. 'Take my belt and hold on to it for your dear life.'

Gawain saw an object flying through the air and land a short distance from him with a splatter. He had to react quickly before it disappeared from view, so he put all his weight forward and stretched out his hand in desperation. He found the belt more through luck than judgement, but although he heard the lady's cries of pain and anguish he remained stuck unable to move. Ragnell tried to attach her end of the belt over her horse's neck but it was too short. So she risked her life by submerging both her hands down into the bog in an effort to help free Gawain's legs, but again it made little or no difference.

The man now realised that his lady was not an apparition and began to warn her not risk her own life. The lady of course did not listen and continued her efforts, but was now in danger of being pulled down with her friend. She felt for the first time her legs begin to sink, despite trying to stay clear of the centre of the maelstrom.

'The sword,' someone cried out.

It couldn't have been Ragnell, thought the young man, for it sounded like a man's voice. Again the he heard it and again the man shouted the same thing. With the mud now up around his mouth it was perhaps with the man's last breath he cried out the name of King Arthur's great sword. 'Excalibur,' he shouted.

The lady thought it was the man's dying wish so she battled her way free from the mire and crawled to where the sword lay. She picked it up and felt an energy or force running through it. Crawling back to Gawain she tried to toss the sword to him only to see it leave her own hand and rest next to the man. Both humans heard a ghostly voice tell Gawain to take hold of the sword and not to let go. Neither the man nor the lady saw anyone else in that desolate place, but a third party saved the young warrior's life. Gawain grabbed hold of Excalibur and felt a strange power from it drag him forth with ease. Within a few moments the sword had done the impossible and had freed the man from the bog. Gawain was stretched out on a less wet piece of ground, exhausted by the side of the pit that had almost taken his life. Ragnell, equally exhausted, put her arms around the man who began to laugh hysterically. Sitting in a solid piece of land together, Gawain and Ragnell looked at each other but saw little of each other's features. They were caked in soft slimy mud from the tip of their toes to the top of their heads. Ragnell had only splatters of mud on her face, but the man's face was totally covered. He tried to remove some of the offending filth, but his hands were too messy so he only made matters worse. Heaving a huge sigh, the man thanked his God, thanked the lady and thanked the ghost for all their efforts in saving him.

Ragnell, whose hands were less caked with the filth, removed some of the clay away from Gawain's eyes and stared at the man. Her bright blue eyes were, he was quite sure, the most beautiful things he had ever seen in his life. 'I can't thank you enough for saving my life,' the man blustered.

'You know fine well I did not save you.'

'Yes you did.'

'You have magic my friend, whether it comes from God or the devil I cannot determine.'

'King Arthur?' whispered the man.

'Not him again,' cried the lady. 'Leave the dead be.'

'If it was not him then who was it?'

'Maybe it's a sign. Maybe we are meant to discover the treasure together.'

The young man agreed and gave the young woman a passionate hug. The mud splashed around them as they started to behave like mischievous children. They threw pieces of the clay back and forth at one and other and screamed with laughter. The lady could not help but comment. 'We must be the oddest looking creatures imaginable.'

Chapter 28

It was the day of reckoning. Lancelot did not have to face a trial as such, but more a formal hearing where he had to listen to a set of charges made against him. He sat beside his father, King Ban, who had travelled from Benoic, in the great hall of Caerleon. It was his father who answered the charges. 'You have no case only the unreliable witness, who has her own reasons perhaps in getting rid of my son. I say you should drop these ridiculous charges and allow Lancelot to return to your side.'

Guinevere sat opposite Ban and got to her feet. 'Perhaps you think a plot to kill the rightful leader of our country is a trivial matter.' The lady glanced at Lancelot and began to mock him. 'Really I am surprised, husband, poison is a woman's weapon.'

Lancelot took his eyes off the wall to glance at his wife. He couldn't help but produce a droll smile. Ban continued to rebuke the charges. 'My son is innocent of any wrong doing. He was clearly not himself and under the spell of the witch.'

Guinevere had remained on her feet. 'He plotted to kill me sir. I am not a vengeful woman I haven't even asked for a trial or for his execution...'

Ban interrupted the Queen. 'Why is that?' he queried.

'I have said already, I am not vengeful.'

Only a chosen few were at the proceedings, which was strange thought Ban. Pelles was the only other King present and two high ranking prefects from the neighbouring areas of Gore and Listinoise. A strange affair he thought these two people, newly wedded, seem to hate each other with a vengeance.

Guinevere continued to mock her husband and called for the man to answer the allegations. Lancelot refused to comply. 'You admit to meeting this witch, who you knew hated me, and yet you secretly made a rendezvous with her.'

Ban continued with his son's defence. 'He did not seek out this woman, she approached him.'

'Let him answer,' yelled the Queen.

Lancelot stared long and hard at his wife. 'We have too many secrets my love, for you to start accusing me of wrong doing,' he stated.

The lady knew what he referred to, but did not stop her attack. 'Do you deny you conspired to kill me and take the High Crown for yourself?'

Again it was the father who answered. 'He was obviously bewitched by this Nemue. She has put a spell on him that even now lasts. Look at him, he is not the son I know, he is a man lost and bewildered.' Ban continued in a similar vein and tried to convince all those present that Lancelot was not competent to defend his actions or his honour. It was a dangerous strategy for clearly his presence in the Celtic kingdoms would still pose a threat to the Queen.

Guinevere saw her chance to save face and to keep her husband quiet at the same time. She took up the lie and put it to good use. 'If what you say is true then he is still a danger to me and the crown.'

Ban listened to his Queen and saw a chance for a compromise.

The Queen continued. 'If we believe he is still under the witch's power, then he must be banished from all our kingdoms.'

It was just the compromise Ban was hoping for, but he had no idea how Lancelot would react to the proposition. To his relief his son seemed quite happy to go along with the charade. With the principle now accepted it was only the fine detail to be discussed.

All parties signed an agreement to the effect that Lancelot of Benoic was to be forever banished from the five kingdoms. The man further agreed that if he ever returned he would willingly stand trial for treason. So it was done, he was free of the monster at last.

So it was done, thought Guinevere. The fool had saved her from any future embarrassment while allowing her to keep her promise to her sweetheart. It wasn't the most satisfying outcome possible, yet she felt justice was only temporary on hold.

The Lady Polyxena had pleaded for leniency personally so that she could take her revenge on the man. She promised to follow Lancelot to the east, or wherever he travelled, with the aim of killing him secretly without creating a fuss.

Guinevere thought this was a clever idea, but was worried. She couldn't get his words to her beloved out of her mind. If Lancelot was beguiled by magic, it was clearly not by Nemue, but by Polyxena. His words stung her, like a hot iron across her back, *'when shall we be free, my love?'* That was what he had said. Could she be so sure that Polyxena was true? Love was a strange animal, full of joy but equally full of pain. It all came down to trust. Did she trust her special one, or was she playing the role of the clown and did not realize it?

The Queen had other matters to attend to also. Despite all efforts to the contrary, by her advisors and even Polyxena, she was convinced that Lady Morgan was behind the assassination attempt. She had no intention of letting that lady off lightly. She had already decided on a spectacular course for her revenge.

With the arrangements for Lancelot's departure over, she could turn her attention to her real foe. The weapon she had at her disposal would inflict the greatest pain imaginable to Lady Morgan.

*

Lady Morgan had been true to her word and had given Yvain and Nemue a small house on her sister's estate at Wedale. This was where young Nemue waited patiently for her lover to return. She was making the place ready by cleaning and fixing what meagre furnishings they had. She was doing something she would never have dreamt of and that was preparing for a matrimonial life.

As Yvain watched the preparations for the wedding that would take place the following day, his mood turned darker. The busy scene only made him feel a terrible sadness. It was as if he felt a premonition that this was the last time he would ever see his mistress again. He knew he couldn't leave without saying his goodbyes so he waited hoping Lady Morgan could find the time to see him.

He wasn't the only one hanging about and looking a little lost, the men of family all congregated together in one room away from all the commotion. It was a strange sight that greeted Yvain when he entered, for all the men were drunk. He was warmly welcomed and made to feel that he was their equal. It was true that he was no longer a servant, a member of the lower classes, but a privateer set upon a new exciting life. Gaheris came towards him and gave him a big hug. 'It is the end of something, isn't it?' he declared. His speech was slurred and he almost fell over Mordred's feet as he advanced towards Yvain.

'It is a strange day full of mixed emotions,' declared the servant.

Many agreed and said so.

'They'll be preparing the dress for the new Queen as we speak,' announced a reflective King Lot.

Gaheris glanced at Lot and swore for the first time in his father's presence. Everyone present looked away, but Lot got up from the ground where he had been lying and came towards his son. Yvain moved out of Lot's way and many wondered if there was going to be a confrontation, but the King only put his arm around Gaheris and led him away from the others. They moved over to a window and spoke in whispers. Yvain's stay with the men was short lived as a courtier sought him out to inform him that Lady Morgan would see him now.

To be given such an honour made the man feel important and he left with the barrage of well wishes. For privacy, Lady Morgan entertained Yvain in an antichamber attached to her own bedchamber. As he entered the room Morgan came to meet him and offered him a warm embrace. He didn't hesitate to hold the woman close to him. She had replaced her wedding gown and was wearing a white shirt with dark breeches. She looked at her most beguiling, probably because she was at her most relaxed. It was at that moment the sadness came upon him. He had loved this woman like a son and had been her protector for all his adult life. Unable to control his emotions he found he could not stop the tears from streaming down his face. As he pulled himself clear of the lady he saw that she too had tears in her eyes.

'This won't do,' said the lady. 'This is supposed to be a happy occasion.'

'Are you happy, my lady?'

It took Morgan a little while to reply. 'My happiness is dependent on the people that I love being happy. Despite the tears I can see you are happy. It would appear I was mistaken about your young lady, she has pleased me greatly with her change of heart.'

Yvain admitted his happiness was and probably always would be tied up with the lovely Nemue. 'She has agreed on a date for our wedding,' announced the proud man. 'She wanted to wait until after winter, but spring isn't so far away.'

'I wish you well and if I can ever be of service...'

'You have done so much already, my lady. I would like to invite you...'

'Of course, I wouldn't miss it.'

As the young man was about to leave, Morgan reached into drawer in her desk and brought out a bundle. The contents she said were no longer of any use for trade, but if he was to melt down the gold and the silver it should fetch a good price. Yvain complained that the lady had already been generous and embraced her once more. As he left he turned one last time to see the lady wipe a tear from her eye.

After saying his farewells Yvain mounted his horse and rode west towards Wedale. The night had arrived and the darkness suddenly fell from the sky. The dirt path that he started on disappeared to become a green and muddy field of which he could not find his way out off. Not used to the route in the gloom of the night the man had somehow managed to get himself lost. He saw two figures, through the mist, come towards him. As they came closer, Yvain slowed his animal to a walking pace, and peered through the haze in the hope of seeing the men's faces. What he saw immediately made him feel uneasy; one man had an eye patch on his left eye, while the other had a large scar across his right cheek, both men looked like cutthroats.

Yvain was old enough to know that in times of danger one should never show fear, so the young man put on a smile and greeted the men warmly. 'I am glad to see you friends, I was hoping you could tell me the quickest way to Wedale?'

The men slowed their horses and came along side, one on either side of him. Yvain was unarmed for all he had with him was a knife that was more used to peeling potatoes than sticking into people. The actions of the men further made him anxious, for they did not acknowledge his address and only stared in his direction.

The man with the scar addressed his travelling companion. 'Do we know the way to Wedale?' he asked. His friend laughed and shook his head. 'No, but we do know the way to hell,' he screamed. As he said this, both men withdrew their swords and plunged them into the hapless body of Yvain. The thrusts were forceful and took the young man's life in an instant. He sloughed forward before slipping off his horse onto the ground.

The man with the patch then got off his animal and with his sword still bloody thrust another blow through Yvain's body.

'He's dead,' complained his companion. 'How many times do you want to kill him?'

Standing over the body the man looked up at his friend. 'It's always best to make sure.' As he was about to return his blade to its sheath, he noticed it was covered in blood so he thought to clean it with a rag.

'Stop,' shouted his friend. 'Don't touch the blade.'

The man looked up at his companion. 'What the devil do you mean?'

'The blade is garnished with a deadly poison. Both our blades were coated in this way.'

'Why wasn't I told,' the man protested.

'The job had to be done and done correctly.'

'Who is this man anyway, he appears nothing more than some lowly servant or tradesman.'

'He is just that, but his woman is someone of importance.'

The man with the patch stared at his sword and looked unsure what to do next. His friend gave him instructions which amounted to the man putting his sword back into his sheath with great care. Once this was done he stared at his colleague again and asked for more answers. 'Why use poison? He's just a normal human...'

'There can be no doubt of his death, our benefactor stipulated this.'

'Only the Gods could revive him now.'

'We must make it look like a robbery, so search his body for any treasure.'

'Oh, not me, I'm not touching him.'

His companion examined Yvain's horse and found the bundle of treasure given to him by Lady Morgan. 'This will do,' he acknowledged. The man looked inside and saw silver and gold coins aplenty. He laughed and stated they were rich.

The man with the patch remounted and after one last look rode away from the scene with his friend in a hurry. After awhile the men discussed what they had done. Neither man could explain the reason for the murder, but with a fat purse and some additional booty it didn't really matter.

The man with the patch was still worried and complained to his friend. 'I won't trust myself to use my sword again,' he declared.

His friend agreed. 'We must either melt them down in some furnace or throw them in some lake,' he declared.

'Poison,' the man grumbled, 'I don't like it, there's something underhand about that. Who is our benefactor anyway?'

'I never got a chance to see the lady's face, but I was really glad to get away from that place. It gave me the creeps.'

'I suppose it doesn't matter, since she paid so handsomely.'

Both men were content with their night's work, but they left more than just a body behind them, they left two strong and powerful women hell bent on revenge.

It wasn't until the following morning that the body of Yvain was found. The prefect of the area was informed but the cause of death seemed obvious. The man had died due to being attacked by bandits who had relieved him of all his goods and shackles. No one from the local area could identify the man, so his body was buried on the ground where he was found. With no mourners present, only the grave diggers, his place of burial would remain unmarked. In a short time, what with horses and people, the ground would become well trampled upon and any sign of the man's last resting place would be gone forever.

Nemue had spent the most miserable night of her life, as she waited for her sweetheart to appear. When he didn't, she galloped away from their small farm towards Lothian and King Lot's castle. She arrived by midday and sought out her husband, but all the men told the lady he had left the night before. It was only after she spoke with Lady Morgan that a search party was arranged. Every available man would take part in the search of the surrounding area.

A bad tempered Ursien refused to waste more time on the servant, but his forthcoming wife, even though it was her wedding day, declared she would ride at the front of the party. Ursien, cursing under his breath, reluctantly gave his blessing.

Lady Morgan left the castle a short time later and was joined by Nemue and Gaheris to scour the countryside for their lost friend. They looked everywhere and by nightfall all three were worried. A tearful Nemue was ready to admit defeat. 'I cannot feel his presence anymore,' she complained.

Gaheris took Morgan aside. 'Your wedding, my lady?' he quietly whispered. 'The guests will be arriving.'

'Let them wait,' Morgan declared.

The lady would not give up and tried to reassure Nemue that any number of things could have happened. Gaheris suggested that Yvain might have got lost and perhaps had finally found his way home.

'No, he is dead. His heart no longer beats for I would know that it if it did.'

Morgan suggested they rested so they got off their horses and began to stroll along the green pastures, with their animals by their side. Few people were about, but a few children were playing hide and seek close to where the adults were walking. One child came running up a slight gradient to hide from her friends, but rushed straight into the group. As the child tried to get by, Nemue put out her hand and caught the girl by the arm. 'Can you help us child?' she asked.

Looking a little frightened the girl refused to say anything.

'We are looking for our friend. He is about my age, tall, dark haired, pleasant looking. Have you seen a man like that recently?'

The girl frowned but did not answer. Morgan bent down to talk with her and gave the girl a reassuring smile. 'There's nothing to worry about,' she declared. 'It's important we find our friend and we are offering a reward. So if you have seen him you could be rich.'

It wasn't clear if the girl understood what was being said to her, but just as Morgan was about to repeat her address the girl pointed to a freshly turned over piece of ground. At first the party didn't understand where the girl was pointing, but at last the girl spoke. 'A man was buried there this morning,' she said.

'Buried?' queried Nemue.

The girl nodded.

'What happened to him?' asked Lady Morgan.

The girl shrugged her shoulders. 'I think bandits robbed him.'

Nemue had tears in her eyes as she too bent down to converse more closely with the girl. 'Can you show us where his body is?'

The girl nodded again and guided them to where their unfortunate friend lay under the ground. Having carried out her task the girl went to leave, but Gaheris handed her two silver coins. The girl smiled and bowed awkwardly, before running off to play again.

Chapter 29

The wedding should have started long before the sun had gone down, but because of the search it had been delayed. The tragedy of Yvain's death had killed the spirit within Lady Morgan. Despite a suggestion of a postponement, from Gaheris, the lady agreed to go ahead with proceedings. This pleased no one, except perhaps Ursien who was becoming rather excited at the prospect of his wedding night.

The guests, of which they were many, all waited patiently for the ceremony to begin. Some were already full of good cheer, thanks to the abundance of intoxicating beverages that was on hand. Others grumbled at the delay, voicing their opinions that the lady was reluctant to fulfil her role as the new Queen of Gore.

Although it was a time of great unhappiness, it was not just because the lady had lost her friend that her heart was so heavy. It was equally sore because she was also abandoning her instincts. Doubts were creeping into her mind concerning her loyalty to the Lady of the Lake. She tried to convince herself that her supporters were just as many as the Queen's and that her fighting men could match her rivals. She asserted to herself that her warriors were better trained than the Queen's. She fought a battle that she could not win and eventually she had to give in.

Morgan's handmaidens took pleasure in their duty and adorned her, firstly with a blue dress that was made of pure silk and fitted her slender body to perfection, then with a multitude of flowers and garnishes.

A band of musicians played in the Great Hall, in King Lot's vast castle. The sound was pleasant to the ear as they played mostly cheerful tunes. This merriment seemed out of place thought the lady. Suddenly she heard a commotion and turned her head to see who had entered her bedchamber without permission.

King Lot entered the room in a hurry and forced his way past all the lady's handmaidens to stand before her agitated and out of breath. 'The Queen has arrived along with many of King Pelles's men,' he announced.

Looking unmoved, Morgan declared the lady was quite welcome to attend.

Lot screwed up his face and pretended he hadn't heard the lady's remarks. 'She is out to make trouble.'

'The lady is rather good at doing that.'

'She should have been busy taking care of Lancelot. What the devil is she doing here?'

Morgan beckoned Lot to sit with her on the window seat. As they both stared out past the watchtower to the fields beyond, Lot continued to impart his news. 'Lancelot has been found guilty and banished from the five kingdoms so I believe from our informant.'

'That is good news, isn't it?'

'I still have a score to settle with him. But it's good news in so far that a great less of Lancelot's men will join the lady now.'

Morgan saw the look on the man's face and anticipated his statement. 'You think we no longer need Ursien?'

'I think it would better for you...'

'One blow, one decisive battle and we will be rid of her forever. Why take a chance at a stalemate. I will go through with this charade and finish what we have started.'

Lot saw the determination on his sister-in-law's face and felt a renewed admiration. 'What about Guinevere?'

'Keep an eye on her and Pelles, if they are up to no good we'll soon find out.

'Don't worry, my men have eyes like hawks, they'll be ready to quell any trouble.'

Part of the wedding celebrations took place outdoors in accordance with the ancient rite and despite the variable weather. A great throng of people came from miles around to witness the colourful event. The crowd completely blocked the two winding streets leading all the way up from Northgate and Eastgate to the very entrance to Lot's great castle. Boys, who were not held up high by their fathers, could not see anything but a sea of heads covering the whole area. There was an abundance of people all present including; tradesmen, matrons with their offspring, cripples on crutches, servants, apprentices, soldiers in shirts of mail and beggars in rags were all crowded as close together as peas in a pod. The light-fingered pickpockets were applying their trade with the glee of a brood of mischievous sprites. The cold and damp of the early morning dew had inflicted some water damage on the canopy that hung above the proceedings as Ursien and Morgan stood in close proximity to one another.

King Lot stood in front of Lady Morgan with his hands outstretched. In his right hand he held two rings which he gripped as tight as he dared, while in his left hand he held a cup that contained a little wine. Standing next to Lot and in front of King Ursien stood Lady Ygerne. She likewise held two rings in one hand and in the other two ceremonial crowns made of fresh wild flowers. The wind blew gently across the small group that surrounded the couple; they included everyone of note amongst the hierarchy, Queen Guinevere and all the family members of King Lot and Lady Ygerne.

The powerful voice of King Lot announced the reason for the gathering. 'The two people gathered here today do so in the presence of our community to take their marriage vows.' He glanced to his left to see Lady Ygerne open her hand to reveal her two rings to King Ursien. This gesture was to prompt the man into starting his rendition. The man did not hesitate and in a voice that was clear and vibrant he declared his vows. 'Here I take thee, Morgan to my wedded wife, to have and to hold, at bed and board...'

There was probably more than Gaheris in the crowd who felt ill at ease at the proceedings, but only one who had announced his own marriage to a lady the day before. He turned to look upon his future bride to see her face aglow in admiration at the beauty of the ceremony. Why did his gut churn inside of him so? Why was his whole body aching at the sight before him? Was it just the thought that Ursien was unfit to touch the lady or was there something more to it? He contemplated his feelings and found to his great surprise that he was jealous. The thought of any man touching the lady made him squirm in displeasure. How this could be so he pondered, after all wasn't he the most fortunate of men in having the angel that was Lady Olwen for a companion.

'...for fairer for fouler, for better for worse, in sickness and in health...'

Guinevere was affected by the proceedings also, but not emotionally. That lady was ready to inflict her revenge and was extremely pleased to see so many people in attendance.

'...till death us do part...'

King Lot found that his hand gripped ever tighter around the rings that he would shortly present from Ursien to Lady Morgan. What strange thoughts were swirling around in his head and what terrible premonitions lay behind them? He was not a superstitious man, yet his foreboding was so gripping that it seemed like a reality from the past. He knew something was going to happen as he glanced in the direction of Guinevere.

'...and thereto I plight thee my troth...'

Lady Ygerne placed the first ring on the smallest finger of Ursien and declared that it was a token of her daughter's devotion; she then placed the second ring on the next finger and declared that Morgan would cherish her husband always. King Lot mirrored this action by doing the same for Lady Morgan. He placed the rings on her left hand and bent forward to whisper something in the lady's ear. It was not the words of the oath. 'I have a good poison if you are of need of it,' he joked.

Morgan smiled and the man continued with the ceremony by placing Lady Morgan's left hand onto King Ursien's left hand. 'In the name of our God...

The man got no further for Guinevere, Pelles and Galahad raced forward to make an announcement. Many in the crowd thought the wedding ceremony was over but it was not. Pelles's men had surrounded the wedding couple and although Lot's men were close on their heels a bloodbath was the last thing Lot wanted in what was after all a ceremony celebrating happiness.

Lot thundered his disapproval at his Queen. 'What the devil is the meaning of all this?'

Guinevere wasted no time in explaining her actions. The lady had a powerful voice and she used it to good effect now. 'Listen to me everyone,' she shouted. 'This marriage is a sham; I cannot allow it to take place...'

'What right do you have to stop it?' questioned Ursien.

'The lady has no right to a Christian wedding, for she has broken one of the most sacred of commandments. She has lain with her own brother and committed an incestuous act that led to issue. I have the proof of birth, signed by a priest but more importantly I have the child of that issue.' Guinevere pulled Galahad beside her and declared that this man was in fact the son of King Arthur and Lady Morgan.

What never occurred to the Queen at the time, but it did to young Galahad, that she was in effect announcing the rightful heir to the throne of the five kingdoms. The young man was attracted to the idea, but he did not reveal anything along those lines to Guinevere. In time he would rule and in time he would show his true colours, but for now he was content to play the sorrowful abandoned son.

A chaotic scene ensued with questions and accusations being thrown back and forth: Ursien looked bewildered; Lot looked enraged, Guinevere triumphant, Gaheris relieved, Galahad wounded, and Morgan's family embarrassed, as for the rest of the crowd they were all completely in shock. The only person present who didn't react was Lady Morgan herself.

This was a day she had dreaded, but now that the secret was out, she felt strangely relieved. She still could not see the young man's features clearly, but with his black curls and his noble looking profile the lady had no doubt Galahad was her son. She waited patiently for him turn his head to look upon her, but he did not. The shame she could take, but the young man's total indifference she could not.

She was becoming aware that soldiers had surrounded them and that perhaps a confrontation was about to take place. She was not alone in fearing bloodshed, for she heard Lot's powerful voice address the Queen.

'Your grace, I hope it is not your intention that blood should be spilt this day.'

Guinevere looked all around her and saw that the conflicted parties were ready to do battle. She gave her orders to her soldiers to pull back. The men did what their Queen had ordered and a confrontation was avoided. Lot acknowledged Guinevere's action with a nod of his head. After all the lady had won, there would be no wedding and no alliance.

People moved away, many of them complaining about the late King's behaviour and many feeling let down and disgusted with Lady Morgan's. She was their ideal, their matriarch. They would never quite feel the same way about the lady again.

*

Perceval had tracked down Abdur's father to the city of Antioch. Expecting to find the man a King or at least a man of importance he was surprised to find that he was nothing more than a common criminal. He made inquires at the gaol to find out what the charges were against him. The official only laughed and gave him a catalogue of misdemeanours, ranging from the trivial; pick pocketing, to the most serious charge of the thief of a historical artefact. 'He is an orbital criminal, my lord. '

'This leaves me with quite a problem,' admitted Perceval.

The official looked unconcerned.

'I have rescued his son, a boy about the age of twelve. I wished to reunite him...but now...'

'I suggest you take the boy to the authorities ...let them deal with him.'

'What would they do?'

'I suspect they'll find some work to keep him out of trouble. I wouldn't worry if he's anything like his father you'll be glad to see the back of him.'

There was something in what the man said. Abdur was nothing but trouble, ever since he set eyes on him, yet he was reluctant to just hand him over to a complete stranger.

Feeling that his trip had been wasted he returned to the rented room to find Abdur no longer asleep where he had left him. He waited all morning but the boy did not return. He searched the centre of the city and returned to the gaol, but could not find any trace of him.

Most people would have left it like that, but Perceval was not like most people. He had a great sense of duty so he continued to search Antioch and after dark waited in the room to see if the boy would return. Two days past before he received word from a law official that the boy had been caught attempting to steal from a rich merchant. He visited Abdur in the same prison as his father and made his case for the boy's release.

He saw the same official as before. 'There's nothing I can do my lord, for charges have been brought. He will get a chance to defend himself tomorrow when the Magister hears his case.'

'Where will that be? I mean to be present so as to help the boy if I can.'

The official looked at the young lord and thought it was his duty to persuade him from his course. 'If the boy is not a relative, my advice is to leave this matter to the proper authorities.'

'I feel the boy has been led astray by his criminal father...'

'No doubt this is so, but be careful my lord, the Magister is a hard man. He might think you have another reason for helping the boy.'

'What other reason?'

'He might think you want him to carry out some other criminal activity, or worse that you wish to use the boy in some other way.'

The suggestion made by the man was an insult and Perceval told the man so. Still if he thought along these lines, perhaps others would too. The Magister might think his involvement with the boy was strange. Yet his resolve remained. He would not abandon his troublesome companion.

'The magister will hear the case in the building next to this one. It might be first thing in the morning or it might be last thing at night. It is up to him what case he hears first.'

Perceval said he understood and thanked the man for his trouble.

'I will be there first thing in the morning,' he told the man.

The Magister wasted no time in dispensing his quick and severe punishments. As chance would have Abdur's case was the second case heard. The charges were read and the Magister asked Abdur if had anything he wished to say. The boy shook his head, but before the Magister could pass sentence, Perceval rose to his feet and addressed the man.

'Who the devil are you sir?' the Magister inquired.

'My name is Perceval of Listinose. I know I am a long way from home, but I come today to ask for mercy for this young boy.'

Magister looked over the young man and found him to be both well-dressed and well-spoken. He hesitated before dismissing the man out of hand. 'Go on sir, make your case but it will have to be good one. This boy is well known...'

'No doubt his father is too?' suggested Perceval.

'Yes, the man is a nuisance to all law-abiding citizens.'

'I beg you not to judge the son in the same light as the father.'

'It is clear the boy has taken after his father in every way.'

Perceval paused before committing himself. 'I ask for your leniency and hope you will allow me to take charge of the boy from this day on.'

Magister leant forward and asked Perceval to repeat his last statement.

'Give the boy to me to look after and I promise he will never get into trouble again.'

'You are bold sir, but what guarantees do we have that you can fulfil this miraculous deed.'

'None,' replied Perceval. 'But if you give him into my care I promise we will leave these shores never to return.'

'And where are you thinking of taking the boy?'

'I have already made plans to take him home with me, back to Britannia.'

Magister sighed and contemplated for a moment. The day would be long if he lingered over each case, so the man decided to get this one out of the way. 'Very well I put the boy into your care. Leave your name with the clerk and be warned if he gets into trouble again, you too will be held to account.

Perceval thanked the man and within a short time, Abdur was given into his care.

The boy looked annoyed at seeing Perceval and was anything but grateful for his rescue. 'Why did you do such a stupid thing?' he asked.

'I suppose you would rather being rotting in a filthy prison right now?'

The boy screwed his face. 'As a matter of fact, yes I would.'

'Why you ungrateful little...'

'Frog,' offered Abdur.

They both laughed and the boy began to tell Perceval the reason why he wished to be jailed.

'So you think your father is the only living person who knows the location of this sacred hoard?'

'Yes. You probably think I'm mad, but he found it quite by chance...'

'Why didn't he loot it? By all accounts he is a thief...'

'He meant to, but the tunnel was so small he couldn't escape with any of the treasure. He was getting supplies to widen the tunnel when the authorities caught up with him.'

'I gave my word to the Magister,' Perceval reminded Abdur.

Abdur laughed, but saw that Perceval did not. 'You surely not going to let a small thing like that stand in the way of a great adventure?'

Perceval smiled. 'My word means everything to me.'

'You cannot be held responsible for what another will do...'

'Oh yes I can.'

'Well allow me be arrested again. Once I speak to my father I'm sure I'll find out where...'

'Now wait. I'm sure I could arrange for you to see your father before we leave without you getting yourself arrested again.'

Abdur looked stunned. 'Really, I could speak to him without others around?'

'Yes, I'll speak to someone today. I'm sure it can be arranged.'

Chapter 30

Lancelot was escorted from the Celtic shores to his new life as an exile in the cosmopolitan city of Constantinople. He led a miserable existence there, waiting patiently for Elaine to join him and for their happiness to begin. He visited the famous cathedral of Hagia Sofia everyday knowing that one day she would come to him.

Still unsure of his way around the busy metropolis this day he found himself in the middle stretch of the Mese by the great mall known as the Markos Embolos. He took a wrong turn and found himself on a street that divided into two branches; one went north towards the Gate of Polyandrion, while the other went south towards the Golden Gate. Unsure what path to take, the man saw the Church of the Apostles ahead and walked north towards it. Before he reached the church he passed a dirty looking beggar who tried to block his way. The beggar stuck out his hand and in a voice that sounded vaguely familiar appealed for money.

Lancelot pushed the beggar to the ground, but the man grabbed hold of his arm and gave him a warning. 'Do not go this way my lord, thieves and cutthroats await.'

'This is the way I know.'

'Take the other path it will lead you through the Forum of the Ox to the Golden Gate.'

Looking down at the filthy beggar, he thought he looked familiar. 'You mean to lead me into your own trap,' he announced, as he tugged his arm free from the man and walked away.

Lancelot increased his pace towards the Church of the Apostles, but never quite made it to its sanctuary. Three men came to block his entrance. They wore hoods, despite the heat of the day, and produced knifes of various shape and sizes. Lancelot thought about making a run for it, but as he turned his head, he saw another figure appeared behind him. 'Here, take my money,' he cried, as he cut open his purse and threw it down in the dirt.

None of the men even looked at the purse as it lay on the ground. Lancelot had his knife now in his own hand and swung it in the direction of the group in front of him. It made a swishing sound as it travelled through the air but made no contact. The middle figure of the group let down their hood. To his surprise it was Queen Guinevere that stood before him.

The lady took a couple of paces forward and smiled. 'You didn't really think I'd leave it like that, did you?' she asked.

The figure behind Lancelot also removed her hood, to reveal the slender figure of Polyxena.

Lancelot was the first to acknowledge the lady's presence. 'Elaine my love, it appears you have brought with you a few undesirables.'

Guinevere stared at Polyxena. 'A betrayal from you I cannot stomach. Not after all I've done for you.'

'I am not your paid assassin. I am Elaine of Gorlois...'

'You are nothing but a murderer and you shall die like the scum you are,' yelled Guinevere.

With these words the two men beside the Queen rushed forward with their knives and attacked Lancelot. The man from Benoic was used to fighting against greater numbers, but when two more men from the crowd joined in the attack, he knew he was in trouble. It was then that Elaine decided to join the fight alongside her true love. She was a woman of gentile birth, but because she was housed inside the body of a paid warrior, she fought like one. The first two men were stabbed by Lancelot, before the man received his first blow against him of any note. It was in his left arm and did not inconvenience too much, but as the two men fell to the ground their places were filled quickly by two others. The numbers were stacking up against them, but still Lancelot and Elaine fought bravely.

A small crowd watched in horror as the knife fight progressed towards the inevitable. The Queen's six men wounded Lancelot and Elaine with a barrage of blows but still they refused to die. With their arms tiring and their bodies blooded the couple were forced into a corner where Guinevere waited to give them the coup de grace.

Guinevere had her own weapon under her cloak. She produced a sword from its scabbard and waited to cut off the heads of her husband and lover. Vengeance was making her blood boil and jealousy was making her act unwisely. Elaine was exhausted and near the end of her tether, but saw a glimmer of a chance. In her eagerness to spill blood Guinevere had left herself open to attack. With her sword down by her side she did not expect the exhausted couple to see her advantage point. Just a few paces away, but out of sight, so the Queen thought, Lancelot and Elaine had crossed themselves and appeared to be ready to meet their maker. Suddenly from the corner of her eye Elaine pounced upon the surprised Queen. With her knife, blooded and in her right hand, Elaine thrust it upwards and around Guinevere's neck.

Guinevere was asked to drop her sword, which she did. The men stopped their attack and looked towards their Queen for guidance. Guinevere pondered for a moment before berating them for not finishing off their duty. 'Kill them, never mind about me,' she shouted.

The men didn't listen to their Queen but looked to Elaine to see what that lady's next move was going to be. Elaine spelled out her demands. 'The Queen comes with us and you do not follow.'

Guinevere began to struggle and Elaine took her arm and bent it back around her back. The Queen yelled in pain. 'Get it over with you traitor,' she screamed.

Elaine continued to give the Queen's men instructions as she and Lancelot retreated from the scene with their prize.

If Constantinople was not far enough from the grasp of the Queen of the Celts, then how far would they need to travel to escape her? The Queen had been taken to old rundown house on the outskirts of the city for safe keeping. She was tied up and attached to a chair, while her captors wandered around the empty shack looking for a way out of their troubles.

'Let's just kill her and be done with it,' suggested Lancelot.

Elaine was pacing up and down, her right hand on her head.

'Is your head still hurting?' he asked.

Elaine turned to look at Guinevere. 'We can't do what you suggest. We would be no better than she is.'

'Then we leave now. Someone will find her in time and she will continue to hurt us down for the rest of our lives.'

Elaine knew what Lancelot said was true. Guinevere was not a forgiving person; she would never give up her quest for revenge.

The smell of decay and urine was precipitating Elaine's already severe headache. She needed the smell of the cool night air and a solution to her problem.

Lancelot decided Elaine could not take any more drama so he suggested she wait for him on the steps of Hagia Sofia.

'No my love, with me gone you might forget your conscience.' It was as Elaine uttered these words that a blinding pain shot through her head and she fell to the floor.

Lancelot rushed to her side, gave her water and pleaded with her to say she was alright. After a short while Elaine looked up at the dark figure of Lancelot and sighed. 'Where the devil am I?' she challenged.

'You're with me, Lancelot. Don't you remember, my love?'

Polyxena studied the man and with his help got to her feet. With her head still hurting the lady looked about her surroundings. Surprised to see filth and degradation she turned her head to see the figure of Guinevere bound and gagged on a chair. She immediately turned to Lancelot for an explanation. 'What is going on here?'

Lancelot's concern was genuine as he tried to make Polyxena understand the last few hours. 'You are making me anxious,' he told her. 'You must recall how she tried to kill us both?'

To his shock, Polyxena did not remember anything of the fight or anything of Guinevere's part in it.

'She is our enemy,' he said. 'We must be free of her...'

Thinking he was in no danger Lancelot had left his sword resting against a wall. Almost in a daze he saw Polyxena go to it, pick it up and advance towards him. It all happened so quickly that the man made no attempt to stop her advance. The point of the sword was now at the nap of his neck. 'Untie her and do not make any sudden moves, I know how to use this.'

There was a subtle difference in the lady's voice, but Lancelot did not pick up on it. Her manner too had changed, she was more forceful, more sure of things. If Lancelot failed to see the difference, Guinevere did not. Suddenly Polyxena had returned, suddenly she was herself again. As her ties were loosened and her gag removed Guinevere studied her favourite and appealed to her to prove her worth and her loyalty to her. 'If it really is you, you shall not hesitate,' she commanded. 'Run him through, kill him now.'

TO BE CONTINUED

Printed in Great Britain
by Amazon.co.uk, Ltd.,
Marston Gate.